MW00462599

The Price You Pay for Love

Destiny Skai

**Lock Down Publications and Ca$h
Presents**
The Price You Pay for Love
A Novel by *Destiny Skai*

The Price You Pay for Love

Lock Down Publications
P.O. Box 870494
Mesquite, Tx 75187

Visit our site at
www.lockdownpublications.com

Copyright 2020 by Destiny Skai
The Price You Pay for Love

All rights reserved. No part of this book may be
reproduced in any form or by electronic or mechanical
means, including information storage and retrieval systems
without permission in writing from the publisher, except by a
reviewer who may quote brief passages in review. Printed in
the United States of America

*This is a work of fiction. Names, characters, places,
and incidents either are products of the author's imagination
or are used fictitiously. Any similarity to actual events or
locales or persons, living or dead, is entirely coincidental.*

Lock Down Publications
Like our page on Facebook: Lock Down
Publications @
www.facebook.com/lockdownpublications.ldp
Cover design and layout by: **Dynasty Cover Me**
Book interior design by: **Shawn Walker**
Edited by: **Cassandra Sims**

WITHDRAWN FROM
RAPIDES PARISH LIBRARY
ALEXANDRIA, LOUISIANA

Destiny Skai

Stay Connected with Us!

Text **LOCKDOWN** to 22828 to stay up-to-date with
new releases, sneak peaks, contests and more…
Thank you!

Submission Guideline.

Submit the first three chapters of your completed manuscript to ldpsubmissions@gmail.com, subject line: Your books title. The manuscript must be in a .doc file and sent as an attachment. Document should be in Times New Roman, double spaced and in size 12 font. Also, provide your synopsis and full contact information. If sending multiple submissions, they must each be in a separate email.

Have a story but no way to send it electronically? You can still submit to LDP/Ca$h Presents. Send in the first three chapters, written or typed, of your completed manuscript to:

LDP: Submissions Dept
Po Box 870494
Mesquite, Tx 75187

DO NOT send original manuscript. Must be a duplicate.

Provide your synopsis and a cover letter containing your full contact information.

Thanks for considering LDP and Ca$h Presents.

ACKNOWLEDGMENTS

First and foremost, I would like to thank God, for blessing me with such an amazing talent. To both of my young kings in training, Torrence and Ethan, everything mommy does, she do it for y'all. Before I leave this earth you will be financially stable, with the ability to run an empire that I leave behind. Now, I have to give credit where it's due and that's to my oldest son, Torrence for coming up with the original title: FOREIGN AND DOMESTIC. You're the reason this book is so special in my eyes and heart. Thank you for exercising your talent and brilliance. I love you so much son.

To my KING, better known as Author Chris Green, I love you so much. Words cannot express the way I truly feel about you. The strength and encouragement you give me is simply unimaginable. I thank God for you every day. Distance is not a factor because our patience will bring us together full force. Just wait on it, baby. Inshallah it will be sooner than later. Now back to my message...This book would've never happened without your help. You've spent countless days and nights, helping me get this done and I appreciate your dedication to me and this project. I know a thanks, is not in order because I have your back the same way you have mine. You've been my support system and not just with the books, throughout my household. You are truly the EPITOME of what a man should be, especially when it comes down to my kids. The way you interact with them gives me such joy. They appreciate you as much as I do. You've been everything I wanted and needed in my life. You came in and filled a void that I thought was lost forever. I've NEVER had a man to pray for me, or open my eyes to religion. Your wisdom, allowed me to see you in a different light. That goes a mile in my eyes and heart. Many will NEVER understand our relationship. But what's understood doesn't have to be explained. That's only for you and I to understand. All I can say,

The Price You Pay for Love

is I am happy about the new journey that we are about to embark on. I couldn't have chosen a better partner to build with. This is our year baby, 2020, will owe us NOTHING because we are taking everything that's owed to us, so let's make the best of it. I love you from the bottom of my heart and NO ONE or NOTHING could sever that. Let's focus and make money moves!! And I'm screaming free KOSA until it's backwards!!! #BLACKLOVE #KOSAGANG #CHRISNDEZZI

And last, but not least, I want to give a special shot out to Tisha Andrews. You were the one who opened my eyes, so that I could see Chris, for the man that he truly is. Thank you for being in our corner and giving me great advice when I wanted to quit. You had faith in him from day one and trust me he knows all about it. Lol!!

And I can't forget, Jane Penella, Daleisha Johnson, April Wright, Loretta Harris-Woody, Helene Young, Shawn Walker and all of our readers, who are rooting for our relationship and projects. We appreciate you greatly. Anyone I forgot to name, please charge it to my head and not my heart. I'm forgetful at times. Lol!! We have so many announcements and surprises for 2020, so stay tuned. This is only the beginning. Thank you to the entire LDP family that supports us and our movement.

Love,
Destiny Skai

Destiny Skai

PROLOGUE
FOREIGN

What was supposed to be one of the happiest days of my life, quickly turned out to be one of the worst days in history, why? Let me explain . . .

My best friend Lexi and I were standing in the bridal shop beaming hard into the mirror. Our cheekbones were so high, our eyes were damn near closed. As I tried on my wedding dress with the final alterations, my heart fluttered with anticipation. The dress was perfect and so was my relationship.

My wedding had been a longtime coming and I dreamed about that very day since high school. Each day I counted my blessings and I was finally headed down the aisle with my first love, to become Mrs. Aaron Young. True love was hard to find, and I felt like the luckiest girl in the world.

"Biitch! I cannot wait for my brother to see you walk down that aisle in this bomb-ass dress." Lexi boosted my confidence higher than the maximum magnitude on the Richter scale.

"You like it?" I replied, as I twirled around in it, admiring the hand sewn Swarovski crystals and glitter on the heart shaped neckline. The bottom flowed freely, and the tail was long. The embroidery details were exquisite and also studded with crystals.

Lexi's opinion meant the world to me. Especially since she was my best friend, Matron of honor and sister in law, wrapped into one.

"I love it. And for thirty grand, so will Aaron. For that price that bitch better give me shelter when I need it."

"You know he promised me a fabulous wedding after he made it. He's just keeping his word." It showed a lot of skin, but I loved it. "I hope it's not too revealing."

She placed both hands on my shoulders. "Calm down, sis, it's your day. Whoever don't like it, can go '*straight to hell Ike,*' with their hatin' asses."

"I want you to stop watching that movie."

"I can't help it. Ike Turner was a plum fool."

"He was, but there isn't anything funny about domestic violence. I swear I didn't like Laurence Fishburne for a long time after he did that movie."

Lexi laughed hard and loud. "I don't know why. Shit, it ain't like he beat her for real." She paused for a split second. "Anyway, back to the dress. You know Aaron loves whatever you wear. His ass would marry you in your birthday suit if that's what you wanted to get married in."

"Lexi, you so stupid." I giggled. "I'm saving that for our honeymoon to Dubai."

"I hear you." She unzipped the back of my dress. "I'm praying I get a niece after them seven days of sex."

"We're going to do more than just have sex, Lexi. For instance, enjoy the country, partake in some excursions, and do a little shopping. We've had enough sex to last us three lifetimes."

"Yeah, I forgot. That's all y'all wanted to do back in high school."

"Don't judge." I waved my French tip in her face. "You started early."

"I know, right."

Quickly changing back into my clothes after I looked at the time, I paid the remaining balance and we left the store. "I'm going straight there so you can follow me."

"Okay."

***

My Bentley coupe was sitting pretty in the parking lot waiting on me. Aaron had bought it a few months ago for my birthday. Gently, I hung my dress on the loop, stretched the tail across the seat, and closed the door. Every time I drove that car or pulled up to our million-dollar mansion, it reminded me of where we'd come from and how blessed we were to be so accomplished. One thing I could say was that Aaron never allowed the money to change him. After obtaining his fame and fortune through hard work and dedication, he remained humble and helped others in need, such as close family and friends.

The Price You Pay for Love

It had been a long day and I couldn't wait to see my future husband. Tonight, we were meeting up at his parent's house for our weekly dinner. As I drove through traffic the harmonious sound of Anita Baker's *Just Because* filled my ears and touched my heart. I sang along and reminisced.

Aaron and I met in high school through Lexi, and I swear I couldn't stand him because he was so annoying and immature, as a freshman. Every single day he would take my backpack and run. I was fast, but he was faster. One day after being his victim for the majority of the school year I was ready for him. I had my jump rope wrapped around my hand waiting for him to try it. When he snatched my bag and tried to run, I slung my jump rope in his direction and caught his feet. Aaron went tumbling down headfirst onto the sidewalk skinning his head in the process. Immediately, he jumped up and rushed in my direction. I thought he was going to hit me, but he didn't. Instead he kissed me, and I was blown away. That was our first kiss of many more to come. We lost our virginity to one another and the rest was history. We've been in love ever since.

As I drove through the evening traffic, I occasionally glanced in the rearview mirror to admire my beautiful dress. It was still surreal that I was finally getting married to my high school sweetheart.

Aaron and I wanted to get married after we graduated, but our parents had talked us out of it. They said we were too young and needed to wait until we had both finished college and found jobs. I can still hear my mom's words replaying in my head . . . *"If it's meant to be it'll happen."* And now here we were four years later preparing to take that step in a few days.

Halfway through our junior year in college, Aaron was drafted to the NFL by the Tampa Bay Buccaneers. We moved to the area and of course he moved my parents there as well. My mom and dad were reluctant to leave their home at first, but I was able to convince them to sell their house and move closer to me, considering I was their only child. Being a doting housewife was far beyond my plans, so I pursued a career in real estate. The business was very lucrative and with Aaron's team-mates purchasing homes, I was able to clear out some pretty hefty commission checks.

The music chirping from my work phone dismissed my thoughts abruptly. Fumbling through my purse, I pulled it out. "This is Foreign Hamilton speaking."

"Hey, Ms. Hamilton, this is Anna Sawyer, Frank's wife."

"Oh, hi, Mrs. Sawyer. How are you?"

"I'm good and you?"

"I'm good. So, what can I do for you?"

"I'm calling about the property we're purchasing. Is there any way you can scan over the agreement, please? It's urgent."

"Yes. Give me about thirty minutes to get home and I'll send it over."

"You're a lifesaver. Thank you so much."

"No problem."

"Have a good evening."

"Same to you."

Once I ended the call, I took the drive to my house. It was almost six, which meant I would be late for our dinner, but Aaron would understand my tardiness. Then I thought about it a little more and felt it would be better to just give him a call, to give him a heads up. I dialed his number and put it on Bluetooth. The phone rang until the voicemail picked up.

"Oh well. I called." They were probably playing music and didn't hear the phone ringing.

Twenty minutes later, I was pulling into our driveway. Confusion settled in, as I scrunched up my face. Aaron's car was in the driveway, when he was supposed to be at his parent's house. Emerging from the car, I approached the front door and unlocked it. When I dropped my keys and purse on the credenza, I noticed that the house was extremely quiet.

"He must be sleep," I mumbled, as I took the winding staircase up to the second floor.

Our bedroom door was closed which was odd because we never kept it closed. Pushing the door open, I was surprised to see he wasn't in bed or in the shower for that matter.

Spinning on my heels to leave the room, I called his name. "Aaron."

Walking towards the west wing of the house, I came up on the guest bedroom and reached for the handle. My ears perked up, as I eased the door open.

"Aaron . . . Aaron . . .," she moaned.

My eyes grew as wide as the back of a linebacker, as I watched some bitch ridin' my husband's dick, and in *my* house. The nigga was truly enjoying himself. All into it and shit. I mean, his eyes were closed, and he was caressing her ass the same way he'd do mine when I was the one ridin' the dick. Pure rage took over my body and I charged towards them.

"You disgustin' son of a bitch!"

At the sound of my voice, Aaron's eyes popped open. His face was ridden with panic. He and his hoe froze when they saw my face. They were in such shock, they couldn't move.

Grabbing a fistful of the tramp's hair, I snatched her off of him and slung her to the floor. Aaron jumped up.

"Baby, wait. Let me explain."

His apology meant nothing. True enough, I was supposed to check my man first, but I had to check the hoe first because I knew I would never see her again. Standing over her, I struck the bitch in the face repeatedly. She tried to fight back, but my anger brought the beast out of me and she couldn't hang or block my vicious blows. The more she attempted to fight back the angrier I became. With my hand balled in a tight fist, I drew back and proceeded with a quick hard jab right in her top lip. Blood spewed from her mouth, but that didn't deter me from pounding away at her face.

"Foreign, stop!" Aaron shouted, as he grabbed me from behind and pulled me off of her.

Screaming like a maniac, I tried to wiggle my body from his grip. "Bitch, let me go."

Aaron's hoe pulled herself from the floor and almost fell, as she rushed to get her legs in the pink thongs that had been lying on the floor. There was a lot of pinned up aggression in me and I still wanted to fight. The closest victim to me was my deceitful-ass nigga, so I twisted my body around to face him and punched his ass in the face. Pounding his face with a two-piece combo, he attempted to move his head, but my hands were too quick. In the midst of our fight, the bitch ran out of the room. I could hear her feet hitting each step as she made her escape down the stairs and out the front exit, slamming the door behind her.

Aaron pulled me close to him and kissed my face. "I fucked up. I'm sorry."

"You fuckin' a bitch in our home?" My voice was high pitched and laced with anger and hurt. "How could you do this to me? We're about to get married."

"It was an accident, Foreign. I swear."

"Let me go!" I screamed. "You did this on purpose."

"No, I didn't. She was at the pool party last week and left her glasses. I helped her look for them and one thing led to another. It wasn't intentional. You have to believe me."

"Well I don't."

He pushed me onto the bed and towered over me with his five foot nine, one hundred seventy-pound frame. "Stop fighting me please."

Just the thought of laying on that nasty-ass bed made me want to throw up. Once again, I tried fighting him. My arms were flying wildly, right along with my legs.

"Get me off this crab infested bed."

"Not until you calm down."

My face was soaked with tears and I could feel the taste of salt surface in my mouth. Remaining calm was nowhere in my future, but I knew he wasn't going to let me go. Instead of fighting, I took a deep breath and closed my eyes for a brief moment. When I opened them, he was staring directly in my face.

"I'm calm."

"You sure?" He needed reassurance.

"Yes." My head moved up and down.

Aaron freed me and stood straight up, wearing nothing but a pair of boxer briefs. To my surprise, I didn't slap his ass. Instead, I walked out of the room, heartbroken and crying. I could hear him taking quick steps behind me. But I didn't allow that to dissuade me from my mission. Stepping into our bedroom, I disappeared into our walk-in closet and stepped back out with my rolling Chanel suitcase.

"What are you doing?" Aaron asked.

"I'm leaving. So, you can cancel the wedding and tell your family and friends why I left you." Tossing the suitcase onto the bed, I opened it and proceeded to the dresser.

"No. Foreign, I can't do that."

"Well, tell them whatever you want to. I don't care." Pulling clothes from the drawer, I tossed them on the bed.

"Our parents would be crushed. We can get past this. Our wedding is days away and I love you." Aaron grabbed my hand, but I snatched it away from his grip.

"We can't get past this. I'll never forgive you and you wasn't worried about our wedding while you were in here slaying the next bitch."

We continued to go back and forth. Just as fast as I'd place a piece of clothing in the suitcase, Aaron would take it. Growing tired of the games, I walked out the room without my clothes and rushed down the stairs. Refusing to give up, he was hot on my trail. By the time I made it to my purse, Aaron had already snatched my car keys.

"I'm not letting you leave."

"You clearly don't want me. Your actions proved that today. Just let me go, please."

"No," he replied before walking away.

***

Needless to say, I didn't leave that night. Nor did we make it to dinner. Aaron ended up lying to his parents about our reason for not showing up.

In the wee hours of the morning, I was awakened by extreme pleasure. My eyes fluttered, as I looked at the clock on the nightstand. The time read 4:44am. Aaron had taken it upon himself to crawl between my legs and he was nibbling on my clit. It was

15

absurd because he wasn't big on oral. Whenever he went down without cause, it was usually because he felt guilty about something.

As bad as I wanted to push him away, I couldn't resist the tender, euphoric touch of his tongue. My body craved him, but my mind despised him. The mixed emotions I was having was weird as fuck. Realizing I was awake, he climbed on top of me and slid inside. Stroking me slowly, he kissed the tears that streamed from my eyes.

"I'll make it up to you. Just don't leave me. Please, I'm begging you. There's no me without you," he whispered lovingly, as he sucked and kissed on my neck. His thrusts were passionate and slow, and each out and in was served with long, deep strokes.

Refusing to reply, I turned my head and allowed him to please my body. As angry as I was, I couldn't stop nature's flower from reacting to the sensation. My wetness was evident of that. Meanwhile, my heart was aching and dying to be healed. Our love making lasted a little over thirty minutes. I knew that because my eyes were zoomed in on the clock the whole time.

Aaron lay beside me and took me into his arms, allowing his leg to rest on top of mine. He had fallen asleep with no problem. Sleep for me was a little harder because I couldn't stop crying. Eventually, my eyes grew tired and I was out like a drunk on a Friday night.

The following day, I woke up to a set of baggy, bloodshot, red eyes. Aaron wasn't in bed, but beside me was a white envelope. My curiosity got the best of me, so I opened it without hesitation. There was a card inside that said: *I'm sorry*, along with a check for fifty thousand dollars. Dropping the check on the bed, I read the contents of the card out loud.

"Please don't make me cancel our wedding. Accept this apology gift and let's move on with our future. I know that no amount of money could repair your broken heart, but I hope this gesture shows you how sorry I am for betraying you. Go downstairs. There's another surprise waiting for you."

Tossing the duvet back, I jumped up from the bed and rushed downstairs. Careful not to trip, I took the stairs one by one until I was standing in the living room. It looked as if we had opened up a florist shop in our living room area. There were dozens upon dozens of Hyacinth, bell shaped, white flowers, which symbolized an apology. Aaron was truly begging for my forgiveness. To the left of me sat the cordless phone. Snatching it off the base, I dialed his number.

"I take it you received your gifts?" Aaron asked.

"Yes. I appreciate the gesture, but that doesn't make what you did disappear or make me forgive you."

He sighed. "I know, but I need to show you how sorry I am from the bottom of my heart. After practice I'm coming straight home. I'm taking you out tonight, so find something nice to wear."

"Okay."

After I disconnected the call, I ran back upstairs to take a shower and get dressed. Before I started my day, I was going to the bank and deposit the check into my secret account. My mama and daddy didn't raise no fool, so I had money stashed away for a rainy day. And the way Aaron was moving, I was certain that day wasn't too far away.

CHAPTER 1
FOREIGN

Three years later . . .

As I nibbled gently on my acrylic nails, nervousness took over my body. Facing the window of the skybox, I watched Aaron fight hard for the Buccaneers to win the Super Bowl. My anxiety was through the roof while glancing at the score board. Aaron and his teammates were facing off with the Dallas Cowboys. The score was tied 32–32 and there was less than a minute left in the fourth quarter. Aaron was the quarterback, so the team was depending on him for the win.

The next few seconds had my heart in a frenzy. Aaron had the ball clutched tightly in his right arm, as he took off from the fifty yard line. Placing my hand on the glass, I jumped up and down as he leaped over and dodged his opponents.

"Run baby. Go!" I shouted in excitement.

Just as he approached the twenty yard line, I froze as I watched a big dude give chase and try to take him down. Aaron juked left and sent his opponent crashing to the ground. Running full speed, he crossed the line and slammed the ball down onto the turf.

"Touchdown, Buccaneers!" the commentator shouted. "Aaron Young has done it again, ladies and gentlemen. The Tampa Bay Buccaneers have won the Super Bowl!"

The entire team rushed my baby and raised him up in the air. A wide smile spread across my lips as I watched my husband gain a victory for the team.

"Yasss, sis! My brother did that." Lexi smiled and picked up her purse. Aaron and Alexis were twins and they looked so much alike with their caramel skin and chestnut eyes. "Come on, let's go meet him in the locker room."

Just as we stepped from the elevator, we spotted him. "Aaron," we screamed.

He turned around and looked in our direction. Once he saw us, he walked towards us. "Congratulations, baby. I knew you could do it."

He picked me up and held me tight. "Thanks, baby." We locked lips before he put me down.

"Good job, bro." Lexi hugged his neck.

"Thanks, sis."

"So, where's the after party?" she asked.

"At a teammate's house."

Not feeling his answer, I butted in. "That sounds like a no invite, if you ask me."

"Y'all can come. I don't care, but you know you hate the after parties." Aaron grinned.

"Yeah, because it's always a bunch of groupies flocking around in bikinis," I replied.

"Aye, yo', Aaron. Let's go, bro," one of his teammates shouted.

"I gotta go. I'll see y'all later." Aaron planted kisses on both of our cheeks before running off without giving us the details of the party.

"He think he slick, but I'm about to text his boy. His ass will tell me."

"Who?" I asked, as Lexi pulled out her cellphone.

"Twan."

"Aaron gone kill you if he find out you been fucking with his boy, and on top of that, fishing for info behind his back." He was against her dating any of the players considering they were all the same. 'Cause everybody knew birds of a feather flocked together.

"Girl, I'm grown. He can't tell me what to do."

Rolling my eyes, I giggled. "Yeah. That's why you sneakin' around with him."

On our way back to my car, Lexi received a notification. "Girl, I got the address. We about to crash this mufuckin' party."

"Hell yeah. But let's wait for like an hour or so before we crash it. Let him get all comfortable and shit. I'm telling you right now, I'm beating his ass if he try me tonight."

Popping the locks on my car, we climbed inside. Lexi put on her seatbelt. "Shit, I'ma help you beat his ass."

"Damn right."

The Price You Pay for Love

***

Exactly an hour and a half later, we pulled up to the mansion where the party was being held. The driveway was packed, so we had to park alongside the road.

"Damn, bitch, they got every hoe from the Bay in here, huh?" Lexi stated, as she closed the door.

"Hell yeah. Your brother better be in the corner with his boys or it's gon' be a problem. God, please don't let me have to act like a plum fool in here."

Lexi stopped in her tracks and looked at me. She had a smirk on her face. "Bitch, are you praying?"

"Hell yeah. I need guidance and a slew of angels to order my steps."

"Come on, girl."

We gained entrance to the mansion and walked inside. The place was packed and as suspected, there were half naked females everywhere. My first mind told me to find my husband and watch his ass like a hawk— I would keep my distance as long as his ass remembered he was married. Never in my life had I been insecure, but his cheating ways had damaged that. It always made me feel like I wasn't enough to satisfy him sexually.

At twenty-four, I was in top notch shape and pretty as hell. My hair was naturally long, and my pecan-tan skin was flawless. Yet, it wasn't enough for the man I had given my heart to.

Lexi tapped me on the arm, interrupting my thoughts. "The real party is by the pool. Let's go," she said, grabbing my hand.

We pushed through the crowd until we made it out back. The moment my sandals hit the pavement, my jaw hit the ground and shook it like an earthquake. Trampy females were participating in some sleezy game called *the cucumber challenge*. They were deep throating it with no problem. However, that wasn't the worst part. A few of them were laying on the table with their legs spread open, while the men rammed the stiff vegetable inside their vaginas.

Just as I was about to turn around and leave, I spotted Aaron. He had the audacity to be one of the men fucking a groupie with the cucumber. They were shouting and laughing loud, when they should've been embarrassed.

"I'm beating your brother's ass." Shoving my purse into Lexi's arm, I pushed my way through the crowd until I was standing beside him. "What the fuck you doin'?"

Aaron's eyes stretched open as wide as the bitch's pussy he was playing in. "Bae, what you doin' here?"

"No. What the fuck are you doing?"

"Nothing. I'm just having fun."

The girl sat up on the table and tried to pull Aaron closer to her. That's when I lost it and slammed my fist into her face.

She jumped off the table and we started fighting.

"Girl, she fighting your sister," I heard somebody say.

That didn't stop me from wrapping my hand around her hair, while upper cutting the bitch. Next thing I knew, someone had punched me in the back of the head, then I heard Lexi.

"Un-uh, bitch! It ain't going down like that!" She jumped on the girl's back and began punching her in the side of the face. The girl spun around in circles trying to throw Lexi to the ground, and the entire scene looked like something out of a circus. Aaron tried to break up the fight, but he got hit too, and a big-ass brawl broke out. The fight lasted a while before the players separated us.

Aaron's dumb ass had the nerve to try and grab my hand, but I snatched away and slapped him in the face, hard.

"Let's go. Now!" I screamed.

The three of us left the house; however, the fight wasn't over just yet. As soon as we made it by the road . . . *Bop! Bop!* I hit his ass with two haymakers. He tried to block them, but his reflexes were too slow, and my hands were too quick.

"You always embarrassing me. You don't give a fuck about this marriage."

"I wasn't doing shit. It ain't like I was fucking the bitch."

Lexi stood in between us. "Aaron, you were wrong and you know it. Daddy never did mommy like that."

"Fuck you, Aaron," I shouted, before storming off and dropping my keys. Bending down to pick them up, I felt a sharp pain shoot through my stomach.

"Foreign, are you okay?" Lexi rushed over to me. "You have blood on your pants."

My heart dropped to the pit of my stomach when I heard those words. Tears surfaced quickly and slid down my cheeks. When I stood up, Aaron was standing beside me. "Bae, are you okay?"

"No!" I screamed. "I'm pregnant, Aaron, and I'm sure I'm having a miscarriage right now. Thanks to you."

"Come on, I'll take you to the hospital." Aaron helped me inside the car and drove me to Memorial Hospital.

***

The hospital room was bitterly cold. My body shivered, as I snuggled underneath the thin blanket they provided. Aaron sat across from me with a dumbfounded look on his face. Disgust was the most fitting word to describe how I felt about him at that moment. Torment squeezed the life out of my heart. Here was another child that would never make it to see to the light of day. *Why did he have to be so selfish and inconsiderate?*

The previous week I had found out I was pregnant, but I had chosen not to bring it to his attention because I didn't want to jinx it. Truthfully, I was terrified at the thought of being unable to carry a child and give birth. *And guess what?* I was absolutely correct, and it was all because of Aaron and his triflin'-ass ways.

After being silent for a while, he finally parted his lying lips. "Foreign, I'm sorry. This is all my fault."

Now I felt like he was provoking me. A stronger feeling of hatred and annoyance added to my anger. The sight of his deceitful face made me want to vomit. Deep down I wanted to hurt him the same way he had continuously hurt me. It was hard to fight back the tears when you had been damaged beyond repair— remaining in the marriage was hard enough.

"You're right. It is your fault. If you would stop being the ultimate hoe, none of this would've happened."

He got up and casually walked towards me with his head hung low. Grabbing my hand, he attempted to place a kiss on my knuckles, but I pulled away.

"Don't touch me. I hate you for what you did to me."

"You don't mean that." His eyes were cloudy. "I love you and I'm sorry I hurt you."

"How many times have I heard that same empty-ass apology? You don't love me. You can't possibly love me. Your weak-ass apologies are as worthless as a penny with a hole in it." I hit the bed with my fist and swallowed the saliva that made its presence inside my mouth. "If you loved me, you wouldn't constantly do the shit you keep apologizing for."

"I'm trying. You have to believe me. I didn't consider what I was doing tonight as cheating."

Swiveling my head around to face him, I gave him the meanest and coldest stare. "Then what the fuck did you call it? How would you feel if I had my legs wide open while another man plunged a damn cucumber in and out me like it was a dick?"

"You wouldn't do no shit like that," he grumbled. "That ain't ladylike."

"Ladylike? You wasn't worried about that when you were doing it. Admit it. You love hoes. That's what you do."

Before Aaron could respond the door flew open and the female doctor walked in. "The labs came back and you are having a miscarriage. I'm going to discharge you and prescribe you something for the minor pain you may feel. If the blood clot doesn't pass within the next day or two, be sure to come back to the emergency room so we can conduct a D&C. A D&C is sometimes needed to clear the lining of the uterus after a miscarriage," she explained.

Choked up on the reality of it all, I nodded my head. "Okay."

"Do you have any questions for me?" she asked.

"No."

"I'm sorry for your loss."

"Thank you," I replied somberly.

When the doctor left the room, I climbed out of bed and got dressed. Using the jacket Aaron had given me, I wrapped it around my waist so no one would see the blood on the back of my pants. Once again he tried to help me, but the touch of his hands made me cringe. Biting down on my bottom lip, I closed my eyes slightly.

"Please, please don't touch me. And when we get home you can sleep in the guest bedroom. I don't want to be near you right now."

"Foreign, please. I just want to hold you."

I looked him directly in the eye. "Aaron, I'm this close to killing you," I said through clenched teeth. I held my index and pointer finger together as an indication of how much patience I had left for him. "So, if you don't want to end up residing in the nearest cemetery, my advice to you would be to stay out of my way." I turned my back on him and exited the hospital room with my head down.

Aaron strolled behind me in silence, like a lost puppy. I walked out of the emergency room and into the parking lot, feeling as though I was less than a woman.

Destiny Skai

CHAPTER 2
FOREIGN

When I woke up the following morning, the brightness of sunrays shone through my window causing me to squint. I sat up and rubbed my eyes. To my surprise, Lexi was sitting on the edge of my bed watching a rerun of Love and Hip Hop. She was so tuned in she didn't see me rise off the bed until I was standing on my feet.

"Hey, girl." She smiled. "Are you feeling better?"

This wasn't my first miscarriage, so of course she knew the routine. Check on me, laugh a little, and get back to the usual fuckery with her brother, nevertheless, I knew she was being sincere.

"Yeah. I'm alright. Tired of losing children that's about it."

Sensing my stress, she picked up the remote and turned the TV off. "Aaron is stupid and that's the one thing I'll never understand about him," she said, with her face scrunched up in a scowl. "He loves you but insists on doing dumb shit, but I know he doesn't want to lose you. It doesn't make any sense because our father didn't raise him to be a womanizer. He must've gotten that shit from Dog 101."

With less than a little pep in my step, I walked over to my closet to find me a fresh set of clothes. "Your brother loves being a hoe." I frowned. "He's so sure of himself he thinks I won't ever leave him. Aaron wants his cake at the beach with a side bitch to help him eat it. I'm not about to keep settling for his BS. I've put up with it long enough."

With her usual strut, Lexi made her way over to the side of the room I was on. She posted up against the wall outside of the closet. "Foreign, I know he's my twin and all, but you're my best friend. We've been family since high school, so I understand your pain more than anyone else. If he can't respect you and give the love you deserve, ditch his ass. You see the way I toy around with all his little friends, right? I do it because I know commitment ain't for me. My guts need all types of different shapes and sizes for my bad days. I don't need strings because strings create love. And from what I can see, love is something these niggas just don't live by anymore."

Smirking, I shook my head, "You mean *never* lived by, to be exact. I know one thing . . . This marriage is hanging by a thread. He's going to come home one night and it ain't gon' be shit here but a Dear John letter," I spat.

"Well, he's surely waiting for you downstairs. I told him you bought a gun last night, so he's down there shaking harder than a stripper on eggshells." Lexi laughed before walking out of my bedroom.

As I headed for the bathroom, I couldn't help but laugh myself. That bitch was crazy, but I was sure of one thing. No matter what problems her brother and I continued to go through, she was a diehard friend, and for that I loved her dearly. I would never let anything come in between that.

After jumping in the shower, I blow dried my hair, pulled it into a high bun and applied my makeup. Glancing at myself in the mirror, I couldn't help but smile. The woman staring back at me was still beautiful, no matter what I went through. Regardless of how selfish Aaron was to me, I knew I was worthy of being loved properly.

I grabbed my fitted Alexander McQueen dress, a gift Aaron had bought for me not too long ago. Being that I wasn't a fashion-type chick, I had let it catch a few dust bunnies in the closet— today, it didn't matter though. I felt horrible, and the only thing that was going to cheer me up was getting fresh and catching some fresh air with Lexi.

Heading downstairs, I made my way around the large living room until I ended up in the kitchen. Aaron was sitting at the table with Lexi. As soon as I crossed the threshold, his eyes landed straight on me.

"Hey, baby. Are you okay?" He rushed over to me as if it hadn't been just one day ago when he assaulted another bitch's pussy with an overgrown pickle. Then, he reached around me attempting to pull the chair out for me.

"I don't need any help, Aaron. It's okay." The nigga still followed me around to my seat like a fly on a ball of shit.

"I made you breakfast. You know I be wanting to throw down for you every chance I get. I thought we could eat together before I headed out to practice."

Looking down at the plate in front of me, I smirked. His bean-head ass knew I loved bacon, and especially with some crispy hash browns. Picking up a slice, I bit it while giving him a sour look.

"Listen, baby, I know we have our differences from time to time, but I'm truly sorry for my actions. I even told the guys I wasn't interested in anymore parties. From now on, I'm just gonna focus on whatever makes you happy. It seems like I haven't been doing that lately. You know I love you."

Without saying a word, I stared at him with a piece of hash brown between my fingers, hoping my eyes reflected the coldness I felt toward him. Trying to butter me up with his fake-ass apologies was definitely not about to cut it.

"Don't you get tired of running this same ole' tired game, Aaron? You've been at it for about three years now. Your time been up," I said, glancing at my wrist as if I was really wearing a watch.

"Come on, Foreign. You have to give me a chance, bae. I know shit be rough sometimes, but it gets better. You ain't got no faith in me no more."

"Nigga, what? You ain't got no faith in yourself. You the one who can't control your body parts and hands, and it's quite pathetic if you ask me. How you think I feel knowing my man slanging his lil' meat in all these infested-ass little monkeys?"

As usual, Aaron's facial expression looked as dumb as he probably felt. And Lexi's crazy ass didn't help the situation because all she did was sit in the corner laughing at him.

He sat down at the table next to me and looked into my eyes. "I'm not gonna let this petty stuff ruin us. You know I'm not gon' ever turn my back on you. And, baby, I know it's the actions that matter and not the gifts and apologies. . . . So let me prove my love to you by changing my actions."

He leaned in and kissed my lips as he stood to his feet. "I left the bank card inside your purse. You and Lexi can go out and have a little fun while I'm at practice. My treat. I promise after I'm done,

I'll head straight home and start on dinner for you. Hopefully, I'll see you when I get back."

Before Aaron could leave, Lexi stepped out in front of him. "Uh . . . You can pause on that 'cause mama and daddy want all of us to have dinner at their house tonight. I'm just the messenger." She smiled.

Taking a deep breath, Aaron froze and twisted his face up in a slight frown. I resisted the urge to laugh out loud, but a huge smile spread across my face as Lexi and I waited for his response.

"I guess I'll see y'all there then," he said, after a few moments of hesitation. Now we were going to see exactly how many lies he'd been running on his parents.

After he walked out Lexi joined me at the table. "You know it's about to be a war when my mama finds out what he's doing. Are you gonna blast him out or what?"

I pondered on the question for a second since I truly didn't like to put people in our business. However, Aaron's parents were the main source for his success.

They had been sure to place him in the best scouting camps, and they made sure his priorities with funds were intact. Not including the support they showed regarding his games. When he was still in high school, his father had donated a healthy check to the school for uniforms, trips and whatever else the principal needed assistance with. It was all to make sure that Aaron received the best— in his classes, and on the field. Even as of today the help from his parents was still paying off. He was about to become one of the highest paid players to be signed in the past five years.

"Nah. I'm not gonna say anything," I finally answered. "I know your parents mean everything to him, so I'ma see if he keeps it real and speaks the truth when the question presents itself."

"We all know how that's gonna go. How much did he say we could spend from the card he left you?" she asked, looking at me with a devious smile.

Laughing out loud, I already knew where her mind was. "Let's go find out."

The Price You Pay for Love

Rushing to grab my purse, we left the house and jumped straight into my upgraded Bentley. Maybe riding out for some fun would make him realize his apology meant nothing. It may even soften his hard-ass heart. *I sure won't be here to find out*, I thought, before smashing out of the driveway.

* * *

After hitting up every shoe and clothing store we could find, me and Lexi strolled through the massive mall looking at all the new trash high-end designers were coming out with. We spent nearly twenty grand off of Aaron's card, just on the humbug. Shit, I even gave a few things away to some people who just happened to be standing around. It made me feel better, and besides, money didn't mean shit to me. The sooner Aaron changed his mentality and truly understood that about me, the better off we'd be. Maybe then his thoughts would be sincere and from the heart, and not materialistic from his pockets.

Walking out to the car, Lexi ran to the driver side door. "I'm driving bitch. You ain't the only one who finna be looking all flashy in this Bentley. I'm about to post this on Instagram."

Glancing to my right, I happened to look at the billboard on the other side of the street. The words *Super Bowl Champs* were in big letters and Aaron's big-ass picture was staring at me like he was posing for a porn audition for all his little sluts. It fueled my anger even more.

After pulling out of the lot, we headed straight over to Aaron and Lexi's parent's house. It didn't take us long to get there. It was always a beautiful scene when entering their property. The exquisite home was one unique piece of a space to reside in. From the spacious balconies to the large swimming pool that aligned across their backyard. Not only was it a gorgeous sight to see, but the tennis court and full size basketball court made the mini mansion one of the most expensive homes on the block. And it damn sure wasn't off of Aaron's NFL money. These rich-ass people had enough money to sponsor athletes by the dozen.

"Girl, let's go see what the resolution gon' be for this war that's about to start." Lexi knew shit was about to get real.

It was unusual for his family to call us all over for dinner, outside of our regular day, so it had to be something up. All I knew was that I damn sure hadn't ran my mouth to anybody. As far as Lexi was concerned, whatever their reason for summoning us remained a mystery. When I spotted Aaron's car, I already knew he was probably in there juicing some sad-ass violin story to make them feel sorry for his triflin' ass.

We got out of the car and made our way inside. Of course, his ass was all buttered up underneath my mother-in-law like he was the baby of the family. Aaron knew how to get his way, but I also knew how to work my magic too.

"Foreign, how is my baby girl doing?" Aaron's father walked down the steps with his arms open towards me. He was always so kind and gave me everything a daughter-in-law could ask for. It was also my way of getting what I wanted.

"Oh, I'm okay, dad. Aaron is just being Aaron. I'm still trying to push and stand firm as a wife."

Holding my shoulders, he leaned back to look in my eyes. "What has he done? Talk to me."

Something told me to blast that ass out the water but I decided to keep my composure. "Some days are better than most but I know Aaron will talk to you if you ask him. I'm just really hungry." I lied with a straight face.

"Foreign, you know I requested your favorite, baby. I got us some of the best catered steaks and potatoes that'll melt right in your mouth." His mom smiled with joy.

"You know I'm always down for that." I smiled and placed a kiss on her cheek.

"Dang. You rarely eat my food, yet you can come eat the catering from my mom's restaurant," Aaron interjected.

Of course, I looked at his stupid ass like he was a frog on a lily pad in the Sahara Desert. He wanted to make conversation with me so bad it was killing him. He was nervous than a muthafucker and his eyes pleaded with me not to expose his recent affairs. I don't care how tough he *thought* he was, I knew he wasn't tough enough to wanna risk his mom and dad cutting his ass off. Not the major support team who felt that he was an all-out angel.

"Aaron, the last time you cooked for me was this morning when you cooked me breakfast. I thought you were cooking for the women at the afterparty for the Super Bowl game."

"That's different than cooking for my wife," he said, while simultaneously nudging my arm.

A devious smirk crept across my lips. Now he was the one strutting across the walk of shame. The nigga was trying his best to keep our recent drama on the hush.

Leaning inward, closer to my ear, he whispered, "Please, baby. Don't do this to me right now. I told you I'ma make it up to you, Foreign. Please."

"You should've thought about that before you started sharing your cock with the entire cheerleading squad, Mr. Cucumber."

I walked off, headed to the kitchen, and left his ass in the living room looking dumb as hell. Little did he know, I truly loved his punk-ass. I had always come to his rescue during the worst times ever and I would probably do the same this time. But, of course, I had to let him sweat for a while.

We all sat down at the kitchen table. Aaron came and took his place beside me to make it look good. The questionable look and raised brow on my father-in-law's face showed his suspicion that something was up between us. He continued to question if I was truly okay. My lying ass said I was fine.

"So, Mommy, are you going to ask Aaron what's been on his agenda lately? I know you rarely get to see him anymore." Lexi was trying to rib some shit up and I definitely wasn't about to stop her.

"Yes, you're right. We haven't had a chance to catch up lately," her mother said. "So what's been going on with my superstar? How are things at home?" she asked, turning her focus on Aaron. Following suit, everyone diverted their eyes over in his direction, as the silence fell over the dining room.

"Uhh . . . Yeah. I mean, things have been wonderful, Mama. We just pushing to be the best couple we can be. I'm even shooting for another large wedding to renew my vowels."

"Wonderful. Your father and I are here to help with anything you kids need. You know I can't let my babies fall short on anything, especially anything pertaining to a wedding."

Mugging his ass, I crossed my arms. This nigga really was filling his mama up with a fat juicy lie. The only thing he was renewing was a bitch pussy every other night. But it didn't surprise me 'cause his ass would say anything to cover himself. Regardless of how much he boasted about this renewal lie, I wasn't putting up with the deceit much longer and that was a promise.

CHAPTER 3
DOMESTIC

The custom twenty-two-inch Giovanni rims on my black Maserati cruised smoothly down Fletcher Avenue. Rick Ross' voice bumped hard through my Alpine speakers shouting, *"Where my money at, I need, I need, I need cash."* Bobbing my head to the hardcore beat, I eased into the Supreme Touch parking lot and slid in the empty space that read, *owner.*

Stepping out of the vehicle, I adjusted the Cartier frames on my face. Swiftly, I headed towards the entrance looking dapper in an Armani dress shirt, slacks and suede loafers. The Bulova Octava two-tone crystal watch on my wrist twinkled and glistened against the sun.

Two years ago, being a businessman had never been on my radar. Now, I was the proud owner of not one, but three upscale car washes, with the exception that one was a bikini wash. The clacking of my shoes caused one of my workers, Tony, to look up.

"What it do, boss? How you feelin' today?" Tony stood and squeezed the water from the rag he was holding.

"Blessed and highly favored. Busy day?"

"We had a midday rush, but we handled it all in a timely fashion."

"That's good to hear. You know I hate for my clients to be kept waiting for an extended amount of time. We don't need any complaints from disgruntled customers 'cause that's bad for business."

"Yeah, I know."

Glancing around, I didn't see my other three employees. "Where is everyone else?"

"They in the back getting more supplies."

"Bet. I'll be in the office if you need me."

"Cool." Tony got back to work, as I stepped inside the cool building.

Pulling my chair from underneath the desk, I flopped down onto the soft, mahogany leather and turned on my computer. Each car wash was booming, so I was looking into investing some of my funds into a profitable business or two. The subject was a bit foreign to me, but I was definitely going to do my research.

The time on the clock moved at a rabbit's pace but my workday would be coming to an end shortly. Coming and going as I pleased was one of the benefits of being the boss. Whether I showed up or not, money was being made. However, that wasn't the case because I always made sure to show my face. My businesses were my life, so I put my all into it. Besides, I didn't trust anybody with my money, so my presence was detrimental to the business.

A light tap on the door caught my attention. When I looked up, a ghost from my past was staring me hard in the face.

It had been months since I'd last seen her face, and even longer since we'd had any type of dealings with one another. See, Emilia worked for the Tampa Bay Police Department, as a detective. Two years back, I'd caught a case that could've landed me in prison for life with my priors. Without her, I wouldn't have been able to begin living like the king I've always been destined to be. For that, I was forever grateful.

"Mr. Demerius Payne." She smiled and entered the office.

"Emilia Flores. How are you?"

Emilia didn't wait for me to offer her a seat. She took it upon herself to sit down and get comfortable. "I'm good. How about you?"

Leaning back in my seat, I extended my arms to show my good fortune. "I can't complain. I'm my own boss, so that's major in my book."

"Mine too. I must admit I'm extremely proud of the way you stepped your game up. This is the man I knew you could be all along."

"You definitely had faith in a nigga. Even when I didn't have it in myself. I appreciate you for that."

"You're more than welcome." Emilia blushed hard causing her cheeks to turn blush-pink. Shorty was a Spanish chick I had crossed paths with when my life was tumbling down a two-hundred-foot cliff. When I needed her the most, she stepped in and saved the day like Superwoman.

"So, what do I owe the pleasure of this visit? I've known you long enough to know that when you appear, something is either going down or it's about to."

Emilia crossed her legs. Although she was wearing a pair of slacks, there was no hiding her womanly shape. The fabric gripped her thick thighs and childbirth-hips just right. Her dark brown, long hair was pulled back into a ponytail. The sparkle in her light-brown eyes confirmed my suspicions before she even opened her mouth. My hands had been clean for years, so I knew it wasn't anything I'd done that summoned her knocks on my door.

"Well, I stopped by because I need your help with a job. Of course, there's a pay day for you, so don't worry about that."

Grinning, I looked around my office. "Seriously, does it look like I'm hurting for money?"

"No. It doesn't look that way, but I was there for you when you needed me. So you owe me, and the risk is not a factor. You'll be safe at all times. I promise."

Based on our history, I knew she would never put me in a compromising situation. That wouldn't be a good idea on her behalf. As a man who stood on principles, I felt compelled to help her. When it was time to help me, she hadn't hesitated or batted one of those long lashes. Then, on the other hand, something was telling me to dismiss Emilia all together. My curiosity was getting the best of me, so I needed all the details of whatever plan Emilia had up her sleeve.

Just as I was about to open my mouth, my cell vibrated hard against the oak wood desk. Taking a hold of it, I opened up the text message from my son.

Young King: Hey dad. Mom has a man over here. Come quick.

Dad: I'm omw

Young King: Don't tell her I told you

Dad: I will handle it. Sit tight.

I closed my phone and sat it back down and proceeded to shut off my computer. The thought of Casey trying me with a nigga in the house made me so hot under the collar, I had to loosen the top button on my shirt. Without a doubt, the anger I felt inside was filled with energy I couldn't control. The scowl on my face caused Emilia to shift in her seat.

"Are you okay?" The sound of her voice was a tad bit shaky.

"No. I'm sorry, but I have an emergency to tend to."

"That's fine. I'll be in touch once I'm ready," Emilia said, as she rose to her feet. The tight slacks she wore were cutting deep into her pussy, exposing a fat-ass camel toe.

"Cool."

We left the room at the same time. By the time we'd made it outside, Tony had started washing her car.

"Tony, I have to hit a corner, but I'll be back soon."

"No problem. I got everything under control," he assured me.

Pleased with his answer, I dashed across the parking lot, hopped in my ride, and darted out into traffic at damn near sixty miles an hour.

***

The drive out to the suburban area in Carroll wood was merely twenty minutes. With my heavy foot, I was able to get the time down by driving like a bat out of hell.

Sliding up the driveway, I parked beside a blue Nissan Maxima and put my vehicle in park. Opening up the glovebox, I pulled out my gold Dessert Eagle.

"This bitch got me fucked up," I said aloud. By now, my anger had surpassed its boiling point.

After getting out of the car, I rushed towards the door like I had a fire blazing underneath my ass. Gaining access with my door key, I walked in and slammed the door to make my presence known. Just like my son had stated, his mammy was sitting on the sofa with her company. The second we locked eyes, fear covered her pupils like contact lenses and her shoulders slumped once she caught a glimpse of the cold steel grasped in my palm.

"Yeah, bitch. You busted."

At lightning speed, I darted across the room until I was up close and personal. The nigga sitting beside her was speechless. Casey stood up and tried to grab my arm.

"Domestic, please don't do this."

Casey didn't stand a chance at compromising with me, so she was wasting her breath. As we stood face to face, I grabbed the back of her head and wrapped her hair around my fist. Tugging on it, I growled in her face. "What the fuck you doin' with a nigga in my muthafuckin' house?"

Her eyes became saturated with water. "He's just a friend," she uttered softly.

The nigga who sat comfortably on my sofa stood up. "Aye, bruh, don't do her like that. All that ain't even necessary."

I pushed Casey onto the sofa and raised the hand that gripped the steel. "Sit'cho muthafuckin' ass down before you leave out in a body bag," I said with my piece aimed in his direction.

Obviously, *fool* wasn't in his vocabulary. With his hands up, he sat his punk-ass down and zipped his lips. Now that he was sitting and following orders, I turned my attention back to the bitch who betrayed me.

"I'm trying to figure out what made you feel comfortable enough to bring this busta-ass nigga to my house? And I don't want to hear shit about y'all being fake-ass friends."

"He just came to keep me company. I wasn't expecting you to show up here." Casey could say the dumbest shit at times and this time was no different.

Company? That couldn't be what this bitch just said, I thought. "Company," I repeated out loud to see if it sounded just as dumb when I said it. "You don't get to have company."

Casey was scared shitless, she positioned her knees in front of her and wrapped her arms around them in a protective position. It didn't matter what she did though. Unless she somehow became invisible in the next five minutes, she was definitely getting her ass kicked.

"Check this out my man." My focus was back on him. "I'm not gon' hold you accountable for your presence here today. But, if I catch you in here a second time, I won't be this nice. And, there *will* be consequences."

He nodded his head to let me know he understood.

"Before I let you go, let me fill you in on Casey's situation because I'm sure she didn't enlighten you. This house . . . belongs to me. I pay every bill in this muthafucka and do you know why?"

Scary dude's eyes were wide in the sockets. "Umm, because she doesn't work?"

"Exactly. So see you're not as dumb as you look. But didn't it dawn on you that there was no way she could pay for any of this shit?"

Scary dude shook his head. "I never thought about that. But from what she told me I thought she was single."

"Well, I'm here to drop some knowledge on you. You're correct about one thing, we're not together. However, if you want to date Casey, you need to find her another place to live."

My gun was still clutched in my hand, but my arm rested down at my side. "As long as I am taking care of her, she's not datin', fuckin' or suckin' nobody, but me. I own her until she's out of here. You understand that?"

"Got it, bro."

"Good. Last question, did y'all fuck?"

"No. I swear we didn't."

"You're free to go, but don't let me catch you over here again. Remember what I told you."

"I will," dude said before he got up, raced towards the door, and slammed it behind him.

Casey stared at me for a long time, but didn't bother to part her lips. So, I did it for her by slamming an open hand into her mouth. *Whap!* On contact her head snapped back and forth like a bobble head doll. When it stopped moving, I delivered a solid fist to her eye socket.

"Ahh," she shouted to the top of her lungs.

"What the fuck is wrong with you bringing another nigga into my house, around my son?"

40

"I'm sorry. Please don't hit me again." The sight of blood on her lip didn't faze me one bit. She deserved everything that was headed her way.

"Fuck you apologizing for? You should've never brought that nigga in my shit. Now you gon' pay."

Grabbing her by the arm, I pulled her towards me. Casey knew what time it was, so she tried to avoid it. "Domestic, please don't beat me. I promise I won't do it again."

"Get yo' ass up and go in the bedroom, and don't let me have to say it again."

She slid off the sofa slowly and stood to her feet. She made sure to take baby steps as she moved at a snail's pace. No sense of urgency whatsoever.

"All you doin' is prolonging this ass whoopin'. Speed up so we can get this shit over with."

Walking down the hall behind her, I stopped and peeked inside my son's room. "DP."

"Hey, Dad." DP walked towards me and hugged my neck.

"Wassup, Son." My junior was damn near as tall as I was. I was a tall six foot three inches, but he was only fourteen. "Did you eat?"

"Not yet. I was hoping you would take me out."

Passing him the keys, I held his hand firmly and told him, "You wreck it, you bought it."

"I won't wreck it, Dad." DP smiled, exposing the expensive set of gold train tracks in his mouth. "I'll be right back. You and mama want something?"

"I'm good. Bring your mama a can of soup back."

"Okay."

DP grabbed his wallet and ran out of the house. That was always his reaction whenever I allowed him to push the whip. It was materialistic, so I didn't mind letting him bend a few corners. Besides, I didn't want him to hear the screams coming from his mother while I was whooping her ass.

When I got to the bedroom, Casey was sitting on the bed dressed in only a bra and panty set, with her hands folded in her lap. She knew the routine. After closing the door behind me, I placed my gun on the dresser and unbuckled my shirt. Tossing it on the dresser, I loosened my belt buckle and freed it from the loops. I stood in front of her and using my left hand, I traced an invisible line on her cheek.

"You know what you did was disrespectful right?" Casey nodded her head up and down like a child being reprimanded. "So, why in the fuck would you try me like that? That shit don't make no sense to me. Then you sittin' in here with some peon-ass nigga."

"I'm so—" Before Casey would finish her sentence, her mouth caught the back of my hand, twice. *Whap! Whap!* The second time she screamed and covered her mouth with both hands.

Towering over her, I wrapped my hand around her neck and applied extreme pressure to her trachea. "As long as you muthàfuckin' live don't you ever bring another nigga to my residence. I'll kill yo' ass, bitch."

She tried to free herself from my grip, but she was too weak. The hold I had on her was too tight. After watching her struggle to breathe for about a minute, I freed her. Hungrily, she gasped for air, while rubbing the base of her neck. The belt was still in my hand, so I wacked her with it across her smooth, brown thighs. *Pop! Pop!*

"Oww!" Casey screamed while simultaneously rubbing her legs.

"Shut up! And you better not move," I shouted, while bringing the leather across her flesh several more times.

Pop! Pop! Pop! Pop! Pop! Pop!

"Domestic, please." Her screams were high pitched and filled with agony. She bolted to the opposite side of the bed to get away from me.

"Casey, get yo' ass over here now." My tone was low yet laced with malice.

Standing in the corner, she rocked from side to side, while rubbing her arms. "Nooo!" she whined.

"Don't make me come get you."

"Promise you won't hit me again."

"That depends on how fast you get over here."

"I'm begging you to stop. Please." Her tears fell from her eyes like a waterfall, dripping onto her breast. "Is this the type of man you want DP to be?"

Casey's words hit me dead in the chest. The belt slipped from my hand and hit the floor. Once I was disarmed, she strolled towards me slowly. Now standing in my face, I was forced to look at the dark ring that began to form around her eye. Breaking our staring contest, I looked away.

"You can't look at me, huh?" With extreme caution, she gently placed her hand on the bottom of my chin and swiveled my head in her direction. "This is the aftermath of what you did to me. I don't deserve this treatment from you."

That was the first time I was silent. There was nothing I could say to make her feel better nor could I make what I did go away. And even if I could, the fact remained, Casey had disrespected me.

"You made me do this to you," I said, because it was what I believed.

"How, for having company? I didn't fuck him. We're only friends." Casey wiped the tears from her eyes. "I don't understand you at all. You don't want me, but I can't date. You didn't want Demerius living in the hood, so you moved us to the suburbs. I did what was in the best interest of our child, but now I'm starting to think it was a mistake. All you want to do is watch my every move and make sure no one else can have me."

She was wrong. I did love her. Just not enough to be in a relationship with her. That part of us had ran its course. When she agreed to move in my house, she knew there would be stipulations, and her laying up with a nigga just wasn't happening. That thang between her legs was on reserve for me only.

"I'm sorry, but you know how to trigger me."

Placing my hand on the back of her head, Casey flinched. Her reaction made me feel a certain way even though it was all my fault. Gently, I placed my lips on top of hers and slid my tongue inside her mouth. As we kissed, I backed her up against the bed and laid her down. Love making was my way of apologizing and I planned on going a few rounds before I went home.

Destiny Skai

CHAPTER 4
FOREIGN

It had been a week since Aaron began spoiling me with his little gift spree. He'd been moving better than a prostitute on probation since Lexi and I had nearly exposed his dirty little secrets to my in-laws. The common dirty dog could please a woman with expensive little toys, but it took a real man to stand firm on his words and actions. For some reason I just couldn't trust anything he said anymore—no matter what the eyes may have perceived me to believe.

When he strolled through the threshold, Lexi and I were sitting in the living area watching the New Curve, 80-inch flat screen, mounted on the wall,

"Hey, baby. I got late practice tonight, so I'll be getting back around one."

"What type of practice lasts for six and a half hours?" I could already feel the lie about to escape his lips.

"You know I got an hour drive. Plus, me and the team was gonna pick up a few beers after we were through. Nothing major. A beer at the sports grill and I'll be heading straight home afterwards."

"What type of athletes wanna watch other athletes play a sport? You sure about that, or do you wanna pull a trivia card from the mystery box?" I was anticipating the next fiction-ass lie that was sure to come from his mouth.

Aaron grabbed me by my arms and pulled me in close for a hug. He snuggled his face against my neck. "Foreign, please don't get angry with me for no reason. We been doing great. What's the problem?"

"We been doing *okay* for a week. Not a decade. You'd lie to God even if He told your ass it was gonna be your last breath."

"That's some deep shit. Maury needs to hear this, or maybe Steve Wilkos," Lexi said, adding her two-cents. She was all ears as she sipped on some wine with a juicy-ass smile plastered across her face.

"Shut up, Alexis! You can't speak on nobody and this ain't got nothing to do with you anyway," Aaron said in a raised tone. "Don't you got a sex scheme to be plotting on right now?"

"Nope." Lexi smirked. "All of your teammates are about to go to practice according to you."

I could tell he was on the verge of getting angry. Lexi and I was on his bumper and he didn't have nothing to say. A hit dog was always bound to holler sooner or later.

"Don't yell at her. She just keeping it real. If you don't want your business out in the streets you shouldn't put it out there, Aaron." I got in his face so he could understand me clearly. "If I catch your ass in one more incident, I'm leaving for good."

The same smirk always crossed his face whenever he was about to reply with that same ole' bullshit line of his. I had heard it so much I mimicked every word that came out of his mouth. "Baby. I'm your husband. You gotta learn how to trust me. I'll make sure my ringer is on just in case you call." He headed for the door.

Sitting my ass back down, I eyed Lexi with a funny grin. "How many lies does it take for you to walk away?"

Finishing her wine, she shifted in her seat. "One. See, I'm not the oracle from the matrix. If I can't tell where my man's Slim Jim is going, then I don't need to be trying to build the Cosby family. Women are going global with the sloppy relationships and there's only one resolution."

True enough my bestie was past crazy, but I still decided to listen. Half the stuff that came out of her mouth was real spit. "And what's the resolution?"

"Give as you receive, baby girl. If a man can be whorish with every dirty butt that walks pass him, you should be able to sniff every stiff sausage that tingles your nose from a ten-mile radius."

Her comment made feel as though I would die from my own laughter. This bitch had my stomach turning circles. Truth be told, Lexi wasn't wrong at all. I just didn't think two wrongs made a right. I always felt like I was enough woman for any man, but apparently Aaron was addicted to ass. It was quite sad because my behind was beyond voluptuous. I had booty for days. Gorgeous was my middle name, so I didn't understand how I could be a second choice for the man who decided to put a ring on it.

"You right. It's hard for me to even think about cheating on Aaron though. I give my heart with every situation, and not to mention I'm nothing like him."

"Listen. Aaron is my family and I will never give up on my twin. But if you're wrong, you're wrong. Just because he's winning for the family doesn't justify him pulling his sleepover stunts. Imagine if the shoe was on the other foot. Do you think he could forgive you for letting some random big cock dude rearrange yo' walls?"

"Hell nah. His ass would probably try and commit murder for the first time." I grabbed the bottle off the table to fix me another glass of white Carlo Rossi.

"My point exactly. Relationships are easy. If he can't accept it, why dish it out? If you know he wouldn't do the same for you, why even try?"

The wheels in my brain started to twirl, as I began to ponder on the shit my girl was schooling me on. Without a shadow of a doubt, I wasn't able to respond. I was done stressing, so there wasn't a reason for me to spazz out with some big speech to influence myself to leave him. I just had to face the fact that my marriage might have been a mistake.

"Guess what, Lexi. My mind is already made up. One slip and I'm packing my shit to take that trip."

"I know his little teammate Calvin is a professional freak, and that nigga spits it to me like he would love to build a miniature football team inside my belly. Please! They probably got hoes twerkin' on them at practice right now," Lexi replied.

"How can I compete with that? A female who's willing to do anything for a small amount of attention." I shook my head from disbelief.

It didn't take long before the dumb-ass image was running through my brain. Glancing at my cell, it read 9:23 p.m. The atmosphere tonight had been a little too laid back. It was definitely the kind of night when a freaky-ass husband could sneak some fishy pussy and get away with it. Strapping on my Black Valentino heels, I grabbed my car keys.

"Where you 'bout to go?" Lexi questioned me with her head tilted to the side, curiously.

"I'm about to go see this long-ass football practice that he just pranced off too."

Rushing to pour another cup of wine, she slid her tiny feet in her sandals. "I know you don't think I'm about to just sit here and wait."

We had rushed out the front door and into the driveway when Lexi stopped me. "Don't take your car."

"Why?" I asked and stopped in my tracks.

"Because everybody in the damn arena knows you're the crazy wife who drives the Bentley."

Lexi had a point. I just wanted to get a little space where I could slide in to see if his story checked out. Sliding inside her Mercedes, we rolled out like Thelma and Louise.

Our city was one of a kind. It was the life. The city of sins and trickery. Finessing was a tradition and most people played their cards to their advantage.

I had been married for three years now and my luck with love was still scraping across the floor. It was sad, but I couldn't blame anyone but myself. I was really on my way to play another night of lady CSI, in order to see if my man was flexing with more deceit. Yes, I was crazy, but I had the right to be. A lot of bitches were scared to get down to the nitty gritty when it involved their spouse. Not me. I was a different breed. I would pop it off on your ass in the blink of an eye. It was just the way my people brought me up. There were two things I wasn't letting anybody try— my honor and my heart. You could slide with the extra shit.

Turning up the stereo, Lexi nudged my shoulder. "Ain't this a bitch girl? This my shit."

TLC's *Creep* pumped through her speakers. It was so weird because that was the way I was feeling at the time. I didn't know whether I was coming or going. Something told me to turn my ass around and just let things be, but of course I was hardheaded when it came to things like that.

It took us about forty minutes, even, to arrive at the arena where the football team practiced. The lot was packed, so it took another five minutes to find a parking space. It looked like a game was about to start out that bitch. The practice cover-up had to be the stupidest shit he'd ever pulled. It was obvious something else was going on, and it wasn't a bunch of sweaty men tossing around a football.

After we finally parked and headed towards the entrance, I spotted the slim Spanish chick, who was one of the female ticket operators. Even after I had told her over and over that my husband was the quarterback for the team, she still always tried to cut me a deal on the games. Eventually, she spotted us one day when we were exiting the arena. The girl acted as if she hadn't heard anything I'd ever told her about Aaron.

"Hey, girl. How are you?" she asked upon seeing me.

I spit out the dry gum I was chewing on and tossed it in the trash before responding. "I'm fine, sweetie. I don't wanna distract you from doing your job, but I have a quick question. Could you tell us where the fellas are practicing at?"

"The team?" Her brow shifted downwards. "There is no practice today. Everyone is at the new club that just opened, about a mile down the road. They say it's the new hype of the town. Everybody who's somebody will be there tonight."

Her reply caused me to swing my stupid expression around in Lexi's direction. "If you beat his ass tonight. I'm not gone say shit," she said, looking just as slow as I was.

"That's mandatory." Rage took over my body, as I stormed off back to the car.

This was like lie number six thousand. The nigga claimed to be handling business at practice, but he was really out sporting his face for a new club opening.

Lexi jerked her neck back and forth after we climbed back into her whip. "Today is the day you need to step up. He needs to give you a good explanation as to why he made up this bogus-ass excuse to play you to the left like a Beyoncé single."

"It don't even matter no more, Lexi. I swear if this man is doing anything out of pocket with a bitch. I'ma shank his ass like an actress in a Michael Myers movie. He's so immature and lying is a natural habit for his sick ways."

I was tired of being tried like a side piece. The opportunity had presented itself once again and I was ready to put my foot down. Even if it meant sleeping in my bed alone from now on.

Aaron . . .

Ever since I walked through the club about a cool hour ago, I had spotted more than fifty beautiful women who had shown up to tonight's new opening. The place was exquisite. From the lights to the furniture, down to the waitresses who were sliding across the floor, serving us drinks. The entire team was here tonight, and, of course, you know my face was the main attraction. There were over thirty women in my section, and I knew for a fact, twenty of them were hot in the pants for some action.

After arriving at the arena earlier, I headed to the men's locker room and changed into my Louis Vuitton two-piece suit. My loafers were crispy with a suede bottom where I could just breeze straight across the floor as if I were gliding.

"So, how you vibin' tonight, nigga?" Calvin, my close friend of three years asked me, while he grabbed on some lil' honey's ass. The nigga had on so much jewelry, he looked like a walking icebox. It was normal. I knew he lived for the wildlife. Foreign hated his ass, but what could I say? This was the first person who had actually rocked with me since becoming a part of the team.

"I'm vibin' good, bro. This definitely has to be the new spot. It's ducked off and we ain't gotta worry about no intruders plotting to rob our asses when it's time to leave."

Quickly ditching his little freak, Calvin came and took a seat next to me on the VIP sofa. I could tell he was about to say something crazy by the silly-ass expression he wore. "So how many of these lucky ladies sliding out to the hotel with the team?"

"Hotel? You never said anything about us hitting the telly. I gotta be back to the house around one."

Watching him break out in a fit of laughter, he slapped my shoulder. "That was a good one, Aaron. You need to try that comedy shit out, for real."

Waving his hand, he motioned two women to come over to the private section with the team. As expected, they didn't hesitate. One was a full course chocolate stallion with red hair. Her dress was hugging her ass so tight you would think she had that bitch laminated on. The other little breezy was a red slim bodied, but beautiful. Really, one of the most gorgeous women I'd seen since I arrived. I watched them both as they moved forward and took a seat next to me.

"Ladies, this is my brother. He's the quarterback of the team . . . the man that makes it all happen."

I guess the chocolate girl took his statement as her cue to make her move. As soon as the words left the crazy-ass nigga's mouth, shorty dug inside my pants and pulled my shit right out. Before I could deny her, the chick had me resting in between her lips. Luckily, the sofa was large enough to block the view of the other teammates who were sitting down with us. Otherwise, they would've been watching a true flick going down right in the mix of this club night.

I leaned back, and grabbed her head, while she maneuvered and handled her business. After a few seconds of slow, sloppy head my eyes closed. When I opened them bitches, it was to the scariest shit I had ever seen in my life. Foreign and my sister were walking through the club, as if they were heading straight to the VIP section.

Jumping up from the couch, I watched the girl stumble to catch her balance. I pushed her head so hard, she damn near caught whiplash.

"Where you goin', nigga?" Calvin asked, looking at me with a dumb expression.

Ignoring his ass, I made my way down the backside steps and smoothly blended in with the crowd. I couldn't help but to turn around after I got a good distance away from the team's section. I could see Foreign and my sister talking to Calvin. I could tell she was flippin' the script because her hand gestures were going crazy.

All I could hear was the Plies song that blasted through the pro speakers. At this point, it was pointless to even try and intervene because I wasn't supposed to be inside a damn club from the jump. It was gonna be the same results. Foreign would ask me why I was there. After that, she was gonna punch the fuck out of me. My only hope was to make it out of that bitch and get to my car before she spotted me.

Sliding towards the exit, Coach Williams slid directly in front of me. "Aaron, I wanna thank you for sponsoring this little event here for the team. This is wonderful. Not to mention all the sweet women walking around in here." He proceeded to stand in front of me, vibing to the beat, with a cup of Patron dangling in his hand.

"Oh. No problem, Coach. It's all a part of being with the team."

"Where you going? Let's hit the bar and grab a few more drinks. Practice isn't until Monday."

I glanced back and watched Calvin turn Foreign and my sister around. I knew it was time to bounce my ass up out of there. "Look, Coach, I'm not feeling too well. I'll catch you guys another time."

"Sure, Aaron. Tell the wife I said hello."

I ain't tryna tell her nothing right now, not in here, I thought. Especially since he just happened to be the one standing at the front door when she pushed her ass inside this club.

Leaving out the front door, I quickly strolled over to my whip. Hitting the auto start, I put that bitch in drive and smashed out of the parking lot. My phone started vibrating and I was quite sure it was Foreign. My only mission was to make it back to the crib before she did.

CHAPTER 5
LEXI

Antwan answered the door wearing a pair of boxer briefs and a thick gold chain. His golden frame and chiseled chest is what turned me on the most. He was skinning and grinning like I was a representative from Publisher's Clearing House, bringing his ass a check. All I had for him was a fat pussy to eat and beat. Pushing past him, I stepped inside the house. "What the fuck you grinnin' for?"

"Well damn. Hello to you too."

"Yeah. Yeah." I removed my trench coat and tossed it on the back of the white leather sofa. "I need a drink," I said, with my back facing him. When I turned to face him, he was right on my ass. Literally. It was like he was undressing me with his eyes.

"Damn!" He gripped my ass. "This the surprise you got for a nigga?"

"Yeah. You like it?"

"Hell yeah. This what you bought with the money I gave you?"

"Yeah." Antwan drooled, as he took in the view of the purple lace bra and panty set I picked up from Victoria's Secret.

"I knew you would." Placing my hand on his chest, I licked my lips. "Now fix me a drink so I can unwind."

"What's going on with you?"

"It's that damn Aaron."

Antwan grabbed my hand and escorted me to his wet bar. "Tell me all about it."

"It's nothing really. He's just a fuckin' lying-ass cheater and I don't understand why. He has the perfect woman at home and he steady fuckin' up."

"That's Aaron for you." He was nonchalant with his reply, as he fixed me a glass of white Remy.

Sitting down on the barstool, I took the glass from his hand and sipped my drink. "Y'all know what he be doing. You probably condone that shit too."

"Aaron is a grown-ass man. We can't make him do shit he don't wanna do."

"Yeah right. All y'all asses are hoes."

"Nah. Not me. So, stop comparing me to them niggas."

"Boy bye. You are a young, rich hoe."

Antwan sipped on his drink as he approached me. Standing in front of me, he pushed my legs open so he could post up between them. "Just because I'm young doesn't make me a hoe. Have you ever seen a bunch of bitches over here?"

"Nope," I replied, sucking my teeth, "but I never popped up on you either."

"How many parties have I had here?"

"A few."

"And how many times have you spent the night here?"

"A lot. Why? What's your point?" He knew how to aggravate my soul. That was for damn sure.

"That should tell you something about me. I'm not a hoe. I don't bring bitches to my house because I don't trust these hoes. And you've never seen another female at my place. I'm trying to fuck with you, but you be tripping."

Taking another sip, I sat the glass down on the counter. "It's not that. I'm trying to avoid being involved with someone like my brother. I don't wanna have to kill you."

"Listen, I ain't shit like your brother. I don't know what that nigga problem is. To me, it just seems like he wasn't ready to get married and now he draggin' your friend."

There were no lies detected, but he knew more than he was telling me. "Let me ask you a question."

"What?" His brow slanted downward. Confusion was plastered on his face like Maybelline foundation.

"Like, does it ever cross anyone's mind to tell him what he's doing is wrong? Or do y'all *not* care?"

"It's not my place to say anything to him. I'm not married to Aaron and who's to say he'll listen."

"You have more influence than you know. Dudes listen to their homies before they listen to their woman."

"Bullshit." He chuckled and put the glass back to his full, pink lips. "I ain't listening to nan muthafucka who don't pay my bills."

Cutting my eyes at him, I sucked my teeth. "You'll listen to me."

"Maybe."

"Would you tell me if Aaron was fuckin' up?"

"Nah. I'm staying out of that and you should too. We have our own shit going on and getting into marital affairs ain't one of them." Antwan caressed my thigh while looking into my brown eyes. "I mean, unless you trying to let me lock you down."

"Nope! Not happening."

"Damn, you hard on a nigga. You better lock me down before it's too late. Don't miss out on your blessing."

"Yeah, whatever. You won't have me around here looking stupid and fighting off random-ass groupies."

Lifting my glass, I downed the remainder of my drink and sat it back down. With my hands planted firmly on his waist, I pulled him closer to me. Our lips connected, as we engaged in a deep, sensual lip lock. Antwan had pussy pink lips. They were soft and I loved the way they tasted. A true prize. Those vacuum lips could suck an egg from a bitch's fallopian tubes.

The liquor I consumed earlier, on top of what I just drank, had me aroused. My hands took a slow drive down south, inside his boxers, until I came in contact with his semi-stiff, warm rod. Stroking it slowly, I placed tender kisses on his ripped midsection. He pushed his boxers down past his thighs, then pulled my panties to the side. Eager to please me, he moved my hands and guided himself inside of my sacred place. That first push was life.

"Shiitt!" Closing my eyes, I wrapped my legs around his waist, all while keeping a death grip on the counter. The last thing I wanted to feel was my ass crashing against the ceramic tile.

Antwan was packing nine inches and he worked that muthafucker like a professional porn star. It was something about them ninety babies. Those young niggas would break a bitch back. It had to be the milk they drank as babies.

Before a bitch could let another moan out, he dipped inside my guts like a gynecologist. I couldn't help but to watch, as he slid back and forth. I was so wet, it actually felt like a pool was falling out of me. "Slow yo' young ass down!" I was scratching the nigga back like a deranged tiger.

"Hold my neck," he whispered into my ear.

Of course, I obliged. The little cock diesel he-man raised my ass off the barstool and held me in the air as I watched the nigga piece pumping in and out of me. It was deep. I could hear my ears popping as if I were dropping off the freefall at Six Flags. My pussy was speaking in four different languages and he was my tutor.

"You feel me in there?" he asked, while biting my bottom lip.

"Yesss!" My words were his fuel. He turned into a jack rabbit instantly. His rod thrusted inside of me forcefully. My head was leaning backwards, feeling that rough pleasure, as I felt my first orgasm spilling out of me.

"Please, slow down!" I was panting like a fat bitch trying to swallow a piece of chocolate cake.

Antwan's hands were palmed around my ass cheeks beating the kitty unmercifully. It was mesmerizing. It hadn't even been five more minutes in when the feel of my second nut began to build up— that real feeling like I was losing my breath. This nigga was truly my young porn man.

Holding the bottom of my back, he moved through his hallway until we ended up in a large bedroom. I could still feel his manhood swirling around in me with every step he took. Whatever smart-ass comments I had made before I walked through his bedroom door, I knew I was about to eat that shit."

My eyes were trained on him as he laid me down. He stood over me stroking his piece. His shit was glistening with my juices and I knew his ass was nasty when he wiped that shit and stuck his fingers in my mouth. Like a heartbeat, my pussy began to pulsate off that shit.

"Why won't you let me lock you down?" His voice was thick, but sensitive at the same time.

"Because I'm not into being played or gamed like I'm one of the opponents on the football field. Just fuck me, Antwan." I continued to rub on my juicy kitty lips, as he stared with a look of arrogance.

"You continue to disobey me when I give you so much leeway." Antwan's statement led to him flipping me on all fours. Stroking his erection back to mean mode, he plunged back into my soft spot. All I could was gasp.

"Fuckk!" Gripping my throat, my boytoy whispered in my ear: "This my pussy, and you ain't got no choice but to be with me." His strokes grew longer and harder. My ass was sounding off the way he pumped in me from the back. It was a bliss of euphoria. A drug that was like no other. He was definitely trying to make me fall in love. I knew for a fact if I spent the night with his rough ass, I was probably gonna be hit with cupid's arrow by morning.

Foreign...

Pulling back into the driveway of my home, I spotted Aaron's car sitting in the garage. My rage instantly turned back up because I was certain I was about to kill his ass. Practice clearly hadn't been on his agenda if the entire squad was partying inside a new hoe house in Tampa.

Climbing out of Lexi's car, I silently closed the door and headed inside the crib. I couldn't see any lights on in the living room and I knew for a fact I hadn't cut them off before I'd left. His ass wasn't sleep and if he was, I was about to wake him and the entire goddamn neighborhood up.

After letting myself in, I walked upstairs and barged into the room. The flat screen was on, but I could hear the water running inside the bathroom. Moving closer to the steam that filled my eyes, I stepped in and snatched the shower curtain back. Aaron's ass looked like he seen a poltergeist.

"Where the fuck you been, Aaron?"

"Baby, what the fuck! Why would you scare the fuck out of me like that? I didn't even know you were back."

"I ain't scared yo' ass *yet*. How was practice?" I folded my arms across my chest.

"Fo-Foreign. Just, cal-calm down, baby." Judging by the way he stuttered, I could tell he'd forgotten to practice his fuckin' lie too. "I went to practice, but when I got there everybody was heading out to do some other shit. Even coach. I already knew whatever they had going on wasn't gonna sit well with you, so I just grabbed me a little chill time in at the bar."

"What fucking bar, Aaron? The nearest thing to us is a country-ass hillbilly joint. You damn sure wasn't listening to Tim McGraw while having a beer."

Looking down at the floor where his little expensive suit sat folded up in the corner, I frowned. "Where did this come from? It damn sure ain't what you left the house in?" Ignoring me, he continued to bathe as if I wasn't standing there. "I know you fuckin' hear me, Aaron?"

"Baby, calm down. Can you please just calm down and come enjoy this shower with me. Please."

This nigga had some nerve. The only reason I couldn't kill him was because I didn't have my proof. I knew something was fishy about his fake-ass story.

Storming out of the bathroom, I made my way downstairs and sat at the kitchen table. I don't know what came over me, but I couldn't keep back the salty tears that began to run rapidly down my cheeks. How could anyone ever be with a person who didn't have the capability of being a true companion? It was always something when it came down to him giving an explanation. One lie after another. A woman over and over. I had to fix me a drink in order to calm my nerves because I was on the verge of a real breakdown.

Just as I began to calm myself, Aaron strolled through the kitchen as if he hadn't done shit. With that same dumb-ass expression he wore whenever he'd been caught in a lie.

"Baby, are you okay?"

"No. I'm not okay, Aaron. I'm not happy. Not anymore." My glass of Henny was still cold, and it had me feeling like I was sipping a truth serum instead of liquor.

"What do you mean you're not happy? I thought we were great. We've been bonding more than ever, Foreign." By now, he'd taken it upon himself to have a seat next to me.

"Listen. You been drinking and I don't wanna make you feel uncomfortable with this conversation, but don't you think you're over exaggerating, just a little?"

Sitting my cup down, I sucked my teeth. "You're the exaggerator, Aaron. You married me and you didn't keep up your end of this fuckin' contract. You're a lying bastard and I'm tired of it. Do you hear me?" I stressed, while pushing a finger into his chest.

"Baby, I know I may not be perfect, but I love you. Besides my family, there is nothing in this world I cherish more than you. You and my career come before my own life. You have to stop being so damn selfish and care about somebody else's feelings for a change. Regardless of how you may feel, I provide. I give you everything you want. Is this the way you always have to repay me?"

Hearing his stupid-ass comment, caused my face to ball up instantly. "You dumb-ass dog. You're the reason this is happening. You destroyed your own marriage. I've done nothing but show loyalty. I gave you my love and you spit it back on the floor, as if it was a dried out piece of gum. You never fuck me unless you see something sexual on the TV. This isn't a marriage, Aaron. It's a friendship with benefits. You think I can be pleased by your gifts and money. Like I can be bought. That isn't what I want."

Standing to his feet, Aaron began to pace around like he was contemplating the shit out of everything that dripped from my lips. I was already prepared. Tonight, one of us was about to get that ass beat, and since I wasn't receiving any dick, it couldn't have been me on that list.

"Foreign, I'm starting to feel disrespected as your husband. You don't trust me. It seems like the love we once shared isn't connecting anymore. What are we supposed to do about fixing this?

I love you, and nothing will ever stop me from doing that. Just tell me what you want?"

"I want a divorce, Aaron."

After hearing my response, his facial expression quickly grew into a frown. "A divorce! What the hell are you talking about? We're not getting a divorce, Foreign. I love you."

"You asked and I told you. Simple."

Leaning down closer to my face, he clenched his jaws like a Pitbull. "I don't give a fuck how you feel. Divorce is out of the question. You better sit yo' ass down here and drink on some more of that shit, girl. If you think you leaving me, you got another thing coming. And, have yo' ass upstairs in the next thirty minutes. I'm about to go and lay down. I advise you to get yourself straight before you come up. I want some pussy and I'm not waiting all night."

Aaron kissed me on my cheek after acting like he'd just put the pressure on me. I wanted to hit his ass in the back of the head with the saltshaker that sat on the table. Even though I hated his actions, there was no doubt I loved his ass, but my heart was telling me to leave. Yet, my dumb ass always fell for the same thing.

Turning off the kitchen light, I decided to head upstairs to see how the rest of my night was about to end.

CHAPTER 6
DOMESTIC

A few days had passed since Emilia did a pop up at my place of business, requesting my help. After giving it some thought, I hit her up to see what it consisted of. So, today I was meeting up with her for lunch to discuss the details. The Waffle House was her choice, so I obliged. It wasn't my go-to place, but there was something about the small dirty restaurants. As crazy as it sounds, they always had the best food hands-down.

Stepping inside the small diner with a manila envelope clutched tightly in my hand, I took a glimpse to the right of me. Emilia was sitting in the corner with a young guy. Casually, I strolled in their direction and took a seat beside her, while greeting them both.

"Good afternoon. I'm glad you could join us." She flashed a wide, bright smile.

"What type of man would I be if I didn't show up?" I answered, while sliding the envelope towards him. "Twenty thousand as promised."

Keith took a quick look inside the enveloped and tucked it on the inside of his jacket. "Thanks for looking out over the years and keeping your word in the end."

"No doubt. I appreciate you coming through for me. Without you, I'd be locked away in a six-by-nine, doing life, as we speak."

"Those two years were a muthafucker, but it was worth it in the end. I picked up a trade and I got my mind right."

"Well, that money is your start-up. Find you a place, buy a car and save the rest. None of that splurging and shit."

"Shiiid, I'm trying to run up a check. I heard you the man on these streets." Keith grinned and stroked the peach fuzz on his chin.

"I'm a businessman. That's it."

"I feel that."

Fresh in my mind like yesterday's events, I reflected on our history. Two years ago, Keith was a poor kid on the streets, headed to juvenile for twenty-one days. Meanwhile, I was locked up on a robbery charge— one of many on my record. Having been a repeat offender since being a teenager, I knew I was going up shit creek with no paddle. As fate would have it, Emilia showed up in the nick of time. Back then, she was the detective on my case and told me she could help me. My mind was all over the place. When she approached me alone in the county jail, no one couldn't tell me the shit wasn't a setup. Emilia's words replayed in my mind, *"In order for me to help you, you have to help someone else. If you want to walk out of here and see the light, you'll do it."*

Come to find out, her word was solid. All I had to do was take care of Keith during his incarceration and pay him twenty thousand dollars after he completed his two year bid. Keith was a juvenile, so he took the charge for me and I walked. Emilia helped him get a two year plea deal with the help of a close friend, who just so happened to be a judge. None of that shit was free. It all came with a price. Upon my release, I had given Emilia ten thousand dollars, but my freedom was worth every dollar spent.

Folding my hands and placing them on the table, I cleared my throat. "Now that you're out what are your plans? Will you be looking for a job?"

Keith appeared to be a little uneasy. His eye contact wasn't great and the way he constantly fidgeted in his seat made me feel as if he was lying about something. One of my strongest traits were spotting a bullshitter from a thousand mile radius.

"I mean, yeah. That's the plan. All I need is a set of wheels to get around to find work. That's the main thang."

"Well, there are tons of places that are willing to hire felons. All you have to do is get out and look."

Emilia nodded in my direction. "For instance, you."

Right hand to the sky I wanted to check her. Regardless of what may have sounded like a good idea in her brain, she was overstepping her boundaries. The fact of the matter was I didn't owe him anything else. I held my end of the bargain and now it was over. We didn't have an established friendship, so I didn't feel the need to offer anything further. Besides, I didn't believe hiring him would be a good idea.

"I'm actually fully staffed right now, so I don't have any room for new employees. If something comes up, I'll let you know." I lied.

"Thanks man. I appreciate that. Hopefully, it won't take long for me to find work."

The waiter walked over to take their orders. Emilia glanced at me. "Order what you want. I'm paying."

"Thanks, but I'm good. I have to get back to work."

"I'll walk you out."

"Cool. Take it easy, bro." After dapping him up, I stepped away with Emilia on my trail. We stopped beside my car and locked eyes. Clearly, something was on her mind besides business. "Why you keep looking at me like that? Something on your mind?"

"Who's the woman in your life now?"

And there it was. In the back of my mind I knew that was her main concern. "Nobody right now. I'm focused on business."

"I don't believe you."

Now I was offended. "Since when have you known me to be a liar?" Stroking my chin, I chuckled. "Oh, I get it."

"Get what?"

"I haven't pushed up on you, so you assume it's because I have a woman."

"See, you know exactly what I'm talking about."

"Emilia, I haven't seen you in almost a year. Then you pop up out the blue and you think the first thing on my mind is sex. I'm more interested in what you got going on. You didn't grace me with your presence just because you wanted some dick."

"You're correct, but I already told you I have a job for you."

"But yet and still you haven't filled me in on what you want me to do. That's what I'm waiting on."

"Unlock your doors so we can talk inside." Emilia walked to the passenger side, got in, and sat down.

Taking my seat on the driver's side, I brought the car to life. Leaning over to where she was seated, I unfastened the buttons on her shirt. Emilia's eyes were struck with seduction. Opening her shirt, I glanced at her full breasts before I sat back in my seat.

"Really?"

"No offense, but you popped up out the blue and it ain't because you missed me."

"You think I'm wearing a wire?"

"I just needed to be sure. Now fill me in on this plan of yours."

For the next twenty minutes I listened to a plan that was supposedly fool proof. The entire time she talked, I scratched my head and even gave her the side eye a few times. It amazed me. The lengths women would go to seek and destroy a man due to a broken heart was unbelievable. The tongue was lethal, but sex was a powerful weapon, and deadly if it wasn't used properly.

She took a photo from her pocket and handed it to me. "Do you think you can pull this off?"

Staring at the picture, I nodded my head. There wasn't a shadow of a doubt I couldn't do it. My mind just couldn't wrap around the fact that she was actually going through with such a foolish plan. Under any other circumstances I would've said no, but I was curious to see how it would play out. And even more curious about the woman I was staring at.

"Yeah, I got you. Just make sure you come through with my money."

"Oh, I most certainly will. Thanks. I'll be in touch."

"No problem."

When Emilia got out the car, I folded the picture and placed it inside my wallet. Operation crazy-bitch was in full effect.

"And she wonders why I don't fuck with her," I mumbled. Chuckling, I shook my head and blasted Rick Ross, as I pulled out of the parking lot. Once I did this *one* job for her, the bitch could cancel Christmas, going forward. Emilia had one favor from me and she had just utilized it.

Casey . . .

Pulling into the driveway, I parked behind the blue Maxima and got out. As I walked up on the porch I was greeted by Craig and Tim.

"What's up, sis? Everything good with you?"

"Hey y'all. Yeah, I'm good."

Craig nodded toward the front door and continued twisting up the blunt in his hands. "That nigga in the house."

"Thanks."

Crossing the threshold, I went straight to the back and opened the bedroom door. Shawn was lying across the bed playing the Xbox. When we made eye contact, he tossed the remote and sat up.

"Today was your last day not to call me. Next time I don't hear from you I'ma pop up over there with my brothers."

Removing my shades, I sat them on the dresser, then sat down on the queen size bed. "I know. That's why I'm here."

Shawn looked at me sideways. Although the initial swelling had gone down, it was obvious his focus was on my bruised eye. "That lame-ass nigga still doin' hoe shit, huh?"

"No. He hasn't touched me since the last incident." Feeling somewhat foolish by my answer, I folded my hands, allowing them to rest in my lap. "Did you tell your brothers what happened?" I asked, as I played with my fingertips.

"Should I?" he questioned.

"No. I don't want to start anything. I'll just come here to see you to keep the peace. Especially since it's the only way to prevent an unnecessary war from popping off."

"You sure?"

"Yes."

"You know my brothers don't give a fuck. They'll shut all that shit down."

"I know, and that's what I want to avoid. At the end of the day, that's still Demerius' dad."

Shawn shook his head, then grabbed a hold of my hand. "I get what you sayin', but you can't let that nigga treat you like that. I'm not like my brothers, but if I tell them what he did they'll handle that shit. You know I care about you."

"I know and I truly appreciate your friendship. You're like a breath of fresh air when I need to get away."

"This is what you can have permanently, but you don't want a stable relationship. You want a crazy-ass nigga. I know I don't have his type of money, but I can still take care of you and Demerius. We can move away. My family has an empty house in Tennessee and a legit business. We can go there and start over. All you have to do is say the word."

True enough, Domestic and I weren't together, but I still had respect for him. I knew Shawn liked me, but I had never crossed that line due to the arrangement I had with my son's father. Deep down, I still loved Domestic. Yeah, he had a temper, but there was nothing he wouldn't do when it came to taking care of his woman or his household. There were things in his closet that needed cleaning, but we all had hidden secrets.

Shawn's words were so sincere. He leaned in to kiss me, but I tensed up and pulled away. I reacted as though I was still in a full blown relationship. It was like I was afraid Domestic would smell the deception on my breath. The control he had over my life was insane and I had allowed it to happen.

"What's wrong?" he frowned.

"It just doesn't feel right."

"Why not? It ain't like you cheatin' or nothin'. You already told me the nigga don't want you. Stop depriving yourself and being faithful to a man who don't give a fuck about you."

The second those words left his lips I became embarrassed and defensive. "It's not like that."

"No problem. I'll fall back," he replied, as he scooted back holding his hands up in surrender mode. Don't miss out on your blessing. I'm what you need."

"I just need time to figure some things out."

"Even though there's nothing to figure out, I'ma give you your space. But don't expect me to wait too long though."

Shawn made me feel like the biggest dummy ever. Everything he'd said was valid, but I was so blinded by the way Domestic used to treat me, rather than opening my eyes to the way he treated me now.

The Price You Pay for Love

In the back of my mind, I knew I should've taken what he'd said into consideration. Truth be told, a part of me wanted to wait and see if things would get better between Domestic and I, to see if we could be a family again. Until then, I was holding on to my friendship with Shawn. He was the one person I knew who had my best interest at heart and would never steer me wrong. He sympathized with my situation, although he didn't understand it. Nor did he judge me, and I loved him for that. Shawn was that one friend every female needed.

CHAPTER 7
AARON

I woke up to the sound of my iPhone 10 buzzing off the damn meter. Rolling over, I noticed Foreign wasn't next to me. I wasn't the least bit surprised. Lately, she'd had an attitude that would make the humblest man go crazy. Knowing her, she was probably downstairs waiting on me to come down so she could argue some more. Truth be told, I couldn't fault her. But life could be hard sometimes. Relationships to be exact. They were a part of life and we only had one life to live.

Sliding the green icon on the screen, I placed it to my ear. "Yo."

"Nigga, what the hell are you still doing sleep at 12:30 in the damn afternoon. Are you sick?" There was deafening music playing in his background. "No, I'm not sick. I just let time get past me a little. Why the fuck is yo' spot so loud? It sounds like a fuckin' carnival over there."

"It's not a carnival unless you're here baby boy. You the quarterback. We got some people over here looking for you."

"What are you talking about, man?" I sat up and wiped my eyes. "Did you forget what today is?"

Checking out the date on my cell, I smiled. "Happy birthday my dude. It totally slipped my mind. What you got planned for today?"

"I'm throwing the best party of the century. It's been on and poppin' since last night. I've been blowing your phone up since this morning. I got two sweethearts here who've been dying to meet you."

I already knew where this conversation was leading, so I quickly headed for the bathroom. Dealing with Foreign, was like having an earpiece that could hear all the way from Saudi Arabia. Turning on the shower to drown out my convo, I sat on the toilet. "Who's over there?"

"Nah, nigga. This ain't jeopardy and I damn sure ain't Mr. 21 questions. You need to make yo' way over here and find out for yourself. The whole team is damn near over here."

Thinking about his proposition, I paced around the huge bathroom. Today was really a time to relax with the family and catch up on a few things I had gotten sidetracked on. The last incident was so critical I thought I would never hear the end of that shit. Since the altercations always made it impossible to deal with, I was literally treading softly regarding my habits and problems.

"Get rid of at least half of the team and I'll pull up. I can't be around too many people doing no dirt. I be feeling like all the damn eyes in America watching me."

"All you gotta do is tell me you on the way and I'll leave you be. Speak now or forever hold your peace."

Of course, I didn't want to turn down a free meal with the women. It would be good to party and break out of the cycle of being miserable in the walls of my own home.

"I'll be there in thirty minutes," I finally said, without further hesitation.

"Ladies, he's on the way. The leader of the wolf pack is on the way." The nigga was screaming in my ear like he was promoting an upcoming game. All I could do was smile and hang up.

Jumping in the shower for a quick ten minutes, I found some quick street gear before grabbing my car keys off the dresser. Heading downstairs, I spotted Foreign lying on the couch inside of our grand living room. Moving towards her, I leaned down and placed a kiss on her right cheek. Rolling over, she stared up into my eyes. "Where are you going?"

"I'm just heading out to meet up with Antwan. We're shopping for new clothes today. The new photo shoot for *Sports Illustrated* is in two weeks and we need to be prepared. Why didn't you come get in the bed with me?" Although the answer was a known fact, I still asked to see where her mind was at the time.

Taking a deep breath, she exhaled. "Because I was thinking. I'm trying to mash a lot of things inside of my head, Aaron. Our problems. Your issues. All I want is happiness. I've never seen us so divided. Sometimes I ask myself am I a great wife."

As she spoke, I couldn't help but notice her hand moving nervously. It was something she did often when she was mad or wanted to talk. And of course, swinging on me was also in that category.

Her smooth thighs were sitting so perfectly in the Chanel pajama shorts I'd bought for her a while back. The way she gazed at me caused my manhood to slightly rise. She knew that shit was hard for me to resist.

Getting on my knees, I positioned myself directly in front of her. "You know I love you right?"

Her face frowned up before she folded her arms. "Do you really mean that? Or are you just saying it just to make me feel better?"

Rubbing her bare legs, I began to place light kisses on them. The way she squirmed told me know she liked it. She let out a light moan before trying to push my head away. "Stop, Aaron. I'm serious right now."

"I'm serious too, baby. Now shut up." Before she even knew it, I had her legs folded up in the air with my lips purring against her pretty pussy. I literally stuck my nose in it before giving her a slippery stick and slide with my tongue.

"Aaronnn!" By the time she moaned my name, I had my entire mouth around her clit.

There was a light taste of her strawberry Olay body wash. It actually enticed me even more. Placing her hand on the back of my head, I slid from top to the bottom with my mouth game. Every time I glanced up at her, Foreign would close her eyes in satisfaction. Somehow, I knew this would definitely get me out of the doghouse from the bullshit I had been doing. No, I wasn't the perfect husband, but I was only human.

Foreign's pussy began to flush out her orgasm, wetting up my lips, and I wasted no time lapping her juices up, in a matter of seconds. "Ahhh!" Her mouth hung open, as if it were my turn to receive the oral session.

Pulling down my pants, I released my stiff piece. Sitting up, she smiled before grabbing it with her right hand. Spitting on it, she stood up with a huge smile and whispered to me.

"Go rub that in and have a nice pull session with your hand, baby. It'll feel better than my dry ole mouth."

That shit made me go limp instantly. I thought it was a joke until I watched her head up the stairs. "Foreign! Stop playing with me and come back here."

"Bye, Aaron. When you start showing me you love me every day and not just half of the week, you can have what's yours. I'm tired of being a damn wife for three hours out the day."

"What the hell are you talking about? We already spoke on this, Foreign."

"No, you spoke on it and I listened. You haven't showed me any proof that you're trying to keep this marriage, besides offering me gifts. Throwing a little money in my face like a stripper doesn't make me feel better. So, what's next?"

She was leaning on the rail like an answer would fall from my mouth at that exact moment. "You act like I'm not trying to fix this fake-ass beef with us. Your whack-ass attitude is only pulling us further apart. You don't care whether I try or not because you're too stuck in your own damn feelings. Can I get a little credit?"

I don't know what the hell I said wrong because before I could get another word out, I felt something glide pass my head like a bullet. Luckily, I was quick enough to dodge it. If not, my ass would've been heading to the E.R instead of a damn house party.

"Stupid-ass boy. You hurt me. If you wouldn't have stuck your nasty little dick in every girl you ran across, I wouldn't be complaining."

As she shouted obscenities, another small ornament from our hallway table came flying towards me again. "Stop throwing shit at me! What the hell is your problem? How can you expect to fix this shit if you always find something to beef about? Let's just talk like we're grown please!"

For some reason, I didn't know how I found myself yelling and having to play dodgeball after I came and offered a great plate of head personally delivered. I was starting to face the fact that Foreign was just scarred since the first incident of me cheating. Regardless whether I were to ever deal with another woman or not, she would feel that way until we were six hundred and forty three.

The Price You Pay for Love

"I want a divorce, Aaron. I don't see you being sincere about us, about this marriage. I love you and you take that for granted. Fuckin' other bitches is just your way of telling me I'm no good."

From the looks of her demonic frown, I could see that any more words would surely make things deeper than the six foot grave I already rested in. Turning for the door, I walked out of my home and jumped inside the new Benz truck I had purchased a few days prior.

I wanted to turn back around and try to resolve things before leaving on a bad note. However, I couldn't face the fact that what she said was true— I was a sex addict. Yet, and still, that didn't mean she should forget all the things I'd done sincerely, and from the bottom of my heart. I knew one thing for damn sure: if I couldn't find peace in my own home, I was gonna go out and find it somewhere else.

Aaron . . .

It took me almost an hour to get over to Antwan's spot. Traffic was pumping like a gas station serving one dollar gallons, not to mention, I was three seconds from having a disturbing wreck on the express way. My mind needed to be eased, so before I even got there, I stopped at the nearest liquor spot and snatched me up a bottle of Remy V.S.O.P.

The parking lot of my man's spot was flooded with cars. There were enough cars to start a small dealership. Heading inside, the loud music crashed against my ear drums. People were crowded around the living room, moving to the beat like they were shooting Jay-z's *Big Pimpin'* video. I could see Antwan dabbing to the music, as he bounced over to me with a cute video vixen on his arms.

"Wassup my boy. What took you so long?"

"Little trouble at the crib. I'm here now though." I could feel the liquor biting on my conscience. The shit Foreign pulled had me heated. Handing me a bottle of Ace of Spades, Antwan grabbed my Remy. "Throw this bullshit away. Walk with me."

The halls of his home were covered with African photographs taken by his father who also played in the NFL. After receiving an injury and being put on indefinite leave, he began to spend his time chasing women and traveling the world with a major photography crew.

Sliding through the thick movement on the floor, we headed upstairs to the top of his two million dollar home.

Ending up in front of one of the master bedrooms, he opened the double doors. My eyes landed directly on the two women who were prancing around the room. They were indulging in a pillow fight and their naked bodies screamed super model status. I looked over at Antwan who grinned from ear to ear.

"Who are they?" I couldn't just bounce around with just anybody. Little freaks would get a nigga in a world of trouble.

"These are my friends, Pink and Cherry. They're professors from Florida State University. Ladies?"

Their faces swung around in the direction of Antwan's voice us as if he'd startled them. "Heyyy, Antwan. Is this your friend?" one of the girls asked, with her eyes locked in on me. Her body was pecan smooth and her boobs were perky. After watching her walk towards me, my vision landed on her phat backside.

"Yeah, this is my man Aaron. He's been trying his best to make it this way. He's exhausted."

"Well, that doesn't sound like too much of a problem. I think that me and Cherry can fix that."

Pulling me inside the room, they stood at my side as if they were ready to devour me. Antwan stepped out of the room with a smirk similar to Ronald McDonald. He was the king of starting explicit shit and leaving a nigga for the fire. You could be sleeping with a federal agent and wouldn't know if Antwan had anything to do with the hook up.

After the door closed, Cherry wasted no time squatting to release my buckle. Within seconds I was being gobbled down by two women I knew nothing about, thus my reason for being so addicted. The rush of females did something to me— I just loved different pussy.

"Mhmmm! This is gonna be so fun." Pink stood up and placed a hand on my chest. Rubbing her womanhood, she removed my piece from her friend's mouth and placed it on the lips of her kitty. With no time to waste, I grabbed her left leg, raised it, and pulled her closer to me. Sliding inside of her semi-virgin walls, I stroked at a medium pace while her friend kissed me on my shoulders and back. Pink's soft moans erupted in my ear. She grew wetter by the second and the light strokes elevated to long, deep, rapid pumping.

"Shittt!" My frame allowed me to hold her in position as we stood with our feet touching. Noticing her facial expression, I realized she was releasing her first orgasm. She felt like a pure virgin and her pink hair turned me on all the more.

After allowing her to claw at my back for minutes, I removed my piece and grabbed Cherry by the arm. Placing her on the bed, I made her lie flat with her legs spread eagle. Immediately, I got to my knees and prepared to taste the light feast that lay before me. Not only was she bald down there, her sweet spot smelled like heaven.

"Ahhh!" Her moans sounded like a plea for relentless pleasure. It wasn't long before I decided to get a piece of her cookie. Within a matter of minutes, she'd released her passion juice on my lips twice, ensuring me I was in for another sweet ride on the threesome fun house.

Just as I was about to slide inside that pretty pussy, Cherry's words stopped me like a horse that didn't want to scurry off a cliff: "So, how much you payin' me for this kitty after you done?" Her voice was sweet, but I could clearly see she was beyond serious.

"Uhh . . . No disrespect lil' mama, but I don't pay for pussy." Again, I tried to enter her but this time she placed a hand on my chest and looked at me as if I'd suddenly grown two heads.

"What? I hope you don't think I'm bustin' this bomb-ass vagina open for no reason. Nigga, I'ma bad bitch."

Her friend Pink stood to the side like she didn't know whose side to choose.

"Shit . . . if you feel like that shorty you can dip and leave me with lil' mama right here."

I could tell from the way she jumped up from the king size bed that it was about to be a serious problem. "So, basically you just raped me? I gave you head and let you stick your creepy looking lips on my pussy and I was promised a check whether you're finished with me or not." Now, she was standing in front of me naked with her hand out like a five year old.

I couldn't help but chuckle because the shit literally made my dick soft. Snatching my pants up, I zipped them up just in case some crazy shit popped off. Her last comment had me feeling like a real busta and it was the number one reason why I was careful who I snuck around with. Now, I felt as though I needed to defend myself.

"Hold the fuck up. I didn't rape shit, bitch. Don't ever disrespect me like that. I didn't promise you anything and I damn sure ain't said shit to you about no money. You trippin', ma."

She walked over to the large nightstand and picked up a small black box. "This is all the proof I need, sir. I never deal with none of y'all dirty little athletes 'cause y'all don't never wanna pay up. Pink get dressed. We're not doing shit else until we get our money."

Grabbing my gold bottle of Ace of Spades, I slid back in my shirt. "Listen, you can keep the video, hoe. That shit ain't gonna work sweetheart. I've got lawyers for this type of shit and once they see that you're lying, your ass gonna be the one behind bars you silly-ass trick."

"Oh yeah? We gon' see muthafucker. You think just because you the quarterback of the Buccaneers you can do what you want? I'll make sure the whole world sees this shit. Bet on that."

"Bitch, you don't even know how to spell Buccaneers. What the fuck make you think you can be a slut and use that as evidence to collect a check from me. Shut the fuck up."

My actions had officially led me astray and I had to walk out of the room. Based on the awkward conversation, I could see things were about to get heated.

Heading back down the steps, I moved quickly through the partying guests and found Antwan. He inhaled on a Garcia Vega, while getting a dance from a Dominican chick.

"Nigga, what the fuck's up with those bitches? What you tryna do? Get me cased up?"

"What the hell are you talking about?" Antwan asked, sitting up and releasing a mouth full of smoke.

"The bitch tryna scream that fake rape shit like she about to press me for some money. I don't trick, bro. You know this."

His frown turned into a smile before he busted out in a fit of laughter. "Just pay the bitch, Aaron. You act like you hurting for that shit, bro."

I had to clean my ears before looking at him seriously. "I'm not paying them hoes shit. The bitch Pink ain't even complaining. It's her friend. I'm out, bro, 'cause you ain't got this shit in order. I got enough going on."

Antwan proceeded to push the bitches who had been sitting in his lap onto the floor before following me out of the front door. I didn't stop until I got out to the parking area.

"Listen, bro, if you gon' have set up artists inside the crib, do me a favor and don't call me over."

"Just calm down, my guy. I'ma check them hoes. Real talk. I don't want that to mess ya day up even worse. Your sister been screaming at me about the way you been getting into it with Foreign. So, I know it's rough."

"Ain't nothing wrong with my relationship. We just arguing like a muthafucka. I find myself drinking more. I find myself cheating. I really just gotta clear my mind."

Walking to my car, I got inside and started the engine. Swerving out of his driveway, I dialed Lexi's number. I held on until she finally answered on the fifth ring.

"Hello?"

"What the hell is wrong with you telling Antwan about me and Foreign's problems? He shouldn't know shit about me and my wife."

"Who the fuck are you yelling at, nigga? Tone it the fuck down before I punch yo' ass in the face, Aaron."

"No, Lexi. You know I'm going through enough. I don't need the team talking about what's going on in my home. That's our family business. Don't you agree?"

"You wouldn't have to be worried about anybody saying shit if you was making your wife happy. You're my blood-brother. Not a friend. Not my man. I can only tell you the truth and hope you understand it. How did you know I said anything to Antwan about anything anyway? Because you're over his house, right? Well I know today is his birthday and I also know there's an ass load of bitches over his crib. That means you were probably cheating again. You're not fooling anybody but yourself, Aaron. You're infatuated with women."

Letting my mind meditate on her words, I realized she was right. I knew Foreign was my wife and I knew my failure in my marriage was due to my behavior. My habits. All I could do was ask God for a change and try my best to switch my deeds from bad to good.

"Just let me worry about Foreign, okay? She's my wife and I know I'm not perfect, but I'm the only man fit to be with her. No one could ever love her the way I do."

"Aaron, you don't have to prove anything to me. You have to do it for her. Regardless of you telling me to stay out of your business, she's my best friend, and that makes her my business too. I introduced you to her, boy. I bet mommy and daddy don't know what you've been doing to her. All I can tell you is you're going to push her to her limit until she leaves you, jackass. And, oh . . . don't call my phone preaching about some shit you don't even live by." Lexi ended the call in my ear without so much as a goodbye.

Tossing my cellphone inside the small cup holder, I reached for my bottle and took a large swig. I hated when I felt this way. It was painful enough seeing that I couldn't maintain my own household. But losing all my close relationships in the process wasn't worth it.

A man was nothing without his other half to back him up. It seemed like more pain was being caused than joy. Everyone doubted I would make it into the NFL but I did. The same way I knew Foreign would be my wife. It was destined for me to be happy.

To make my parents proud. And I was going to fix everything by any means.

CHAPTER 8
FOREIGN

As I stood looking in the mirror, I wiped my tears away. My heart was completely torn into two pieces. Mentally, I wasn't okay, and I could feel myself diving completely off the edge. My husband of three years was having another affair, and he had no couth about himself whatsoever. The hoodrats he chose to sleep with were social media attention seekers and would do anything for a buck and a fuck. Over and over, he showed me he had no regards for our marriage.

Despite his fuckups, he was still the love of my life. For the life of me I couldn't understand where I went wrong. Everything had been good with us until he was drafted to the NFL. Not long after, the groupies showed up and sent my world tumbling in a downward spiral.

Although he was the ultimate cheater, I stayed because I loved him and thought he would change. You'd think after two miscarriages he would get his shit together, but unfortunately; he was too selfish to consider my feelings. I was used to the cheating, but what I didn't expect was for one of those thirsty thots to send me a video of my husband feasting between her legs. It pained me to see him giving her oral pleasure when he had a problem with oral sex in the first place.

The door slammed, signaling his return. Opening up my phone, I set it to play. Aaron walked through our master bedroom with a smile on his face, without a care in the world. He dropped his duffle bag and stepped to me.

"How is my beautiful wife?" He attempted to kiss me, but I curved him like a fast ball.

"Keep those unfaithful, dirty-ass lips away from me." I mugged him roughly and rolled my eyes so hard, they could've gotten stuck in my head.

"What are you talking about? I haven't done anything."

"Oh, I beg to differ." I shoved the phone in his face.

He grabbed it and backed up. "What's this?"

"Hit play and you'll see."

Aaron touched the screen with his finger. After a few seconds, he threw the phone onto the bed and grabbed me. "I'm sorry. That's not what it looks like."

"Oh, really?" I reached back and slapped his face with all the strength I had left in me. "Well, I don't know what it looks like to you, or anyone else, but, it looks to me like my husband was eating pussy that doesn't belong to him, or me, since it's clearly *not* my pussy."

"Let me explain," he pleaded.

"There's nothing to explain, Aaron. These are receipts. This is *you* on this video. I'm tired of this, I really am. I'm so tempted to walk away while I still have my sanity."

Aaron sat on the bed and hung his head in shame. "I don't know what's wrong with me," he admitted. The anxiety of knowing he'd truly fucked up caused him to rub his head continuously. It's like I'm addicted to sex. . . .. and I can't stop, no matter how much or how hard I try."

"That's no excuse. You let the money, fame, and the groupie hoes get in the way of everything we built. I'm non-existent in your world. You only need me around to cook your food, clean your house, and wash your clothes."

"That's not true, Foreign. I love you. That's why I married you." He tried to be emotional but his eyes were dryer than the Sahara Desert.

"You married me because you knew I'd never fuck you over. I take care of home and I don't party at all. You wanted a homebody to raise your fuckin' kids and be a maid while you sling community dick all over the place. And why don't we have kids, Aaron?" If he said anything slick, I was definitely gonna go upside his head.

"I should be asking you that. I'm not the one whose body keeps rejecting them," he replied, looking me in my eyes without an ounce of compassion.

I grabbed the closest thing in my reach which just so happened to be a perfume bottle. I threw it at him and clunked him upside the head. "It's your fault we don't have kids! Did you forget about the two miscarriages I had, stressing and fighting bitches because of your lying, deceitful ass?"

Aaron sat still, looking like a deer caught in headlights. "I didn't mean that."

"Don't apologize, because you meant every single word." There was so much rage and anger in my system, I wanted his ass to hurt the same way I was hurting. I desperately wanted to give him a taste of his own medicine. Grabbing my keys and purse, I headed towards the door, then abruptly stopped.

"Just so you know, I'm done with this. I'm done crying and being sad. It's time I start living my life as a single woman. I'm not enough for you, and apparently, I'll never be."

"Where are you going?" he asked, as if he had the right to know.

"That's none of your concern, dear. Why don't you question the bitch in the video? Don't wait up."

My outburst had me feeling like a new woman. It was about time I gave him a piece of my mind. It wasn't like I wasn't an attractive woman. If I must toot my own horn, I had to admit I was fine. I was twenty-four years old, my complexion was pecan tan, my ass was nice, and my stomach was as flat as a board. My body didn't have an ounce of fat on it. Yet it still meant nothing in my husband's eyes.

Today I was flaunting my shape in a casual jean dress that hung off the shoulders, coupled with a pair of nude strappy heels. Fashion Nova was my favorite place to shop. I wasn't big on designer brands and materialistic things didn't mean shit to me. I was a simple girl. Aaron was the only one big on splurging. When he bought me the Bentley coupe for my birthday I was grateful, but he could've spent that money on a Toyota and I would've been just as satisfied.

Anyway, I unlocked the doors on my fancy whip, put on my shades, and took off out of the driveway. Tonight was about me, and I was looking to have some fun, even if I had to party alone. Ironically, that's exactly what happened, and I ended up at a karaoke spot.

Sitting at the bar, I made myself comfortable and ordered a Rum Runner. From my seat, I danced to the music and did my best to have a good time. Aaron called me twice, but I ignored both calls and didn't bother to respond via text. That bastard needed to wonder about my location for a change.

The DJ played *"Twerk"* by the City Girls, and that pulled me right off the stool I'd been keeping warm. While I was dancing, some guy came behind me and grinded against my ass. Normally, I would've objected to it, but not that time. That night was all about me, and it felt good to receive genuine attention from a man. When the song came to an end, I was sweaty as hell, so I went back to the bar.

Dude was on my heels. He was handsome, to say the least. With his chocolate skin and white teeth, he resembled Morris Chestnut.

"You got moves out there on that dance floor."

"You not too bad yourself," he complemented, while flashing me a million dollar smile. "Let me buy you a drink."

"Okay. Let me go to the ladies room and freshen up."

"I'll be waiting." He grinned, showing all thirty-two.

The restroom was near empty when I stepped inside, with the exception of the female holding a basket full of hygiene items women could use for a small fee. Passing on all her offers, I cleaned my face and went back to the door. Hershey Chocolate was sitting there waiting, as promised.

Damn, he could cover me in his chocolate any day. Of course, it was the liquor that had me thinking that way. Being the gentleman that he was, he helped me into my seat and ordered me a second drink.

"So, what's a beautiful woman like you doing in here alone? Trouble in paradise?" He nodded his head towards my huge wedding ring.

"You can say that."

"I guess he doesn't realize how lucky he is." He sipped his Courvoisier on the rocks.

"You'd be guessing right."

"That's unfortunate. You're truly a prize."

"You don't even know me," I replied sassily, sipping from my straw.

The Price You Pay for Love

"I'm naturally drawn to good people. Besides, for you to be off the market means he saw something special in you."

"That's what I thought in the beginning."

We continued to have small talk and ordered more drinks. On my third cup, Maurice had the waitress bring us two shots a piece. Both of us were tore the hell up. Taking me by surprise, he stood up and gave me a lap dance. It was so funny, and I loved his energy. The room started to spin a little, so I had to sit down for a few.

"You okay?"

"Yeah, I just felt dizzy all of a sudden."

He ordered me a bottled water which I downed quickly before asking for another one. I took a few sips of the second one and thought it best to remain seated a few minutes longer. Once I no longer felt like I was on a merry-go-round, I jumped to my feet and grabbed my purse.

"Going to freshen up?" he asked.

"No, I'm going home now. I need my bed."

"Let me walk you out."

"It's okay. I can manage."

"I want to make sure you make it to your car safely."

"Okay."

My car was parked in the front, so I didn't have far to walk. Stopping beside the driver's door, I placed my hand on his firm chest. "This is me right here. Thank you."

Maurice opened my door and I climbed inside. "So, can I have your number?"

"Is this you shootin' your shot?" I giggled.

"Not really," he replied modestly.

"Well . . ." I paused. "I just feel—"

Cutting me off, he shook his head and filled in the blank. "Guilty?"

"I just don't think that's a good idea. I did have a good time, though. Thanks for that, at least." I smiled.

"Well, take my number just in case you need someone to talk to."

"Okay. I guess." He locked his number in my phone and I pulled off.

Halfway down the street, I started to feel nauseous. I struggled to hold it until I could pull over. However, it was too late because I hurled over the passenger seat, regurgitating on the floor. "Shit!"

Now I had this big-ass mess to clean up. My car was going to be funky as hell once the sun came up. Halfway home, I remembered there was a late night car wash nearby, so that's where I went. Surprisingly, it was still open for service. There were two vehicles being cleaned, so I parked in the guest spot.

As I walked up, I was greeted by one of the attendants. "We're closing in thirty minutes," he informed me.

"Sorry, but I have an emergency. My friend threw up in my car and I need to have it cleaned before it settles in my carpet.

"Sorry, but that's a lot of work and there's not enough time left to get it done."

Just as I was about to walk away, I was stopped by a tall, brown, handsome stature. The broadness in his shoulders stood out, just like the bulging print in his joggers. *Damn!*

"Excuse me, Miss. What do you need?" His baritone voice made my kitty squirm.

"Um- I- Um . . . I need a car wash. My girlfriend had one too many drinks and threw up in my front seat."

"We can take care of that for you. Give me your keys."

He tossed them to his worker. "Wash the lady's car. Be a gentleman, fool." Then he looked back at me. "Follow me."

Yassss! Lead me into the land of the living. I'd follow his sexy ass to the moon if that's where he was going, but instead, we walked inside the building.

"You can wait in my office. I know you don't want to sit out in that humid air."

"Thank you."

"I'm Demerius, but my friends call me Domestic."

We shook hands. "Nice to meet you. I'm Foreign."

"That's an interesting name."

"So is yours and blame my mama for that one."

"It suits you." He pulled my seat out for me. "I'll be back."

"Okay."

The liquor had me a little spaced out and I couldn't wait to get home and dive headfirst into my bed. The air coming from the AC was blowing hard and I needed all the air I could get.

Domestic came back fifteen minutes later and sat down behind his desk. Judging from the way he was studying his computer, I guessed he was doing some work.

The silence was killing me, but I didn't want to interrupt, so I kept myself busy by reading a book on Kindle. After a while he looked up.

"I apologize. I'm trying to log my receipts for the day. I swear I need an assistant."

My eyes met his. "No apology necessary. Business is important. I'm okay."

"Most women don't understand that."

"I'm not like most women."

Leaning back in his seat, he folded his hands. "Why you outside this time of night?"

"Well, if you must know, I was out having drinks with my girlfriend."

"Right," he smiled, shaking his finger, "you did say that, but if you were my woman, you'd be locked down in the house."

"Well, thank God I'm not."

"I'd do something about that slick tongue too."

"And, what exactly would you do about my slick tongue, Mr. Demerius?" The liquor had me feeling bold.

"I'd bite on it and suck it. You'd be at my mercy." He licked his lips and I almost creamed in my panties. I was too excited.

"Hmm. I guess."

His worker walked in. "Aye, boss. We all done out here. I'm leaving. Tony gon' finish up her car. It should be done in thirty minutes or so."

"I'm coming out. I'll be right back." He excused himself.

"Um, where is your bathroom?"

"Down the hall. I'll point you in the right direction."

My bladder felt like it would explode at any minute. Quickly, I hiked up my dress and squatted over the toilet. The release of the hot piss brought on so much relief. Afterwards, I cleaned up with my Summers Eve wipes and washed my hands.

As I strolled down the hall, Demerius was returning to his office. And, Lord have mercy, the man had taken off his shirt, exposing his beefed up muscles. It was definitely time to leave the premises.

"Everything good?" He smiled. That was when I realized he had a dimple in his left cheek.

"Of course."

"Good."

My eyes were zoomed in on his beautiful tattoos and smooth caramel skin. He was most certainly a fine piece of male specimen. Saliva stirred around my mouth. Swallowing hard, I cleared my throat.

"You like what you see?" His ole cocky ass had caught me staring.

"Maybe," I stated boldly.

He walked over and stood in front of me. Grabbing my hand, he placed it on his chest and made his chest jump. The slightest touch of him made my kitty jump around in my panties. I wanted to move my hand so bad, but it was stuck in place. Thoughts of Aaron flashed through my mind. I didn't want to be like him and break my wedding vows.

Picking up my purse, I stood up. "I have to go. Is my car ready?"

"Not yet. Why you in a rush?" Demerius placed his hand underneath my dress and traced my panty line with his finger. Firmly, he gripped my ass and gave it hard squeeze. "I like you."

His hands were quite frisky as he made his way to the front. The tips of his fingers grazed my lips, and I melted fast like butter.

"You don't know me."

"We can change that." Demerius rolled his tongue across the side of my neck. On contact my eyes closed, and I placed my hands on his waist. *Fuck it!* Aaron wasn't faithful to me, so fuck him.

To soothe my curious mind, I placed my hand on his crotch and squeezed it. He was semi-hard. I had to make sure he was working with something worth cheating for. The harder he sucked on me, the wetter the seat of my panties got.

"Fuck me," I whispered.

Placing his strong hands on my ass, he scooped me up and sat me on his desk. He removed my panties and threw them. "Spread them legs for me."

"Close the door first." I didn't want anyone to walk in and witness what was about to go down.

"Don't worry, everybody gone."

"What about my car?"

"It been ready. I wanted to spend more time with you." Pushing my legs further apart, he stroked my whole cat with his hand. "Oh yeah, she shaved too."

Demerius arched his back and came face to face with my plump peach. His nose was all up in it, doing what I assumed to be the smell test. Using his fingers, he separated my lips and sucked on my pulsating bud. It hardened when it came in contact with his thick lips. The flick of his tongue made my body shutter. He confirmed he was a stone cold freak when he put my legs on his shoulder, lifted my ass up, and licked me from the back to the front, stopping at my Hershey Highway.

"Ssss. Mmm. Yessss!"

He sucked on my lips individually and kissed them gently. Removing his joggers, I watched closely as they dropped— the nigga was hung like a horse. Looking me in my eyes, he stroked it. My eyes widened just a bit. Without a doubt, I could clearly see he was packing more than Aaron. Besides, my pipes definitely needed cleaning out since I hadn't been sleeping with my husband every night. I had put his ass on restriction two weeks ago.

"Can you handle all this beef?"

"I guess we're about to find out."

Snatching me to the edge and teasing my entrance, he soaked his head with my juices. Forcing his length inside, he gripped my hips and pushed hard, until he sank deep inside my ocean.

"Ahhhh shit!" I yelped while wrapping my legs around his waist.

"You feel this fat-ass dick in that sweet pussy?"

"Yes. Yes."

Every time he rammed his Mandingo-sized meat up in me, I could feel pressure in my ass, like he was fucking me from the front and the back, at the same time. *This man is about to kill me in here.* Wrapping my arms around his neck, I clamped him tight and held on for dear life.

"Lay back and spread them legs. I'on wanna see nothin' but pussy."

With my back resting on his desk and my legs stretched north and south, Demerius propped one leg on the desk and drove his thick long rod deep inside my snatch box. "Fuccckkk!" I shrieked.

He went crazy and drilled me hard. As he bounced up and down in my shit, his heavy balls slapped against my ass with every stroke.

"Ooooh! You killin' me!" I cried out.

"Take this fat dick." He put his hand on my stomach and pushed down on it. My moaning got louder. "Say my name while I beat this pussy up."

"Demerius," I shouted.

"No! Call me Domestic."

"Domestic!"

"Uh-huh. Just like that."

He grunted from deep within as he continued to fuck me like a madman. "I don't give a fuck who you married to . . . This my pussy now."

What! I thought.

Domestic played with my clit, rubbing her fast. A pleasurable amount of pressure built up inside of me. Yep, my orgasm had surfaced, and I was ready to erupt.

"Ooh shit, I'm cummin'. Sss . . . it's cummin'. Shit. Keep going. Beat this pussy."

"Whose shit is this?"

"Yours," I complied.

"Damn right. Say that shit."

"Domestic. Domestic . . . I'm cummin'."

"Bust then."

We came at the same time and just like that, my little sexcapade was over. However, I didn't want it to end. There would be more where that came from.

"Your husband done fucked up now. You ain't going nowhere." Playing hard, I smirked. "Oh really?"

"You goddamn right." He got dressed and helped me off his desk. "Lock my number in your phone. You'll be hearing from me tomorrow morning," he ordered.

I did as I was told. He kissed me on my cheek and escorted me to my vehicle. "Get home safe, baby. Shoot me a text so I can sleep comfortably knowing you made it in one piece."

"I will."

When I got home, I was cheesing my ass off. All I wanted to do was shower and go to sleep. My body was tired and needed some rest.

Aaron was sitting up in bed watching television. Deep down I wanted to laugh so bad because he looked just like me when I waited on him to come home at night. Pitiful.

"Where you been?"

"Out."

"With who?"

"Why? You don't get to question me."

"I'm the man of this house and you will tell me where you been," he barked angrily.

"I'm not telling you shit. How about that?" I walked off and went in the bathroom and sent Domestic a text message just as he'd requested.

CHAPTER 9
AARON

The recent situation with me and Foreign was like the top news between all of our friends. I never thought I would be caught down so bad. That foul ass bitch Cherry had the audacity to upload that disrespectful ass video to Instagram and Facebook. I was so lucky my mom and dad weren't social media type people. Otherwise, my ass would've been picking out a casket right about now.

The pain I'd seen on Foreign's face was the last strike for me. It was hard to run across a woman who would have your back through whatever, one who stayed by your side after the deceit and betrayal. She wasn't a hoe from the streets. Neither was she a sack chaser. Foreign was my queen, and I had finally come to the realization that I was the reason my marriage had gone downhill. I had made excuse after excuse and I had never stood up for the actions I'd taken as a man.

After reaching my destination, I parked my car and looked over at Lexi sitting in the passenger seat. She removed her Chanel glasses before glaring at me. "Keys, Aaron. Let me have them."

"Why do I have to do this, Lexi? I can work out my problems another way. Don't you think this is a little too much?"

Crossing her arms, she smirked. "Do you think losing your wife is a *little too much*?" she repeated sarcastically. "Or what about you dying alone at the age of sixty-three while she's married to a billionaire carrying around a 12-inch cock? That wouldn't be pretty either, Aaron."

The sun was bouncing off the windshield into my eyes. Even the air smelled disturbing, and I could tell that it definitely wasn't the place I needed to be at that moment. My stomach began to slightly bubble and before I knew it, I was hanging out the door, releasing vomit all over the concrete.

"Look at you, Aaron. You've been cheating so much, you're the one who's gotten pregnant."

Lexi laughed in my face like the shit was funny. Everyone knew I didn't have it in me to stand in front of anyone and talk openly about my problems. I was more on the hush side about my business. Now, I was being pulled out of my element due to my continuous mistakes which I needed to fix badly. Foreign meant the world to me. My family was my life. But there was certain shit I just couldn't do.

"I don't know about this. Suddenly, I'm not feeling so good."

"Listen to me. You're my brother and all, but I don't feel sorry for you. We're grown now. Our life is very easy, Aaron. You either stay single and do as you please or find someone who you truly love and lock it down for the sake of that person. No one is forcing you into commitment. You have your own free will. So, what's it gonna be? Do you want Foreign and your marriage, or will you slut for the rest of your pathetic life?"

This crazy twin of mine wasn't going to let up and her speech continued to eat at me. Even though Lexi was a pain in my ass, she always spoke nothing but the cold hearted truth. She was heartless when it came to emotions and I knew her ways could cut a person deeper than a fresh box razor. I had to do what I needed in order to save my love.

Climbing out of the car slowly, I was sure to avoid stepping in the puke I'd released earlier.

As I closed my car door, Lexi slid over to the driver's seat. "I'll be back to get you in one hour. All you have to do is last for sixty days and you'll see a change. Trust me." Lexi waved before backing out of the lot.

I knew there was no other option, so I decided to go ahead and face my present reality. Strolling inside the building, I made my way to the small meeting referred to as *Communication and Healing*. Proceeding in, my eyes landed on twelve people— eleven were different men and women who were obviously dealing with something similar.

The counselor was a small pecan skinned woman who sported her hair in a neat French roll. She seemed to be in her early forties. The image resembled a young college student who had graduated with a diploma for any and everything, dealing with talking somebody to damn death.

"Class, I want you to welcome a new member of our group. We've been waiting for him. My name is Ms. Anderson. Would you like to come introduce yourself and tell us why you're here?"

I knew before stepping in the room, I was going to be put on the damn spotlight. This bitch was ready to expose a nigga. Walking in front of everyone, I cleared my throat.

"Uhh, hi. My name is Aaron Young, and I'ma quarterback for the Tampa Bay Buccaneers."

"Hi, Aaron!" Everyone said the shit in unison as if they were singing in a fuckin' choir.

The woman waved her hand for me to continue, so, I did.

"Today, I'm here because I wanna save my marriage. I'm a sex addict and I cheat." It killed me to say this shit in front of a bunch of strangers I didn't know. I still couldn't understand how I'd let my sister convince me into doing this.

The counselor looked at me for a moment as if she were trying to see inside my mind. Then she asked, "Why do you cheat, Aaron? What drives you to do these things?"

I looked at her ass with a stale face because she was sho' being too damn nosy. I still replied though. "Sometimes I don't know what it is. I just love different women, I guess. I love my wife more, of course. But sometimes, I just lose control. . .. women are more like a weakness to me."

"Is there something your wife doesn't have that another woman does? Maybe she's mean to you. Can we know about her? Share your pain with us so we can feel you, Mr. Young."

"My wife is amazing. Her name is Foreign. She's a beautiful person, inside and out. . .. unless I'm cheating or eating up her favorite foods." The members shared a quick chuckle with me. "My wife is the most supportive woman I've ever known. She's been the direct key to my heart ever since we met in high school."

I hadn't gotten more than thirty minutes into my story before I had a few people in tears. Some gave me the mean face, as if the blame was specifically because of me. I had to respect it since I knew it was the truth.

As the counselor cleared the session, she stopped me at the door. "Mr. Young?"

"Yes, Ms. Anderson?"

"I know it took a lot of heart to stand up there and give your secrets away like that. Can I give you some advice that carried me a long way throughout my life? It helped me stay firm on my feelings and it also helped me pick the right husband. It was to trick someone into thinking my love was real, that my whole life was sincerely for them. They aren't the ones who lose in the end. You are. If someone lives their whole life feeling like their lies won't rise, then you have another coming."

"What do you mean?" I asked, curious to hear her perspective.

"I mean, if you don't want to be with someone you should set them free so they can make choices to better themselves. When you cage a person into having no options while you do as you please, you begin to birth a monster you're not going to be able to stand. It'll be your exact actions flipping back against you because that's the only kind of love you were able to show. Don't become a statistic in your own game, Mr. Young."

Her statement was so thick it had made my flesh crawl like a breeze with invisible thorns. I never knew the other side of emotions could make someone feel beyond guilty. My feelings were so much in the gutter because I'd never given Foreign a correct chance at love.

"Thank you for that, Ms. Anderson. I'll be sure to apply it to my own relationship."

After I'd made it out of the center, I stopped and posted up in front of the building with my mind running like a paper mill. Taking a seat on the bench, I glanced up at the sky. I knew for sure, nothing was more important than my role as a husband. In order for me to achieve that, I needed Foreign's forgiveness.

Lexi honking the horn of the Benz broke me from my reverie. "Boy, you need to come on. It stinks out here."

I walked to the car and got in. Reaching over, I gave my sister the biggest hug I could.

"What the hell. Get off me. What did those people do to you in there?"

"They helped me. I actually wouldn't mind dedicating my weekend to this type of class. It could actually help me in the long run."

"Well, I'm glad somebody has had a change of dick." She laughed.

I couldn't help but laugh with her. She knew how to find a way to break my stress when I was feeling down.

"I know you're probably feeling better and all, but you have another problem on your hands."

I could tell by the way she was looking, she wasn't joking.

"What you mean? What's going on?"

"Foreign is at our parent's house and they're waiting for us to get there. Lucky for me, I had to leave the boiling, flamed pot to come scoop you. In other words, you're in hot water."

"What happened?" As I waited for the answer, I prayed silently, hoping Foreign hadn't said anything to my parents about the video.

"She's waiting to grill you about your porn video. Daddy is pissed, so I hope you're ready. Foreign is looking like the grand champ right now."

The shit Lexi had just told me was like an uppercut straight to the gut.

The entire day had gone so smooth, yet it still ended with a knife to my throat. My mom wasn't a friendly person when it came down to disrespecting women. If it angered my mom, then it was surely going to move my pops right to her side.

Sliding out of the center's parking lot, we hit the dash heading towards our parent's crib.

"What all was said? I'm not about to try to argue with three people. I ain't got no win like that."

"You need to ask them what was said when you get there. You know what this is about so just worry about that."

I kept to myself for the rest of our ride. The shit was like a trip to the Hostel hotel. By the time we pulled up, I had my reasoning down pack. At the end of the day, I was a husband. I deserved another chance.

Lexi and I entered through the front door and headed straight for the living room. My eyes instantaneously landed on Foreign, who sat with her face full of tears. My mother walked directly over to me and landed a hard slap to my cheek before walking out. Judging from her initial reaction, I knew there would be no reasoning to debate my wrong doings. At this point, there was nothing I could say.

Lexi took her seat next to Foreign, leaving me standing by myself.

"Girls, give me and Aaron a minute alone." My father's voice was laced with disappointment.

They didn't hesitate to get up and walk past me without the slightest hint of empathy for my current situation.

My father strolled over to where I stood ensuring we were face-to-face before he spoke. "What the hell is wrong with you, Aaron? Explain yourself."

I truly didn't know what to say, so I just kept it real. "I slipped up, Pop."

"What the hell does that mean, Son? Have you lost the meaning of family? I've shown you this since you were a small child. Why the sudden change when you're at the prime of your life? This is when you should be an example, Son. What in the hell were you thinking? A sex tape, Aaron."

"It's not a sex tape, Pop. Some dirty-ass female is just trying to play me for some money because of my status!"

"Lower your tone in my home. There is no excuse for your behavior. You are my only son and I've never raised you to act like that. Your mother is crushed. We stood behind you through your entire career. You brought this woman home to me as my daughter in law and I accepted your choice. I felt like you were ready to take another step towards your success with this family. Marriage is a contract, Son. Your vows are your life. If you can't stay true to the simple things, you're going to cause so much hardship in your life, it'll be beyond imaginable."

The Price You Pay for Love

"I'm not perfect, Dad. You speak on this family like everything you did for me was from the bottom of your heart. You didn't teach me how to be a man because you were too busy working toward your own success. The only time I could get your attention or make you proud was with a trophy or an MVP status. You speak on my mistakes but you were never even there to warn me about this life. This is the son *you* wanted."

"I worked to make sure you could do what you love, Aaron."

"No! You worked to support me in the things *you* loved. I'm not uptight and bourgeois like you and mom. My life has problems, but you and her can't make decisions about what's best for me and my family. I'm not a baby anymore, Pop. I'ma grown man."

Shaking his head at me, he took a seat on the sectioned off couch. "Aaron, I never wanted you to feel like I haven't been here for you. I had no choice but to work when you were a teenager. My time was dedicated to making sure you didn't have to want for anything. It wasn't to make you live out my dream. It was to make you strive hard to see your own talent.

All I want you to do is realize all the things you have at stake. You're an icon now. These type of things will destroy your reputation for the people's eye. No matter what this family thinks, regardless of how you feel, you're a reflection of this family. Things you do will affect us all. Once you learn to understand that, you can grow out of your own selfish actions. You owe that woman everything in this world. Do you want to know why?"

"Why?" I asked my father.

"Because you made her your first choice. Don't be like the rest who made that decision just to say they could, Son. Please. I'm not telling you what to do. I'm giving you advice to keep your happiness." My father turned and exited the room.

Dad left me by myself for a good ten minutes allowing me to drop a few tears from the words he'd doused upon me. Truth be told, I hated feeling like everything was my fault. I had never experienced an altercation like that with my father, and it displeased me to see him so upset. Being the star of the household put certain obligations on me. Even if I felt like all of them weren't my responsibility.

For the remainder of the night, I felt so distant from my mother, especially when we gathered to eat dinner. She couldn't even look at me and her hands would slightly shake every time I called her name. Foreign wasn't even at the table sharing dinner with us and she still kept her lips sealed where I was concerned.

"Am I banished from this family or something?"

"You should be!" my mother snapped. Her voice grew loud and shaky. "I refuse to support you doing something so foolish and childish. Does cheating on a woman make you proud, Aaron? How would you feel if your father did those things to me?"

I couldn't help but to glance at Lexi and my Dad. I could tell it was time for me to leave just from the frown on my mother's face. Standing up from my seat, I stood there momentarily before making my statement. "I'm gonna take some time to try and mend me and Foreign's marriage. I know I can't take back my sins, nor can I make you all forgive me. At the end of it all, I'm still gonna be your son."

"If my daughter in law is in pain, it troubles me. I need to see growth between you two, not a disaster. We never said you weren't apart of this family, but maybe you need to do a self-check," my dad said, before lowering his gaze.

Nodding my head, I wanted to check them about their recent situations, but I decided to take my admonishment and keep it pushing.

Leaving out of my parent's home, I spotted Foreign, sitting on the hood of her Bentley, with her back towards me. I thought she was already gone, but I now realized she had been sitting outside the entire time while my family and I discussed the same story, over and over. Now that my heart had been unveiled with my problem, it was time to iron things out.

Taking a seat next to her, she looked over at me. "I never wanted to tell them. It just came out, Aaron. You hurt me."

"Foreign, you don't owe me no explanation, baby." I grabbed her face to make her look into my eyes. "I screwed up bad and I get it, you're hurt. The only thing I can do now is take my classes seriously and start to elevate toward happiness for us again. In order for me to be successful, I need you to forgive me."

"Aaron, my heart is ripped to shreds. I just don't know if I have that in me anymore. Forgiveness isn't used on a daily basis. It's when you make a mistake and fix your actions for better choices in the future. You're a dog, Aaron. It's naturally in you and I don't think I can just forgive that," she replied, with a gloomy sigh.

I honestly didn't know how to respond. Not only did she have a reason to feel this way, but my parents made her feel I was no longer worthy. It was the very reason I never wanted them in our business in the first place.

"I don't think we're meant to be anymore." Her eyes let me know she was ready to abandon the situation completely.

"Baby, please don't say things like that. I married you because I love you. We aren't like couples who end up separated, with two different families. You're all I got, Foreign."

Rising off the car, she took a step back from me. "I'm gonna fill you in on something, Aaron. When I dedicated my life to you, it was wholeheartedly. I didn't come in with a fantasy of fuckin' other men. I didn't even have the guts to look at another man and that was because of you. The day I gave you my hand, I cut the rest of society off and focused on building my life with you. Because you were the only one I wanted. This right here," she pointed at herself and then me, "it's not what I signed up for. Maybe we just need a little space."

Climbing inside her car, Foreign started the engine and pulled off. The shit she'd just said to me crushed every bone in my body, but there was no blame I could put on her. I was literally stuck and didn't know what else to do.

Lexi . . .
An hour later

Pulling in Antwan's driveway, I left my car running and got out to ring his doorbell. He opened the door, meeting me with an intense gaze with those fake-ass romantic eyes. Unfortunately, sex was the last thing on my mind. My mission was strictly business.

"Wassup, my queen. You came all the way over here just to have a conversation?"

"Yes, I did, but you don't have to worry. It'll be very brief."

"What's the problem?" Hearing the anger in my tone, his look turned serious and the stupid-ass grin quickly vanished.

"Aaron is three seconds from losing his entire marriage. Whatever little freak you introduced him to aired his business all over social media. The entire family is in this big-ass rampage because of this bullshit. Not only that, you mentioned something to him about our conversation which is some real pussy shit!"

"Wait! Watch ya' mouth, ma. You ain't gotta be disrespectful. I'm listening to you."

I had to catch myself before I slapped the spit out of his mouth. I had to remember the nigga was only twenty-four.

"Antwan, my brother is about to lose everyone who loves him over this drama. You were part of that influence. Instead of pushing your friend to be a husband, you tried to make him live a fake-ass bachelor dream. This bitch has a video of my brother and I want it back."

"How the hell do you expect me to get it? Those bitches are from Tallahassee, not Tampa."

"That's something you have to figure out for yourself, Antwan. I'm gonna fill you in on a little secret . . The pussy I gave you was a token of appreciation for being a hot little athlete. But when it comes down to my family, I'll be your worst nightmare.

If that video gets in the wrong person's hands, it could end my brother's career. It's called blackmail. You either get that video back, or I'll put an end to your little dream in a month's time. I'll strip you for every coin and I'll prove beyond a shadow of a doubt that you sabotaged this family to receive a check. I don't think the NFL would take kindly to finding out you smoke tons of weed. Or what about your pill habit?" The dumb expression he wore, told me I had gotten his attention.

"I'll get in contact with them myself and have it back to you by tomorrow," he said, suddenly realizing I didn't give a damn where them hoes were from, or what he had to do to get it.

"Great. After that, we can let this little mishap slide. And for future references, next time you decide to have a slut party Antwan, make sure my brother has nothing to do with it. That'll keep you clear of his personal problems. Capiche?"

Instead of giving me an answer, he nodded before closing his door in my face. I didn't care about him getting mad because I wiped my ass with feelings. Family was first and that was the way I implemented what I knew. It was my way of winning and staying true to my bloodline. Before I let my brother crash out with his stupidity, I would alter it by any means. That's what family was for.

Destiny Skai

CHAPTER 10
FOREIGN

After I left Aaron standing in his own sorrows, I drove around aimlessly, listening to slow music. Every song that played had me in my feelings, and the tears wouldn't subside. To say I was broken hearted was an understatement. I was damaged, ruined beyond repair. The man I had given my heart to had stomped on it repeatedly and constantly treated me like I was one of his random thot pockets of the week.

If I had to choose between the old Aaron and the new one, I would take the old one any day. I would rather live a regular life and be happy, instead of living in the limelight on some rich shit. If my husband worked a regular nine to five, we wouldn't be in this predicament. I would take that any day over the life we had now.

So caught up in the moment, I didn't realize an hour had passed. Nor had I even noticed that my gas needle had dropped a notch. The more I thought about it, the angrier I became. Men could be so stupid at times. They could have a queen at home, but still cheat with a Bed Bug Betty ass bitch. For the life of me I just couldn't figure out why a man could be so selfish and ungrateful.

Even if you stood ten toes down with him, sometimes love wasn't enough for those bastards. A woman could suck, fuck, lick his balls, cook his food, wash his dirty drawls, and the nigga would *still* fuck another bitch. Instead of stepping to a woman and simply giving her the common courtesy by telling her he's unhappy or needs a break, most men prefer to drag a woman till the end. But me? I quickly learned that this new generation of men didn't give a fuck about commitment and staying true to their significant other.

Aaron had ruined a great thing, and quite frankly, I was over trying to repair it. My eyes were tired of releasing tears. Tired of being faithful to a lying-ass cheater. It was time for me to dish out the same treatment and get even. In my book, an even swap ain't no swindle. So, I decided it was time to do me.

Ten minutes later, I found myself pulling into the car wash. Ever since my very first fling with Domestic, I couldn't get him out of my head. I'd find myself fantasizing about him, dicking me down on his desk and sucking all of the negative energy out of my body, on the regular. Until my recent encounter, Aaron had been the only man I'd slept with, so when I finally experienced something new it was hard to ignore. Another man had finessed my soul with no effort, yet his touch felt so genuine, and my body reacted like a moth to flame.

Before I stepped from my vehicle, I gave myself a once over in the mirror. Domestic didn't need to know that I'd been crying. My eyes were a little pinkish, but I could easily pass by saying it was from lack of sleep.

Exiting the car, I proceeded to the front entrance and walked inside. Slowly approaching his office, I could hear indistinctive chatter. Not wanting to barge in on his conversation, I tapped on the door to get his attention.

Domestic looked up and smiled. He said a few words to the woman he was engaged in conversing with and leaned against his desk. "I'll be in touch. Thanks for stopping by."

"You're most certainly welcome." The woman walked past me and I caught a glimpse of her shiny badge. Of course I was curious, but it wasn't my business to question him.

He greeted me with open arms. As I held him tightly and rested my head against his chiseled chest, my nostril became enticed by the smell of Creed lingering on his body. It felt so good to be in the arms of a grown-ass man. Unlike Aaron's childish ass. We had only known each other briefly, but I felt safe in his arms. He grabbed my hand and escorted me to his desk.

Straddling his lap, I placed both of my hands on his shoulder. "I couldn't wait to see you."

"Everything okay?"

"I'm just tired." I sighed.

He stroked my left cheek. "You sure that's all it is?"

Engaging in a long discussion about Aaron wasn't what I had in mind, so I decided a watered down version would be just as good. "I'm starting to think my marriage was a mistake."

"How so?"

"If it's okay, I really don't want to talk about it right now."

"That's cool. Whenever you ready, I'll be here to listen."

"Thank you. I just want you to take my mind off of things." I placed a gentle kiss on his lips.

"You tryna bust it open for me right now?" Domestic had the sexiest, evil grin. It was so seductive.

"Actually, I don't have any plans on going home tonight. And, I was thinking I could wake up to you in the morning."

Domestic licked his lips. "Oh, yeah?"

"Yes."

"I can definitely make that happen."

"Good." I pecked him on the lips once more. "Because I definitely need you."

"I'm going to give you all you need and more. Just sit tight while I do some last minute things and we can leave right after."

"Okay." As he stood up, Domestic lifted me into the air. The gesture alone sent a tingle up my spine. I could only imagine what his big strong ass had in store for me that night.

***

Two hours later we finally arrived at the Marriot by the airport, far away from home— the true definition of creeping. I wasn't about to risk being seen by anyone who knew Aaron. To get out of dodge, in and of itself, showed how much respect I had for him. Not him though. He didn't give a fuck who saw him or who he allowed to videotape him.

Stepping inside the room, I headed over to the bed and sat down. Domestic stood in front of me and removed my Nikes.

"I'm sure you can use a foot massage."

"Hell yes. Right after I take a shower."

Removing my socks one by one, he grinned. "Only if your feet don't smell like you've been kicking footballs all day." His eyes had a slight sparkle in them.

Slapping him on the arm, I giggled. "My feet don't stink."

"That's not what it sounds like." Domestic raised my foot to his face and sniffed it. "What's that smell?"

"Shea butter."

"I know that's right."

Domestic surprised me when he rolled his tongue across my freshly pedicured toes. Granted, I knew he was a freak, but his actions threw me for a loop. The man had known me all of five minutes but didn't hesitate to lick every inch of my body. Slowly, but surely, he was becoming my addiction. Easing my tights over my thighs, he removed them and tossed them to the floor. Anxious to feel him inside of me, I removed my shirt and bra, then scooted to the head of the bed.

Removing his clothing piece by piece, Domestic finally came out of his boxers. His thick, chocolate curved stick, sprang to the side and I melted instantly. Sliding between my legs, he pushed them apart and pushed his way inside. The first stroke raised my back from the bed.

I grabbed ahold of his back and whisper, "Domestic."

Gently, he pumped in and out of the sacred spot which was supposed to be reserved for my husband. Each stroke was more sensual than the last. I was like putty in his hands. My eyes rolled to the back of my head, as I nibbled on my bottom lip. Our bodies grinded slowly together to the music playing in my head. Rolling my hips in a circle, my thrusts matched his. We weren't in love, but he made love to my body, which was exactly what I needed. The tips of my manicured nails scraped across his back.

Finally, I was able to open my mouth and moan. "Oh my God!"

"I told you," Domestic whispered in my ear, "I-I'll give you what you need. That nigga don't appreciate you. You're mine now."

Of course he didn't appreciate me. I knew that already, but to hear another man say it put it in perspective. Unable to contain my emotions, several tears escaped my eyes.

Domestic spotted the tears and kissed them away. "Don't cry. You got me now."

In my mind I wanted to say thank you, but I couldn't. He had me hypnotized. My eyes weren't the only things releasing. A powerful orgasm crept up on me and caused my kitty to pour out vaginal tears.

Leaving me satisfied, Domestic rolled over and collapsed beside me in bed. Our conversation only lasted for minutes before we passed out in each other's arms.

Aaron . . .

When I turned over it was seven in the morning and Foreign still wasn't in bed. Pulling myself from bed, I checked every guestroom as well as the living room, only to come up empty. I rushed back to the bedroom, picked up my phone, and dialed her number for the hundredth time. My heart was beating out of my chest like a drum. I didn't know if she was missing or hurt. Sadly, all I'd gotten was the voicemail again. If she didn't answer for me, I knew who she would answer for. That was unless they were together.

"H-hello."

"Lexi!" I shouted.

"Stop screaming in my ear, stupid."

"Is Foreign with you?" Lexi sucked her teeth. Then I heard some rustling in the background. She still hadn't responded. "Lexi!"

"Nooo! She's not."

"She didn't come home last night, and I'm worried about her. Did you at least talk to her?"

"Aaron, I'm tired and sleepy. She probably stayed at a hotel to keep from having to see your face. Just relax. I'll call and make sure she's okay."

"Okay."

Lexi wasted no time hanging up the phone on me. Tossing my phone onto the bed, I flopped down onto the mattress and buried my head into my hands. All I wanted was for Foreign to be okay. To walk through the front door unharmed. If something was to happen to her I would never forgive myself. Just as I continued to think the absolute worst, my phone rang. Quickly, I snatched it up.

"Did you find her?"

"She's okay. She stayed at a room just like I said."

"What hotel?"

Lexi exhaled deeply into the phone like I was getting on her nerves. "I don't know. And if I did, I wouldn't tell you."

"That's fucked up, Lexi."

"No, you're fucked up and you need to fix this shit. Stop cheating on my damn friend."

"I'm trying, but if she's not coming home what am I supposed to do?"

"Try harder. You really fucked up. Foreign wants a divorce, so you better get creative, nigga. These hoes don't give a fuck about you. They only fuckin' you 'cause of your status. My bestie was here before the fame. Get it together, twin. I'm going to bed. She'll be home soon."

"Thanks," I said somberly.

"Don't thank me yet."

Then she hung up again without warning. Lexi always gave me the third degree, but I would be lost without her. Since my wife was on her way, I decided to get up and put myself together. Hopefully, she would be in the mood to go out for breakfast and do a little shopping with me.

It took about thirty minutes for me to shower, and another half hour for me to get dressed. By the time I had put on my jewelry and brushed my waves, Foreign was walking her happy ass in the room without a care in the world. She strolled past me like I wasn't even right there. I knew my cheating had her a little distraught but all that mattered now was straightening my wrongs with a little more love and support.

"Baby. Why didn't you come home? I was worried sick about you? You didn't even answer any of my calls."

The way she rolled her eyes let me know we were still beefing. Instead of having an adult conversation with me, she headed for the bathroom. She frowned and smacked her lips when she realized I was following her.

"Can you please quit following me? I would like to take a shower so I can go to sleep."

"Is there something wrong with me seeing you take a shower? I was hoping we could go out for breakfast this morning. I know we haven't spent much time together lately, but I wanna start changing that."

She huffed at me with a raised eyebrow. "When did you think of that bright idea?"

"I thought about it after we left my parent's house yesterday. Nothing can change the reality of our past. But maybe stepping up for our present can correct our future before it's too late."

I stepped in front of her and she slightly took an inch backwards. It was like my presence alone disturbed her and I could tell she wasn't trying to communicate.

"Are you at least gonna give me a chance to change this for us? The chance to be a husband again? I'm taking rehabilitation classes. I even skipped practice to make sure we bond for the rest of the day."

"Aaron, we ain't gotta do none of this. When I was trying to be your wife, you wanted to be cuddy buddies. You fucked other bitches and treated me like I was your disposal bucket. It shouldn't take me giving you the cold shoulder to get some respect to start flowing around here. This place doesn't even feel like home to me anymore."

Laced with disappointment, her last comment caused me to rub a hand across my temple. I knew I wasn't the perfect man, but what did my wife and I truly have if she no longer wanted to step foot inside the home we shared.

I didn't want her to run back off, so I remained humble. "Foreign?"

"What, Aaron?"

"Do you remember when we were in high school and I promised you I would always be with you forever? I told you no matter what problems happened between us, my love would be until the end of time. That humans aren't perfect, but we have to make choices in our life that would be critical. Some would be for the best and others would have no purpose. I need to be sure you still believe in those words."

Foreign paused before turning on the shower. "Aaron, you don't even believe in those words yourself. They only apply to you. It takes two to build a real relationship, but it only takes one to destroy it. When we got with each other, I didn't do it because I knew your parents were going to send you to the best scouts. And I didn't stay for any financial gain. Aaron, I was there because I really loved you. Please don't speak to me on a matter you never placed your all into."

My face hit the floor and cracked, as I watched her strip out of all her clothes and jump in the steamy shower. I wanted to pull the curtain back, but I decided to just ask my question from our small distance. "Do you still even love me, Foreign?" As I waited for an answer, she continued to bathe as if my question bounced off the walls of our bathroom. "Foreign?"

"I hear you, Aaron. Can we just save the Family Feud questions for another time please?"

"Is it possible for us to discuss this over breakfast? We can go anywhere you like. My treat."

"I'm not really hungry. I just really want to be alone right now, if you don't mind."

Her reply was so dry it forced me to walk out. My wife was no longer my best friend and I could feel us stretching further apart by the day. Lexi was the only person who could truly help me with the outcome of our relationship, but I knew she wanted me to face this battle on my own. I needed to find a way to win Foreign's heart back.

Grabbing my car keys, I left the house in search of my own advice. Some sincere advice could hopefully be the glue to help me mend my marriage back together. There was only one person whose words would be powerful enough to stick with me, and that person was always available.

CHAPTER 11
AARON

The Price You Pay for Love

Making my way through the *Communication and Healing* building, I stepped inside the room and spotted my counselor, Ms. Anderson, sitting at her desk. She looked up after hearing the door close behind me.

"Aaron? Class is not until Friday. Are you okay?"

"Uhh, actually. . . I came to see if I could get a private session today. I'm in dire need, Ms. Anderson. I'm going through something right now and I don't think I'll be able to save my marriage if I don't get some help."

Removing her glasses, she motioned for me to take a seat at her desk. It was already going on eleven o' clock and I knew for a fact, she would be leaving within the next thirty minutes.

Upon sitting down, I quickly noticed her eyes begin to study mine, as if she were searching for the questions I had yet to ask.

"Ms. Anderson, I'm stuck right now, and I don't know what to do. I know it's going to take time to change my girl's frame of mind on forgiving me, but I'm starting to feel like the more time that passes, the more I'm losing her. So far, no one has been able to offer me any significant advice regarding what I should do. Not even my family. What am I supposed to do to convince my wife to forgive me, to give me another chance?"

It was like she analyzed everything I'd said in a matter of seconds. She replied with little contemplation. "Would you allow your girl to have sex with another man today?"

"Of course I wouldn't let her do something like that. She's my wife." The question Ms. Anderson asked me had to be the dumbest shit I'd ever heard. The bitch had jumped the gun already and I hadn't been sitting down more than thirty seconds. *What now*, I thought.

"But you're her husband, Aaron. Do you *really* love her? If so, what's the difference?"

Before I could answer, my words seemed to get caught in my throat. Honestly, I didn't know what to say. I didn't want to be viewed as a hypocrite, so I tried to choose my words carefully. "Well, while it is true that I'm her husband, it's also true that I'm working on making changes within myself, as well as my actions. Not sending my girl out for slaughter."

"So, let's evaluate this situation, Aaron. Your wife is furious with you because you're having sexual intercourse with every woman you run across. This is a habitual problem that you've had for a while, which means it's an obsession."

"I wouldn't call it an obsession," I said defensively.

"Aaron, an obsession is a trait that renders you incapable of stopping on your own. Something you find irresistible. Whether the obsession is a drug or a person the question remains the same. . . What causes you to fiend for a person so much that you become willing to risk the woman you gave everything up for? Is she not enough?"

"Of course."

"Then why do you cheat, Aaron? I want you to picture something for me. Imagine me walking around this table right now and throwing myself on you. Would you like that?"

Ms. Anderson's words sounded like a script out of a 1970's porn flick. That shit would definitely never happen. Even if she was the last person on earth. "Nah, I can't say that I'd be happy with that."

"But why not? You sleep with other women, right? What makes me so different from those other girls?"

"Those chicks are fine honeys, models and actresses. Women with taste and appeal. In my world I deal with nothing but the best!"

"So, from the way you're yelling, I can tell that you're passionate about your obsession right now. It hurts, and it's hard to admit that your wife is unattractive in your eyes. Just like me. She's not your little actress or model. She's just an ordinary woman and you don't want to admit that. You don't want to hurt her, but you're cheating for a personal pleasure. Once you admit those traits, you'll see that you're the one who's ruining your marriage, Aaron."

Ms. Anderson struck the center of my chest with her words. Denying her accusations wasn't a visible choice. Everything she said was the absolute truth. I wiped the tear that graced my eyelid. Foreign wasn't being shown affection and loyalty. Lately, the love was diving off a rocky ship, and I was the one to blame. I couldn't disagree.

"You're right. But my feelings for my wife are real. I love her more than anything that walks this earth."

"So step up and be a man, Aaron. Treat those same models and wild singers like you would do me, and any other woman. But not your wife. If you love her the way you say, stop being selfish and keep your dick in your pants." Her face cringed up like she was the grandmother of a corrupted teenager. I couldn't help but lower my gaze.

"You can survive these faults if you come to the class, Aaron and start thinking about her feelings. If she rejects your gestures, try harder. The only thing I can do is tell you the truth. I'm your counselor, not the woman in the neighborhood who keeps everything on the hush."

I stood and pondered on my next move. "Thank you, Ms. Anderson. I promise I'll be at the next class. I'll wire the usual for your grateful duties."

"No need. Take it as a free game code and run with it." She placed her glasses back on and went back to work.

Leaving out of the session, I called Foreign's phone knowing she might not answer. As expected, she forwarded my call. Getting inside my car, I dialed Lexi hoping I might have better luck.

"What is it?" She answered on the third ring.

"I need to talk to you. I gotta really get things right with Foreign, sis. The idea I have in mind is liable to make her smile for eternity, but I can't do it without you."

"What are you talking about, Aaron? You don't need to be thinking of anything new. You're already in deep water."

"You don't even know what I have in mind, Lexi. That's the reason I need to talk to you."

"Listen, I'm busy. If I don't handle this business yo' ass won't have anything but a mattress and a pot to piss in. Leave all the bright ideas alone until I get this taken care of."

"What's going on? Is everything okay, Lexi?" I could tell by her tone she had something up her sleeve.

"Keep your mouth closed and cater to your woman until I tell you it's clear to talk, Aaron. I have to go." As usual, she ended the call in my ear.

It was hard dealing with different opinions, especially when you valued everyone's thoughts equally. Foreign was upset. And sitting around wasn't going to help at all. I pulled off with my thoughts so jumbled, I needed to clear my mind for what was ahead.

Lexi . . .

After hanging up with Aaron, I stepped out of my car and headed for Antwan's front door. I thought I'd heard slight chatter before he opened the door and allowed me to come in.

"Where is she?" He could judge from my expression and tell I meant business.

Earlier that morning, I was awakened out of my sleep when I heard about Antwan's nasty little prostitute. Apparently, she had made her way back and was ready to speak about the issue at hand. My mind was already made up there would be no debating on the deal I was prepared to make. Aaron needed this handled, and afterwards, I would make sure Antwan was removed far away from him. I could always smell a snake from a far.

Unlike my brother's traits, or the traits of the average female, I was stuck on relations. It was never hard for me to sever ties with anyone when I cut all love tucked under my shoulder. It was just the way the world worked. The ultimate sacrifice on this planet was giving your heart to a person who would destroy it for their own selfish desires— that was a problem I refused to indulge in.

Stepping into his large vestibule Jenny, from the block, stood with her hands folded, while leaning against the wall. When her eyes locked with mine, she straightened up. I could tell she didn't know who I was, or what was about to come out of my mouth. Before I could speak, Antwan tried to introduce me, and I quickly cut him off. However, I wasn't there for the formalities.

"My name isn't important, but my brother's name is. I'm sure you and your little friend got very acquainted the last time you were here. So let's get down to the business. Where's the tape?"

She began to twiddle with her fingers when my question caressed her earlobes. "Umm . . . that's the problem. Red has the video. Not me."

"Excuse me?"

"My friend has the tape. She's so caught up on receiving a check, she's willing to leak it across the internet for a nice price. I can't lie. At first, I needed the extra money for personal purposes, but after Antwan called and told me it was an issue, I came back. Cherry is trying to be slick. She's not trying to come off of it."

My eyes gently rolled over to Antwan who leaned quietly on the wall, as if he didn't know what was going on. At that exact moment, I could see the entire vision of their little play running through my head. I was more on point than either one of them expected. Stepping in front of Bambi the tramp, I folded my arms.

"Didn't you know from the jump that this was a blackmail scheme to break my brother out of some money?"

She tried to speak, but I cut her off again. "You were invited to a party by Antwan specifically. No average girl can just decide to go to a professional athlete's mansion party. So you knew this was a setup, right?"

"Wait. Hold up. What do you mean she knew this was a setup? You saying I got something to do with this?"

This nigga was trying to raise his voice like that shit was about to make me back down.

"That's exactly what I'm saying. You can lower your tone because the level of your voice won't convince me of anything. You're only trying to defile him for whatever duck-ass reason you have in your head. My brother is my only concern. These nasty ass females have a video of him and you know his reputation can easily be ruined in the eyes of the fans. Everyone in the industry knows my brother is married. Foreign has been on the front of several articles with him, not to mention, television."

"You trying to take up for your brother, but you know the bullshit that he do. He's addicted to bitches. No one has ever forced that man to go be with none of these women. Aaron doesn't care about that girl. He has a great woman at home, and he still chose to cheat. Not once in a while, but frequently," Antwan said, while casually pouring himself a drink at the mini bar.

Turning my attention back to Cherry, I pulled out a small contract and placed it in her hand.

"What is this?" she asked, demonstrating her ignorance.

"It's a contract not to disclose anything about the video. I agreed to give you broke bitches twenty grand a piece. But how can we finish the deal if your conniving-ass friend is missing?"

"She doesn't know about the deal. I'm the only one of us who knows. All I can do is try to call her to see if she'll agree."

"Well, it would surely be nice if you could scurry on and make it happen. My patience is running beyond thin."

Watching her step into the kitchen, she dialed some numbers on her cellphone. That's when I turned my attention back to Antwan's dirty ass. "I don't know what the fuck you got going on, but it's not gonna work." My tone was firm and unwavering.

"I don't know what the fuck you're talking about. I hope you don't think I'm trying to get any money from Aaron 'cause that would be very dumb of you, Lexi. As you can see, I own a three million dollar home. I have six cars and a bank account that'll last me for years. I don't need shit from yo' brother."

"Yeah, maybe you don't, but it could be something else, like some personal problems. Just so you know, I'm gonna fill you in on something. I'm Aaron's twin sister and I can feel certain things he can't. I've noticed a few other things about you that my brother probably hasn't. . . .. Like the way you're constantly calling him to participate in your little sexcapades with these little random-ass whores.

You're trying to pull a stunt and I can see it from a mile away. For future references, you need to be aware that I'm well connected when it comes to things like this, Antwan— from the streets to the industry. My brother may not have a gangsta bone in his body, but

118

I can guarantee you my associates are far from pussy. I want that videotape back. If it doesn't come back, we're gonna have a problem."

"Are you threatening me?" He got all puffed up as if that would make me stand down. His feelings were boiling by the second and I knew my statement was eating him up.

"I don't have to threaten shit. You've heard the stories for yourself. I handle my business accordingly. I'm the protector of this family and you can believe I take pride in what I do. When you fuck with my brother, you're fucking with me. I would advise you to calm down and relax before you blow a head gasket."

The scolded expression he'd been giving me faded within seconds. He needed to know I wasn't the one to try. Neither was my family. Him nor his two-dollar tricks knew how far I was willing to take this matter. They needed to understand my only intentions were focused on helping Aaron get out of the sticky bind he was in.

Before I could get my next words out, Cherry stepped back into the hallway. "She wants more than twenty thousand. She feels like Antwan tried to play her. You promised us fifty grand a piece," she said looking in Antwan's direction then back at me. "He knew we had just gotten fired from our jobs. You asked did we want to make the extra cash and we said yes."

Now my attention was back on this dumbass nigga. "What the hell is she talking about? You promised these bitches money to have sex with my brother? What is this really about?"

Making his way over to Cherry, he snatched her phone. "Bitch, you don't even have a voice in this shit. You need to keep your mouth closed." He snarled in her face like he was about to pull an Ike Turner.

Digging in my purse, I grabbed my black 380 snapshot pistol. Raising it towards his leg, he jumped quicker than a bitch on a sack of dope.

"Yo'! Put the gun down. What's wrong with you, Lexi?"

"You acting like you about to pull a stunt and hit that girl. Lower your hands and chill out. I'm not playing that, baby boy. You gotta do that shit on your own time. We got business to handle."

His ass was standing straight like a pencil after realizing I wasn't the average fuck buddy. Hearing Cherry speak, I knew this idiot didn't have control on the mission. Antwan was working against Aaron and it was clear to see.

"Listen, Cherry, Berry, whatever your name is. I need to know where she is, and I'll pay the little tab for my brother's business back. When can we handle this?"

"In two days," she replied. "I need to let her know she's guaranteed to get what's rightfully owed to her."

Cherry was nodding her head like a hurt victim in the courtroom. I despised bum bitches, but for Aaron's sake, I had to do whatever it took for things to remain normal. After taking the phone from Antwan, I placed my number in her phone, and handed it back to her. "Call me in two days. I'll have the money along with the contract. Just keep this between us, and it'll be easy."

"Can you please put that gun up in my house?" Antwan asked, looking back and forth between me and his freak slave. "You see I'm not a threat."

Debating on whether I should or not, I allowed him to plead his case. "First off, I wasn't about to hit her. This slut is lying. If I had a problem with your brother, I would've pulled his card at my party. Ain't shit scary 'bout me."

After that sly comment, my mind told me Antwan was definitely the culprit behind these slick-ass females' little bribery game. It was written all on his face. Lies always happened to find their way to the light, especially when you were dealing with money-hungry people.

"It doesn't matter right now. I'm well aware of what's going on here. From this point on, you have nothing to do with this. I'll handle the issue with the girls, and you can leave them be. Do we have an understanding?"

"Fuck it. I'm not trying to be involved in this shit anyway," Antwan blurted out like he was off the hook.

"Good." Looking over to Cherry, I held up my cell. "See you in two days."

The Price You Pay for Love

Walking out of Antwan's home, I got in my car and headed straight for Foreign.

Aaron . . .

I'd spun around Tampa's expressway about six times since leaving the counselor's office. My mind couldn't leave the thoughts of my decisions alone. I knew retiring from the league would disappoint my father, but if it would make Foreign happy to be away from that life, then it would make me feel joy from the pain that was aching me so badly.

Truthfully, I had the most loyal woman ever. It was hard to find someone who could live up to the standards on striving for one man. A few visions of my deceit had allowed me to sit back and see where I'd gone wrong with my emotions.

I was on my fourth cup of Grey Goose and nothing seemed to calm my heat at the time. Blinking, I adjusted my eyes to see the red light I was approaching. Easing on my brakes, I sipped from my cup and dialed Foreign's number on my car phone. Of course, I received the same response, a dry voicemail. Truth be told, I was scared to go home and find her gone. My worst fear was to discover that my wife had packed up her things with the intentions of never coming back.

Pulling over into the parking lot of a corner store, I parked and leaned my head against the headrest. After wasting so much time on the fast life, I had finally realized it was what slowed me down from making myself happy.

Football was no longer what I wanted. Neither was the fame and fortune. None of it compared to what Foreign was worth. Deep down, I knew I could make things right, I just had to figure out how to do it. After I downed the rest of my alcohol, I decided it was time to head home and face the music.

Destiny Skai

CHAPTER 12
EMILIA

Black coffee was exactly what I needed. Our daily meeting was dragging the hell out of me. It had already been a long morning and, quite frankly, I was tired. The more I squirmed in my seat, the more irritable I became. At that point, I wanted to stab myself in the ear with a pencil. Not even five minutes later, it finally came to an end.

Relieved of the bullshit investigation we were wasting tax dollars on, I proceeded to my office and closed the door behind me. Once I was comfortable at my desk, I cracked open my computer and began my search. Our system had to be the slowest in the district. The government was so damn cheap it didn't make any sense. Instead of 4G, we had 2G in that muthafucker. Finally, the search window produced the results. Using a sticky note to write on, I scribbled down his address and stuck it inside my pocket.

"Mr. Aaron Young, I got you," I mumbled aloud.

There was a knock on the door, so I turned off my screen. "Come in."

One of the older detectives walked in with his hands pushed down in his pockets.

"How can I help you?"

Marshall pulled out a chair and sat down. "The captain wants us to work together on this case."

It was just like the sergeant to pull a dumb-ass stunt like that. Of course, I wasn't pleased, which meant my face displayed my countenance perfectly.

"For what? This is a simple case of an underage girl attending a party she had no business being at. She clearly stated she had used a fake I.D."

"That's what I said. So, take that up with your superior."

"This is ludicrous. I'm not some rookie detective."

"Like I said—"

Before Marshall could get out another word, I interrupted him by holding my hand up to silence him. "Oh, I am. Don't worry about that."

"Well, let me know what he says. I'm not interested in this case, so if I'm not needed, it's all yours." Marshall remained seated. The way he stared at me made him look creepy.

"Is there anything else you need?"

"No."

"Okay. I'll give you an update. I have work to do."

"No problem." He got up and strolled towards the door with his hands behind his back. Once he crossed the threshold, he closed the door behind him.

Today was going to be a short one since I had an active investigation on my hands. Gathering my belongings, I piled them inside my tote bag and headed out. Before I left the building, I stopped by the chief's office. Softly, I tapped on the door and gained access after the third knock. With caution, I proceeded inside and stood in the middle of the floor.

"Flores," he adjusted his glasses. "Although I have a pretty good idea of the issue at hand, what can I do for you?"

Since sarcasm wasn't his native tongue, I let the snide remark slide. My purpose was business related. "I'm curious to know why you've deemed it necessary for me to have a partner on such a simple case."

"Honestly, I believe you should have some type of backup when you go out and start asking questions. This could get very ugly," he stated sternly.

"These are professional football players, not gangbangers, Sir," I responded. "They're certainly not about to ruin their careers based on the lies of a teenaged girl. And surely, they aren't going to harm me because of it. This is not a federal case and I don't need help with minor interviews."

The captain held his hands up in surrender. "Fine. If you think you can handle this on your own without it getting messy, then do it. But I'll be watching you."

"Are you ever going to let what happened go?"

"No, not until you prove you can be trusted and reliable."

"I made one mistake and—"

"And, it almost cost you your badge," he said, slicing my sentence in half with a quickness.

"Got it. I'll follow all procedures accordingly."

"For your sake, I hope so."

Exiting his office, I made a dash out the door. The incident he reflected on resurfaced in my memory bank— an incident I struggled to free my conscious of. A year ago, I'd been investigating a rape case and I interviewed a minor without the consent of his parents. In my gut, I truly believed he was guilty, so I kept pushing for a confession. I pushed until he committed suicide. A few days after his untimely demise the girl confessed, she had lied.

Devastation was only a portion of what I felt. On the inside, it felt like a part of me had died right along with him. The community was in an uproar. The department received so much backlash, the end result was a payout of a million dollars. And, me? Well, I ended up with a desk job. It wasn't what I wanted, but it was better than losing my job all together. After the incident I was no longer assigned investigative cases, however, this would my very first one since then and I was on my way to get some answers.

According to the GPS, my destination was twenty-five minutes away. It was after three in the afternoon, so I fought my way through the unexpected traffic. The closer I got, the more I thought about my approach. Getting a football team to flip on a fellow teammate was similar to the street code. It would be damn near impossible unless the law put their asses in the hot seat, facing long sentences.

Turning into the neighborhood, I spotted a familiar car driving in front of me. I activated my sirens which prompted the vehicle in front of me to slow down, before it came to a complete stop. Exiting the Grand Marquis, I walked up to the window with my hand on my hips. The driver rolled down the window.

"Why did you pull—" He froze in midsentence once he recognized my face.

"Mr. Aaron Young, how are you?"

"I was fine until you pulled me over."

"You should be a little happier to see me." I smirked.

"How did you know where to find me?"

"Relax, don't be so snappy. I'm law enforcement. I know where everyone lives."

"I'm having a rough day, Emilia. What's going on?"

"Hmm. You know, something interesting happened today at the station."

"And what's that?" Aaron appeared to be uninterested in what I had to say.

"You were in attendance at a party where an underage girl was given alcohol, drugs, and having sex." My statement got his immediate attention.

"I don't know what you're talking about."

"You sure about that? Because your name definitely came up."

"You know how those parties are," he said in a nonchalant manner

"Yes, I do. Which is why I'm not surprised. They tend to get really wild and it's rare for anyone to be asked for identification. I know from experience."

Aaron removed his seatbelt and turned his body toward me. "So, who is this girl?"

"Her name is Samantha and she's seventeen." Pulling my phone from my pocket, I scrolled through my saved images until I got to her picture. Then, I handed him the phone. "Do you remember seeing her at the party?"

He stared for a moment before handing it back to me. "Nah, I can't say I remember her face. But for the record I will say this, I didn't touch her. I don't fuck underage girls. I like my women a little more seasoned."

"Oh, I know."

"Well, if you know, why are you questioning me?"

"I wanted to see what you knew. It happened at a party Calvin hosted, and since he's your best friend, I knew you were in attendance."

"Right." He nodded his head. "So, is that it? I really have to get home."

"For now, but I expect to see you soon."

"A'ight."

"Enjoy the rest of your day."

"I'll do my best." Aaron rolled up his window and pulled off.

On my way back to the car, I hummed a sweet tune. He would be seeing me much sooner rather than later.

Foreign . . .

Sitting in the living room area, I sipped on a glass of wine and flipped through the cable channels. It saddened me to know my marriage had run its course. My dream was to have a house filled with babies while being the best wife humanly possible. I wanted us to be together forever just like our parents. Unfortunately, Aaron had gone out of his way to demolish that dream. Internally, I was dying. Now, all I wanted was a fresh start, one that didn't involve my husband.

Seeing the word *scandal* plastered across the screen caught my attention, so I adjusted the volume.

"*It appears that the Tampa Bay Buccaneers are back in the news. Only this time they aren't winning against a team. According to a reliable source, every player of the team is currently under investigation. Recently, an underage girl gained entrance to the Super Bowl after-party where she engaged in drinking and sexual activity. Sources say amongst the crew was the team's main attraction, quarterback Aaron Young. There have been no arrests made in the case as of yet, but we will certainly keep you posted. Back to you Carolyn.*"

Anger filled my body, as I turned off the television and tossed the remote across the room, shattering a glass vase in the process. It was disturbing to hear such a disgusting scandal. It had to be God telling me to pack up and walk away. The trifling behavior he was displaying was unquestionably going to end his career before his retirement and our divorce.

I heard the locks to the front disengage, and Aaron walked through the door. Rising to my feet, I greeted him halfway.

Aaron had a vacant look on his face. That was, until I slapped the spit out his mouth. "You fuckin' underage girls now?"

His eyes widened in surprise. "No! What the fuck you talking about?"

"It's all over the news, Aaron. The entire team is under investigation. Are you trying to ruin your reputation and career?"

"I didn't do shit."

"Well, they're certainly screaming your name from the fuckin' mountain top." Stroking my temple with my right hand, I grunted loudly. "You got me looking so stupid in the public's eye. Every time I turn around you in between a bitch's legs."

As usual, Aaron just stood there looking dumbfounded. The shit was really pissing me off. He never took shit seriously and that aggravated the hell out of me. His reactions stemmed from being young, rich and stupid.

Pushing his head with my finger, I stepped closer to him and invaded his personal space. "I'm telling you right now, if you go to jail, don't call me. I'm not helping you get out of this shit. And for the last time, I want a divorce!"

Turning on my heels, I attempted to walk away but he grabbed me by the arm. "We're not getting a divorce and I'm not letting you leave. So you can get that out your head."

He really had me fucked up. "If you're worried about alimony, don't. I don't want it and you can keep this house. All I want is a lump sum to get me started and I'm out your hair. You can even keep the Bentley."

The wrinkles in his forehead displayed his anger. The glassiness in his eyes showed his sincerity. "I don't give a fuck about none of this shit. You can have it all. None of this shit means nothing without you. I just want my wife back, that's all. I promise I didn't touch that girl."

The love of my life stood in front of me with tears in his eyes, pleading his love for me, and I felt nothing. I had poured so much love into my marriage until I was empty on the inside, empty like an upside down drinking glass. To keep from hurting his feelings any further, I turned and walked away. Still, it didn't deter him because he followed me up the staircase.

"Foreign, baby, please don't leave me. I need you. I'm trying to change. I have a sex addiction and I'm seeking help. I'm taking classes for it." Aaron grabbed me once more and stepped in front of me.

"Do you know how it feels to hear my husband admit he has a sex addiction? Do you even know what that means? I'll never satisfy you sexually. You need a variety of women and I didn't sign up to share you with anybody. Those hoes can have you. I'm done."

"Fuck them hoes. I don't love them."

"Obviously, you don't love me either."

"Don't say that. We can work on us. If I retire would that make you happy? I'll quit all this shit and leave it behind if it means having you."

"That's a weak-ass move and further proves my point. You have no control over your dick. We took vows and you promised to honor them and be faithful to me. You lied and I'm done pretending. Now, if you don't mind, I would like to shower and get dressed."

"Foreign, where are you going?"

"Out."

There was absolutely nothing he could do to make me stay. My body needed love and affection. That was something I couldn't get at home, so I was going out to get it. A good girl got tired of being just that, good. Especially to a man who didn't appreciate a loyal and faithful woman. I was going to do what made me happy and that was being with Domestic.

So, I gathered my things for the shower and went into the bathroom. Before I stepped in, I sent him a text letting him know to expect me in an hour.

CHAPTER 13
FOREIGN

After arriving to Domestic's car wash, my eyes glanced into the side mirror to check my makeup. Usually, I wouldn't wear all the fancy shit to look good. I preferred a hundred percent natural, from head to toe. Tonight just felt different. Domestic's love was needed.

The aching pain of a torn heart was eating at my mind. It seemed like the only thing I could think about was Aaron's deceit. For the first time, tonight he'd shown a small sign of sincerity. The thought always counted, but the time for apologies was over. What he didn't know wouldn't kill him.

Heading inside, I casually strolled to Domestic's office. Of course, my face was known for having being seen around the shop lately. Nevertheless, for the time being, my identity had been kept a secret, but a lot of things were about to change, soon.

When his eyes met mine, he paused. The phone was up to his ear as he engaged in conversation. The thought of his hands caressing me crossed my mind. Our thoughts must have been in sync because he quickly ended the call and moved across the room toward me.

Looking up to him, his Polo Blue cologne cleared my senses. Wasting no time, I engaged in a nasty tongue kiss. The shit felt so good, it was like a Jacuzzi had dropped out of my pussy. Pushing the door closed, he wrapped his arms around my little waist.

"Hey you. Why the nice skimpy clothes? You must want me to rip them off?" He raised an eyebrow to let me know he was serious.

"That depends. Can you do it to me now?" Raising my skimpy black Chanel dress, my apple arched, giving him a view of my depressed kitty lips.

"I want you to stay just like that," he ordered and locked the office door. Before he could make his back over to me, his pants were down to his ankles and the boxers he'd worn were trying to free the monster contained behind them.

He pulled me in his arms and allowed his hands to explore my body. I could feel his fingers spreading me apart. He stroked his piece, and like magic, it grew got thicker than a broomstick.

"Put it in, baby!" At the moment, my craving for him was outrageous. When he slid deeply inside of me, the feel of a real man's body on top of mine enticed my pussy to talk back. "Ahhh-Sss," I hissed before I could stop myself.

Domestic never wasted time when it came down to sex. His fuel was my energy and it forced me to fiend for more. His strokes were firm and solid.

Less than thirty seconds of him spreading my cheeks and thrusting inside of me, I felt my first orgasm rising. My stomach told me to stop, but the nut was screaming for me to let him handle business.

I could feel his shit sliding in, inch by inch. My juices covered his rod giving easy access to glide inside me deeper. Of course, he took full advantage by locking on to my waist. I held my breath knowing the animal was about to be released.

His pounding session was in effect. My ass clapped roughly against the bottom of his stomach. I couldn't scream, though the feeling caused my heart to beat faster by the second. He wasn't sparing me.

"Did you miss me?" he grunted, while shoving his large womanizer into my guts. All I could do was pant desperately. Sparkles formed in my vision and I felt as if I was getting off the next amusement park ride. Placing my head on the desk, I squinted my eyes and shivered as he took total control.

Our quickie turned into a thirty minute session and my thick cream had coated his piece like icing on a cake. His nut erupted like a volcano, and every drop of his lava spilled deep inside my belly.

Domestic was the only person I'd ever slept with who made my body feel as though we'd just walked away from a car wreck. Sex was only a mind thing, but his sex was a mind game. He knew how to work every position and piece with his eyes closed.

Nibbling on my ear, he eased out of me. "Why are you making me fall for you so quickly? I can get very aggressive and overprotective when it comes to booty like yours." His smile and statement sent a tingle through my womanhood.

"You don't have to be aggressive if you don't want to. It's here for you and I love giving it to you. Willingly," I added.

"Do you think you could love me forever? I wanna have what's mine every night, so you could easily become my addiction."

Grinning, I pecked his lips. "You gotta show me you want it forever. You can't just want me for my good sex." My eyes landed back on his dick print. His erections always seemed to last for hours before it went back to soft mode.

"That's easy. A few thoughts have crossed my mind since the last time we were together. Maybe a few vacations, some alone time in Hawaii . . . maybe France. There are a few ways to make you mine for good and we can still have fun in the mix."

"What about your businesses? We just can't run off on trips with no plan. Who's going to run all of this for you?" I asked, while fixing the collar on his shirt.

"That's the least of my concerns. Everyone who's a part of my establishment has a position. I could leave today and stay away for a year and all my priorities and duties would still be taken care of. It's the life of being a boss, baby. Making you happy would be nice though. A couple of weeks with me and your husband will be dead to you."

To be truthful, the feeling was already etched in my brain. Either that, or Aaron would be the cause of my death with all his treacherous-ass ways. If I was to get hurt from fighting or locked up for killing one of his sex toys, he would still shove his shit in the next bitch who passed his presence.

The feelings were mutual. All the love he couldn't give me, I, now, received from Domestic. The attention he placed on me was something Aaron couldn't do. The mere thought of him asking me about my day made me smile. The small things mattered when we were together. It showed me there was someone who could love me better than my husband could. It was sad because I'd wasted my marriage on a man who truly didn't want to be with me. Learning my lesson was easy, but accepting it was the hard part.

"I guess we'll see what you have in store for the future then, Mister. I'd like to skip dinner and go to our room if possible." I gave him that sweet puppy dog look. My pussy was in desperate need of a tutor and he was the man for the job.

"Sure. I'll stop and grab a few bottles of wine to help us relax. Let me grab my coat and give the keys to my employee, out front." After getting his things in order. We made our way to the register.

Domestic removed the keys from his pocket. Looking into his worker's eyes, he grinned. "Don't do anything I wouldn't do."

"You ain't gotta worry, boss. I'll lock up as soon as the last customer leaves."

Receiving the answer he wanted, we strolled out of the carwash. Walking alongside of him, I leaned over and kissed his cheek. "Thanks for being so sweet to me."

"No need to thank me, love. You know I can't go without a taste of that. I can't imagine not having you to feast on and spend quality time with. It completes me."

Cheesing from ear to ear, I gripped his hand even tighter. Those small words warmed my spirit. It felt good to be loved and respected. My relationship was so faded from the limelight and money, I didn't know what real emotions felt like anymore.

My attention was so lost in his freaky smirk, I never acknowledged the black Durango sitting in the center of the street. Within seconds, my life flashed before my eyes. Four gunshots rang out loudly. All I could feel was Domestic's body jump over me. My head thumped against the concrete. The sound of screeching tires echoed through my ears.

"Foreign, are you okay?"

"Yeah, I just bumped my head on the ground." My hand touched the knot that was slightly bleeding. Domestic opened his car door and reached inside the middle console. Pulling out a black handgun, he checked the clip and bounced back over to me.

"What happened? Why would someone shoot at us?" My voice trembled from fear.

"I don't know. This area of Tampa is flooded with gang territory. I had a similar problem a few months back when one of

134

my employees got robbed. Let me get you back inside until I can make sure we're safe."

Lifting me up, he helped me back inside the carwash. I could already see his employee jumping on the phone before we entered so I knew the cops were about to come. Sitting me down in a chair, Domestic made his way back outside to check the area.

The fall had me slightly dizzy, and I tried to analyze what had just occurred. Not long after his worker had hung up the phone with the authorities, Domestic made his way back inside.

"It was probably some fuckin' stupid-ass teenager. I'm going to file a report just in case I have to kill one of they asses. I already warned the police about the drama, so eventually I'm gonna have to take matters into my hands."

Grabbing my hand, he kneeled down in front of me. "I'm so sorry about this, Foreign. Are you sure you're okay?"

"Yes. You saved my life. I could've been killed but you jumped in the way."

"That's why I'm here. I don't ever want you to think you could be hurt when you're with me. I'll protect you by any means."

Hugging his neck, I relaxed and sat back. It took the ambulance and police about five minutes to arrive. They asked me if I needed medical assistance and I quickly denied. I managed with a peroxide clean-up and some antibiotic ointment for the small cut on my head.

Two officers conversed with Domestic, as the detectives ran back the cameras.

Spotting a Spanish looking woman with a badge, my senses went up. I had seen her at the carwash a few times before, but her words were always brief and short. Domestic didn't need any trouble with the police and this bitch looked like she was a major cop. As they spoke, her eyes met mine while I stood in the doorway with a nasty mug. Whispering something to him, she gazed at me again before walking off.

"Who is that woman?" my mouth started running, as he approached me.

"She's just the lead detective over the department. This is her area."

Letting the childish matter bypass my mind, she was crossed out of my thoughts. I hugged Domestic and laid my head on his chest. "Does this mean I can't stay with you tonight?" I was hoping he didn't say no. There was no way to settle myself unless it was being with him.

Kissing my bottom lip, he squeezed my ass. "Are you sure you still wanna stay? I know you're probably shaken up a bit. You can go home if you'd like."

"Going home isn't in my plans for tonight, but I have something that is." I rubbed the center of his six pack and he grabbed his coat.

"Let's get out of here."

Again, we left the building hand in hand and made our way to our cars. I watched him climb in his whip and I pulled out directly behind him. The anticipation of being with him clawed at my skin like a spoiled kitten.

As a young teenager, my womanly nature had always caused me to fall easily for a good game. It was a form of immaturity that every girl crossed in their lifetime. From the looks of Domestic's position, he was exactly what I needed to stay in my happy zone. Those thick arms and abnormal dick could make any bitch lose it. The main attraction was the sweet sincere side of a man I knew nothing about.

Not too much time had passed since I'd started creeping around with my sexual crush. Maybe it wasn't right being that I was still declared a married woman in everyone else's sight. That was the same way I felt when Aaron started to share his penis like a junkie's liquor bottle. I was tired of drunk driving on fake ass excuses.

Tonight, I was putting my pussy power on Domestic. Getting all his loving would show him the reason he didn't want to leave a sweet catch like me.

Lexi . . .

As I looked at my watch for the third time, still waiting for Aaron
to bring his ass downstairs, my cellphone rang. Checking to see
who it was, my finger graced the green answer button.

The Price You Pay for Love

"Hello?"

"We're here. She's with me," Cherry said in my ear.

"Good, I'll be there in about twenty minutes. I wasted no time hanging up. She'd said exactly what I needed to hear.

The hype of the Super bowl controversy was at the top of every news station. Aaron's face was at the top of the charts for the blame and his mind wasn't able to process the drama that lie ahead. The tape we were on the hunt for would only make things more complicated.

Watching him trail down the steps, he moved like a sick slug.

"What the hell is wrong with you? Did you masturbate before getting out of bed? Because if you didn't, you need to turn around."

"I still haven't heard from Foreign." His voice was low and feeble.

"Foreign is somewhere sleep. She's probably trying to get rid of those dirty ass thoughts of you pumping inside these piglets. You got deeper shit to worry about, boy. If this tape gets in the wrong hands, you can kiss your entire family bye- bye." I waved my hand like I was on board a leaving train.

"I understand that, but I don't care about football anymore. My parents don't even want me no more. I'm just a fuckup and it's clear to see."

"I'm shocked. You're just now figuring that out? It's too late to wanna commit suicide. Let's handle this business and scrape up the rest of your pathetic relationship after we're done."

Grabbing his ass by the arm, we made our way out to the car and took off. It was already a good little drive out to Antwan's house, and time being wasted wasn't a good idea considering what was at stake.

"I'm not trying to see that nigga." Aaron wrinkled his face knowing his two-faced friend was about to play him out.

"That ain't my problem. I wasn't the one who decide to make the slime-bucket your friend— I only fucked him. Learn to kill the snakes then you won't have to duck in the grass."

He thought for a second before replying. "If I had known he was in his feelings about something, I would've never got close to him. He said we were brothers."

"And what nigga don't say shit like that, idiot? Stop being so damn green, Aaron. People will let you gain a certain amount of love and fame just to tear it down from under you. The reason my heart is so cold and solid is because my first rule is one I continue to live by: Never let anyone into my life box. It pumps blood for a reason and it surely ain't to pour out over some punk-ass feelings. You're a man. All y'all should know that."

The sound of my phone ringing stopped me from going in on my twin. Seeing it was Cherry, I quickly answered. "Bitch, we on the way. Stop blowing my line up like I'm one of your tricks."

Tossing the Galaxy in my middle console, I nudged my brother's arm. "You gotta straighten up. There's no reason to droop around about something that's already been done."

"Fuck this, Lexi. The media is gonna think what they want to. And even if that bitch wanted to leak the tape, it'll take a major promoter to push something like that. She ain't got no plug to make nothing happen," he said with aggravation in his tone.

"You'll be surprised."

Instead of amping his problem up, we kept the ride mellow and quiet. Aaron was going through a phase that wouldn't be broken until he terminated his bullshitting ways.

We arrived at Antwan's crib, parked the car, and stepped out swiftly. Making our way to the front door, Antwan's dog-ass allowed us to enter. His feelings were so bundled up he didn't even speak to Aaron. I tapped my brother's arm just to put him on game. Hatred was in this man's blood and it stuck out like a sore thumb.

When we entered the living room we saw Cherry sitting down on the couch next to her friend, Pink. Her hair was now back to its original color and the wild party girl was replaced with a sophisticated nerdy appearance. Before I could a get a word out, Aaron and Antwan was down each other's throat.

"Nigga, that's foul. You used these dirty-ass bitches to set me up, Antwan! I thought we were brothers, man!"

"What? Bro, you sound like a bitch. Your sister filling yo' head up and I'm not trying to hear no small talk about this petty beef shit. I don't got no reason to set nobody up. If I had something to say I'd say it."

"Watch yo' fuckin' mouth with the name calling, bruh. I'm not disrespecting nobody so you gon' show me and my sister some respect."

Placing my hand on his shoulder, my fingers tightened, signaling him to calm down. I knew how Aaron could get when he became angry, and it was never a pretty sight.

"Listen, the time for debating is over. Cherry, does she have the tape or not?"

"Do y'all have the money or not?" Pink shot back at us with a curious eye and a tone too sarcastic for my taste.

I inhaled and exhaled deeply before allowing the slick-ass comment to rub off me like oil on water. Otherwise, I would've pimp-slapped that bitch. In my mind, I knew we were dealing with some broke hoes, so that was something I expected.

Pulling out the two manila envelopes, I handed one to each woman. "That's fifty thousand each, just like you requested. Now where's the tape?"

Removing the camera from her bag, Pink passed it to me. "This is my only source of the film, but I have to be honest with you."

Her words penetrated my ears and I knew she was about to say something to switch my mood instantly.

"I think someone else already leaked the tape. It's being viewed on certain social sites right now." Pink shrugged her shoulders like it wasn't her problem.

The news disturbed me, and I could tell it struck a nerve in Aaron because his head dropped in defeat.

"What do you mean, it's been leaked? You two had the only copies to this video."

"No, we didn't," she admitted, with her stare focused on Antwan.

After Cherry blasted out the confession, I saw the anger as it revealed itself on Aaron's face. "Nigga, you set me up!"

Before I could stop the action, it played out in my head the exact way it occurred. Aaron's medium-build frame eased across the small space and landed a right fist into Antwan's jaw. His body crashed to the ground and Aaron lost control of his hands.

"You thought I was something to play with, boy. Huh?" he asked, while feeding him fist after fist.

Of course, I used that time to snatch back our funds for the video. If the tape was already leaked, there was no purpose of paying shit out of the pocket.

"What the fuck are you doing? We had a deal." Pink complained, due to the way the blessing had been taken back within a split second.

Ignoring her, I snatched Aaron off Antwan. The bottom of his lip was split, and the shape of his eye matched the size of a tennis ball. Jumping up from the floor like he hadn't just got a beat down, he started pouring out his emotions.

"Nigga, I leaked the tape! That's right. I did. I'm the one who invited that girl to the Super Bowl party too. I don't have to get rid of you because you killed yourself. Your career is over whether you have the tape or not. You crossed me out and thought nothing was gonna happen, Aaron?"

I continued to push Aaron towards the door because the vain talk was eating at him. He tried to break free three times until I finally got him out.

"Can you please calm the fuck down?"

My mind couldn't go there while trying to control him at the same time. My only choice was to cuss his ass out since it was the only thing he understood.

Recollecting himself, Aaron took a deep breath before we climbed back in our car. Things happened so fast he hadn't caught on to what occurred, but thankfully, Alexis Young was always on point.

"I'm over this shit. The video is out. Foreign is gonna see the shit again and leave me."

"You have to suck up to her and break it down easy. The only thing I can guarantee is all accusations of that young girl will he handled. Focus on the bigger picture. You're winning more than you think right now."

Squeezing together my plan for him was coming along great. I had killed three birds with no stone, but my mission was still at hand. I had to get Foreign back on the same track. It would be the only way any peace could truly be found in my brother's heart.

CHAPTER 14
CASEY

One month later. . .

Things between Shawn and I were awkward these days. He was constantly putting the press on me about relocating to Tennessee with him. True indeed he was a great man, but I was still hanging onto hope that Domestic would change and give our family a second chance. However, he had been quite occupied for weeks now. His pop ups decreased and Demerius Jr. was spending more time away from home. Tired of guessing what was up, I decided to give him a call.

"Hello."

"What's going on with you? Why haven't I been hearing from you lately?"

"I've been busy," Domestic replied dryly.

"Busy, huh?"

"Well, I do have three businesses to run. You must have forgotten I run this solo."

"You had my help, but you didn't want it."

"Your job is to take care of DP. Nothing more, nothing less. Besides, we been down this road before. You're too emotional and jealous."

"That's because you were always flirting with a bitch and being extra friendly."

"That might be true, but it was all business. Not one of those females could tell you I smashed. You knew I wasn't cheating on you."

"Whatever! That's not why I called."

"What's up?"

My heart rate increased due to the nature of my call. I wasn't prepared for the answer to the question I was about to ask. "What are we doing, Domestic? Are we working towards being together or what? This is confusing for Demerius, and I don't want him to have high hopes that we'll be a family if that's not the case."

"Casey . . ." He paused as if he was thinking of a way to break the bad news down to me. "You know that's not what we doing. I take care of you because you gave me my son. That's my job, and it's the least I can do for you after everything I put you through. You were accustomed to a certain lifestyle when we were together, and I want to make sure that lifestyle is still attainable. I don't owe you anything else."

Tears surfaced in my eyes and streamed down my cheeks. Once again, he'd crushed my heart with no remorse. "Why are you doing this to me? I love you and you know that."

"I love you too, but I'm not *in love* with you. There's a difference. Why do you insist on making this difficult? Do you know how many women would be happy with this arrangement?"

"I'm not other women." Sitting up on the bed, I planted my feet on the floor. "How could you possibly think this is fair to me? I'm supposed to live in this house knowing there's no chance that we can be together? How does that sound? You don't want me, but no one else can have me. That's selfish of you."

"Listen, if you don't like our arrangement you're free to leave. I'm keeping Demerius though."

"I'm not leaving my son. Are you crazy?"

"No, but you are if you think I'm gonna let you take him away from me. You can't afford to give him half of the shit I give him. Not even a tiny portion of it. He's accustomed to a good life."

"You think that's what this is? A good life?"

Taking me by surprise, I heard a female's voice in the background. I tried my best to figure out what was being said, but it was impossible.

"Listen, I have to go. I'll call you back later," and just like that, he hung up the phone.

Falling back onto the bed, I let out a loud, painful scream and clutched my pillow tight. Some men didn't give a fuck about a woman's feelings. All they cared about was getting their dicks wet and stringing us along, while playing with our feelings in the process. If I wasn't worried about going to prison, I would kill his ass. The last thing I wanted was for my son to be raised by the foster system while I was doing a life sentence in the penitentiary.

"Mom."

The sweet sound of my baby's voice dried my tears instantly. I never wanted him to witness the way his father treated me. In his eyes, Domestic was a saint, one who could do no wrong. Before I responded, I cleared my throat.

"Yes, baby."

"Are you okay?"

"I'm fine."

"Are you crying?"

"No."

The room grew silent and I thought he'd left the room. But then I felt him sit down on the bed and place his hand on my back. "You are crying. Is it dad?"

He didn't need to see me upset, so I tried to keep the questions from coming. "I just need some rest, Son. Go back in your room and we can talk later."

"I know he hit you."

Hearing those words fall from his lips hurt me to my soul. It just confirmed he wasn't as naïve as I thought he was. Slowly, I sat up and wiped my eyes with my shirt. Grabbing his hand, I attempted to make him understand. Although he had a nasty temper, bad mouthing Domestic was something I would never do.

"Your father and I have a very complicated relationship. It's something you'll never understand, and one thing I don't want you to do is get in the middle of it. Despite what we go through, he loves you and he's a good man."

Demerius had a sorrowful look in his eyes. It scared me to say the least. "Mom, I need to tell you something."

"What is it, sweetheart?"

"Please don't be mad at me."

Staring into his light brown eyes, I stroked his cheek to give him comfort. "I promise I won't be. What is it?"

"That day when Shawn was here, I had called dad. He told me to let him know if a man ever came here. I didn't know he was going to hit you. I'm sorry." He broke our stare and looked down at the floor.

Raising his chin, I fought back my own tears. "It's not your fault. He was wrong for telling you to do that."

"But I should've never said anything. He doesn't want you to have a friend, but he can. That's not right."

Demerius had my attention. "What do you mean?"

"He introduced me to a lady name Foreign. She's always at his house and at the carwash. I think they're dating."

My poor, innocent son had no idea of the type of pain he'd just caused me. In the back of my mind, my woman's intuition told me there was someone else. I just refused to believe it. For Domestic to introduce our son to her meant it was serious. It also cleared up my questions as to why he'd stopped coming over and why we hadn't slept together in awhile. For the sake of not appearing heart broken, I sucked it up and acted as if I didn't care.

"Good for him. That means I can date in peace now. Don't worry, I won't tell him you told me anything."

He nodded his head.

"Let me ask you a question. How do you feel about moving away to another state and starting over?"

"How will I see dad?"

"We can figure that out later. But would you be okay with it? I need to know before I consider it."

"All my friends are here. Dad is here."

"Okay, I just wanted to know."

"Dad's picking me up later."

"Okay."

Demerius stood up and left the room. It hurt to know Domestic had found my replacement. However, that meant that I should move on as well. Shawn crossed my mind and I needed to talk to him face to face. Before I headed out, I stopped by Demerius' room to let him know I was leaving.

The ride to Shawn's house was a quiet one. When I pulled up in the driveway, the first thing I noticed was the other cars were gone. That meant he was there alone. Checking my face in the mirror, I made sure my eyes were clear before I got out. It would be rude to show up distraught over another man. After knocking on the door a few times, the door swung open. Shawn stood there in a wife beater and gym shorts.

"Casey." He appeared to be surprised. "What are you doing here?"

"If you have company I can leave."

"No, no. Come in. I'm just surprised to see you, that's all."

He backed up and let me in. As soon as he turned around, I attacked his lips with mine. Without hesitation, he kissed me back like he had been waiting for the moment. His hands were at the small of back, but quickly made their way down to my cheeks. It felt good to be desired by a man. Our kiss lasted a while. When we finally separated, he looked into my eyes.

"What's gotten into you?"

"You mean what do I want *you* to put inside of me." I grabbed his hand and led the way to his bedroom.

While he locked the door, I removed every piece of my clothing and lay on the bed with my legs spread-eagle. My body craved the touch of a man. It needed love and affection, which was something I was no longer receiving. My eyes were locked in on Shawn as he stripped naked. Ever since I'd known him, I had never seen his package so I was curious to know what he was working with. All I knew was it better not be small, and he better know what to do with it. My mouth had no filter and I wouldn't hesitate to tell him if the sex turned out to be whack.

With great relief, I was satisfied to see he was working with something. He wasn't blessed like Domestic, but he was a nice size. The skin of his wood was an evenly toned brown. It sprung up and down like a diving board when he slid his boxers down. My kitty thumped in anticipation.

Shawn stood on the side of the bed, motioning me to come to him. Grabbing my legs, he pulled me to the edge of the bed and kneeled down in front of me.

The slither of his tongue rocking back and forth against my budding flower sent my insides into a frenzy.

"Ssss . . . Ouuu . . ."

My fingers dug deep into his scalp as he sucked and slurped on my sweet, succulent peach. His fingers fucked me relentlessly. I could only imagine and wait anxiously for what the dick was about to do.

Getting on my hands and knees, I tooted my ass up in the air. He entered me from behind and held my waist tightly. Taking his time, he slid in and out at a steady, yet slow pace. "Goddamn. I'd been dreaming about this day for months," I whispered breathlessly.

Extending my arms outward, I lay flat on my chest and arched up higher. I wanted to feel every inch of him surfing inside my walls. Somehow, I expected him to be gentle, since he some ways he just looked like the type. However, that wasn't what I wanted. I needed for him to beat it down and put me to sleep. My feelings were already hurt thanks to Domestic, so I needed an outlet to release the built up pressure.

Taking matters into my own hands, I threw my ass back on him aggressively. One of two things was about to happen: I was gon' fuck him like a little ass boy or he was gon' match my actions and fuck the shit out of me.

Swiveling my head in his direction, I attempted to demand my request, but I couldn't because I was on the verge of laughing. Shawn had the funniest fuck face I'd ever seen. His eyes were tightly closed and his top lip was curled. I could only imagine the thoughts running through his mind. Maybe fucking me was actually a dream come true for him. Unbeknownst to him, we would be fucking more often, now that I was a free woman.

"Fuck me harder!" I demanded.

He attempted to deliver, but not the way I needed it. He was too busy trying to make love when I was in desperate need of being fucked like a slut. My ass wanted to be manhandled. Damn handling me with care. *Break my back!* I thought.

"Fuck me harder than that."

"Say less." His response had come out so smoothly, I didn't know how to take it, one way or the other.

Next thing I knew, he pulled out, flipped me on my back, and rammed his hard wood deep inside my guts. Grabbing my legs, he placed one of each of his shoulders and went to work. His hard, deep strokes were starting to do damage to my stomach. At times, I thought I would literally stop breathing at any moment. The mercy he had on me earlier was out the window. He was determined to make me pay. Again, he wasn't Domestic, but his young ass knew how to lay some pipe.

Thirty minutes and three positions later, he pulled out and busted a nut on my tummy. All I could do was roll over on my side and look him in the eyes. There was a small dimple in his hazelnut cheek.

"Was that was hard enough for you?" he smirked.

"As a matter of fact, it was. I was a little skeptical that you couldn't hang, but you surprised me."

"If only you knew how long I'd been waiting to do that. I was trying to be a gentleman and make love to you, but you wanted me to WWE yo' ass."

"We'll have plenty of time for that." Moving closer, I placed a peck on his lips.

"What you saying?"

"I've given it some thought, and I wanna be with you. I'm ready to move away and start fresh with you."

Shawn pushed the strand of hair that hung over my eye, to the side. "You sure about that?"

"Yes, I'm positive."

"What about that Fifty Cent looking ass nigga?"

Every time he said that about Domestic it made me laugh. He called him that because he felt like my son's father was a bully and control freak.

"Fuck Domestic. He'll get over it eventually and once he does, we can co-parent from different states. My mind is made up. I'm leaving and so is Demerius."

"You really think he's gon' go for that? I'm just saying, look at your current situation. This not gon' end well."

"He's not going to do anything to you."

Shawn smirked and scratched his head. "Oh, I'm not worried about that. You know my brothers not playing about me. That shit he pulled when I was at your house will never happen again. He caught me off guard, and he had a gun, but I'm ready for whatever now. And he won't be touching you again either, or I'm gone have my brothers handle that too."

"No, they can't kill him."

"They ain't gon' kill him. They gon' teach his ass a lesson though. It's my job to protect you now and I'ma make sure I do that."

For the rest if the night, Shawn held me in his arms while we talked and made plans for our future. Eventually, I fell asleep anticipating my future with a man who loved me in spite of any misgivings regarding my feelings for him. Nonetheless, my heart and mind told me it was the right thing to do.

CHAPTER 15
FOREIGN

Domestic and I had been kicking it heavy, and I do mean in every aspect of the word. Many of my days were spent at his carwash. Instead of hiring a personal assistant, he had me working there instead, and with pay. I didn't need it, but I sure as hell wasn't turning it down. Whenever it slowed down and he could squeeze in a break, he would come into the office and give me the business— on the desk, the chair, or the floor. We didn't discriminate when it came time to get down and dirty. He had even taken me to his house a few times, and it was gorgeous.

The carwash was one of the three he owned. I found that out when he allowed me to accompany him during the pick-ups. Come to find out, he was thirty-eight, which made him fourteen years older than me, with a fourteen-year-old son who lived with him. I was cool with that though. Then he mentioned that he wanted to have another child.

Things at home started to change when I became absent. Aaron was no longer staying out late or attending those wild parties. I knew the sudden shift was an attempt to suck me back in so he could resort back to his old ways. This time it wasn't happening because I was happy with Domestic and what we had going on. I was completely stress free and I loved it.

After a long hot shower, I hopped in bed. Aaron wasn't home yet, which was fine with me. That was my chance to go to sleep before he arrived. What a fool I was, because no sooner than I had the thought, there his ass was coming into the bedroom.

"Foreign," he called out, but I didn't respond. "I know you're not asleep."

He sat on my side of the bed. As bad as I wanted to pretend to be asleep, I knew he wasn't going to move until I said something.

"What?"

"We need to talk."

"I'm sleepy. We can talk tomorrow."

"No, Foreign. We need to talk now."

Opening my eyes, I pouted. Just so he would know how irritated I was with his presence. "What?"

"You're changing."

"You don't say," I replied ironically.

"I'm losing you and I don't want to. We need to fix this before it gets too deep."

That was just like a typical cheating, no good-ass man. They loved to dish shit out but could never take it. "It's been deep, Aaron. Where the hell have you been for the past three years? Oh, I forgot . . . You were too busy fuckin' every Tasha, Kim, and Stacy. I'm tired and I don't want to hear this shit. Now if you don't mind, I would like to go to bed."

"I'm not giving up on us," he implied, as he left the room and went into the bathroom.

Time passed and I must've dozed off. When I opened my eyes, Aaron was between my legs trying to give me head. Closing my legs, I snapped. "What are you doing?"

"I want to make love to my wife."

"Well, I don't want it."

He pushed my legs out the way with more force than necessary. "Who the fuck is he?"

"Who is who?"

"The nigga you been fuckin', that's who. For the last month and a half, you've made zero attempts to have sex with me, and when I try, I get the same reaction each time."

"Let's see . . . Maybe I'm tired of getting sloppy seconds. You out fuckin' these random bitches and then you come home to me like I'm your side chick. I don't think so, Aaron. Not anymore." For the first time since we'd been together, my tone held was one of conviction. I was confident in myself as a woman, and more than anything, I knew my worth.

"Whatever you got going on, end it now. I'm not playing with you, Foreign."

As if he'd just put his foot down and finished scolding a child, he rolled over and went to sleep. Like he what he'd said mattered. Humph, not in the least bit as far as I was concerned. If he thought

I was ending shit with Domestic, he had another thing coming. The man had written his name in cursive on this pussy, and that was who it belonged to. If he thought he was hurt now, his shit was gon' split in to a million pieces when he found out I was pregnant with another man's baby.

***

The next morning, I was greeted by Aaron's wandering, sad eyes. It appeared he'd been watching me for quite some time. He was entirely too comfortable and that was downright creepy.

"How did you sleep?"

"Fine."

"It didn't seem that way."

His comment puzzled me. Covering my mouth, I yawned before I replied. "What's that supposed to mean?"

"You were panting in your sleep. You had a nightmare that you'd gotten shot. I heard you talking in your sleep."

My first thought was I hoped I didn't mention Domestic's name. True indeed, I was over being with my husband, but I still didn't want to rub it in his face, nor did I want to purposely hurt his feelings. Even though he had constantly did those exact things to me. Aaron didn't know I had been in the middle of a shooting the previous month. I never disclosed the information to him. It was something I'd kept to myself. I hadn't even told Lexi.

"Oh, it probably had something to do with what I was watching last night. I'm okay though."

Climbing from the bed, I slipped my feet into my bedroom shoes and proceeded to the bathroom. After sitting down on the toilet, I stared up at the ceiling before closing my eyes. Recently, I'd gone to the doctor and that was the moment I found out I was pregnant. It was Domestic's baby for sure. Aaron and I hadn't been intimate so that wasn't possible. There was no doubt in my mind about my next move. It was already planned out, now it just needed to be executed.

No one knew I was carrying a child, not even Domestic. My plan was to keep it hidden a little bit longer. At least until I moved out. The idea of me being in the house with Aaron and not carrying his child didn't feel right, and it wouldn't be fair to him. No matter what he did to me, I still considered his feelings. Too bad he didn't feel that way about me.

I flushed the toilet and stood at the sink, washing my hands. Staring in the mirror, I raised my gown. My baby bump was small and barely visible. My secret was safe for the time being. In due time I would break the news to Domestic. His reaction was going to be priceless. He always brought up the topic of having another child.

The bathroom door became ajar and Aaron was standing there with a blank expression. There was no such thing as privacy when he was around. Folding his arms, he leaned against the door frame.

"I meant what I said last night," he calmly stated.

Slowly, I turned my body to face him, with my back against the sink and my arms folded across my chest. "And what would that be?"

"I'm not losing you. We need to fix this. I'm ready to be the man I promised to be. No more games. No more lies. No more cheating."

"It's funny to me that you're suddenly ready to settle down and be a husband. Especially since that's something you should've been trying to do all along." Moving closer to him, I dropped my arms down at my sides. "Tell me this, Aaron, why the sudden change? Why fix your fucked up ways after all this time?"

"I'm getting help now. I'm doing this for us."

Pointing a finger in his face, I poked his forehead. "You're not doing shit for me, it's all for you. It's always been about you."

He grabbed my arms and pulled me closer to him. "Foreign, I love you. Please, don't leave me. I fucked up. I know I did, but I need you."

"Aaron, let me go." It took a minute or so for him to comply but he finally released me. "The only reason you want me now is because of all these bullshit-ass scandals you're involved in."

"That's not true. I was taking classes before this popped up. That last time I hurt you was the absolute worst and I knew I needed help in order to save our marriage."

Looking into his baby browns made me want to slap his ass. I was everything he wanted me to be, and all I got in return was his ass to kiss. He made me hate him. Mentally, I wasn't fully detached. The cascade of tears falling from my eyes confirmed that.

"You were everything to me. I used to sit around and picture what our life would be like when we got older. How many kids we would have? Our grandchildren. Our entire lives were mapped out in my head. All I wanted was you. Nothing else. Not even the luxury of you being in the league. I would've been happy with both of us working nine to five jobs. My love for you *was* unconditional and you didn't appreciate me. You constantly displayed that you had no regards to our marriage."

"You said *was*, that's past tense. What are you saying to me?"

Aaron truly didn't get the message, so I grabbed his hand and forced him to look into my soul when I spoke. "Listen to me. This marriage is something I have no energy for. Loving me should've been easy and vice versa. I love you, but I'm exhausted. I'm sorry, Aaron, but I want a divorce. There is no fixing this. I'm going to start looking for a place."

"You're choosing another man over me?" His voice became elevated.

"No, I'm choosing my happiness over you. This has nothing to do with another man."

A debate with Aaron was not what I signed up for, so I quickly threw on a pair of jeans and a button-up shirt. Makeup wasn't an option since I was in a rush. Slipping on my sandals, I grabbed my phone, keys and purse, and headed for the door. Of course, he followed behind me like a love-sick puppy.

"Where are you going?"

"Work."

"You have a job?"

"Yes, I do. And if you don't mind, I would like to be on time." He followed me to my car. Once inside, I started the engine and pulled off without a second glance in his direction.

Before I arrived at the car wash to start my day, I stopped by Dunkin Donuts to get breakfast for the staff and I, something I did on the regular. Domestic was standing at the clerk's counter talking when I walked in.

"Good morning, beautiful." He greeted me with that gorgeous million dollar smile.

"Good morning, handsome. I brought you coffee and a bagel."

"Thanks, baby." Domestic planted a kiss on my cheek.

Tracy, his cashier, sucked her teeth in a joking matter. "Eww! I don't think that's appropriate at the workplace."

"What's not appropriate is you and Tony at the workplace." Domestic chuckled.

"Now you know damn well I'm not messing with that old-ass fool. That nigga could be my granddaddy."

Placing the donuts on the counter, I grinned at her. "Hmm, I think I remembered your special request."

Tracy laughed and opened the box. "Well, since you bought what I asked for y'all get a pass."

"Gee, thanks."

"Let's go, baby. We got work to do. Tracy you get to work too and ain't no leaving early today or you'll be at the unemployment office tomorrow morning."

Domestic freed me of the bag I was carrying and headed towards his office with me right behind him.

Casey . . .

It was a new day and I felt slightly relieved from the majority of the bullshit that was going on in my life. Shawn and I spent hours talking about the next chapter in our lives. It felt good to have someone plan their life according to you. One thing I knew for sure was that he wasn't a bullshitter. Everything Shawn said, he meant, and his actions stood behind it one thousand percent. Truly, I was grateful to have him in my life. I couldn't say I was in love with him, because in all honestly, Domestic still had my heart. Until I could un-love my past, I couldn't love my future.

However, I was prepared to move on without him since he'd clearly moved on without me. As a woman, I knew I had lost him to another woman, but I needed to see her. I needed confirmation of her existence. Confirmation of who had gotten Domestic's attention.

The carwash was a little busy when I pulled up. Stepping from my Acura TLX, I activated the locks and approached the entrance. Tony asked if I wanted my vehicle detailed, but I politely declined it. My mission was to get closure from Domestic so I could carry on with my life.

"Good morning. How can I help you?" the cashier asked.

"I'm here to see Demerius."

"He's in his office. I'll call him for you."

Obviously, she didn't know who I was, and I had no patience to explain. "That's okay, I know where it is."

Continuing my mission, I walked off in the direction of his office. The door was closed, but I didn't care. I just barged in like I owned the place. The moment I stepped inside I immediately regretted it. Some woman was standing in front of him and they were engaged in a sloppy lip lock. It looked as if they were about to fuck on the desk without remorse to where they were. His hands were filled with her ass. It truly hurt me to my soul.

Clearing my throat, I coughed loudly. "Excuse me."

Domestic and the woman stopped kissing, but his actions had no urgency behind them. When he looked at me, I could tell he was annoyed by my presence alone. Stepping from in front of his girl, he glared at me.

"Why are you here, Casey?"

"I need to talk to you and apparently this is the only place I can catch you at."

"If this isn't about Demerius, I'm not interested."

"Oh, it surely is."

"Baby, give me a minute, so I can talk to her in private."

"No problem, baby." His chick walked past me and closed the door on her way out. Whoever she was, she was good because I would've never walked out like that.

"So, that's why you've been MIA, huh? Not coming by the house or—"

Domestic knew what I was about to say. His hand went up immediately to shut me up. "Don't do that. The only thing we have in common is DP. That's it. We're not together. We won't be together, and I need you to understand that."

"That's funny. You should've kept that same energy when you caught me with Shawn. It's all good though. I'm over you. I'm over this entire situation. You do you and I'll do me."

He stroked his beard knowingly, simultaneously biting his bottom lip. Then slowly, he walked towards me. Standing toe-to-toe, he looked down at me. "What the fuck does that supposed to mean?" he growled, angrily.

My heart was racing, but I couldn't show my fear. That was the way he'd always controlled me, by defeating me. That wasn't happening today. "Exactly what it sounds like. I'm done with you."

"You sure you wanna do that?" He laughed, then leaned down closer to my ear to make sure his girl couldn't hear him, just in case she was eavesdropping. "You mad 'cause I ain't been fuckin' you? Fine. I'll come over later."

"Nah, I'm good. I just told you, I'm done."

"Hmm." He looked around the room as if he was in deep thought. Then his dark, piercing eyes landed back on me. "You fuckin' that nigga now?"

"Just as sure as you're fuckin' Foreign."

Domestic's jaw tightened and the veins in his neck began to protrude. "I asked a question. Now answer it."

"I am."

Before I could get another word out, he delivered a smooth backhand to the right side of my face. *Whap!* The sound echoed throughout his office. He followed with snatching me up by the collar and ramming me into the wall.

"That's why you left my son at home alone last night? So you could get fucked by that lame-ass nigga."

My emotions were on deck and at full force. The pain I felt left me sobbing loudly. "He said you wasn't picking up your phone." The salty liquid covered my face as his arm pressed hard against my throat.

"I don't give a fuck what he told you. Yo' ass supposed to be with my muthafuckin' son whenever he not with me or at school. Fuck wrong wit' you hoe."

He proceeded to smack me in the face repeatedly. My screams grew louder and louder. No one was going to help me. Therefore, I had to save myself from his deadly wrath. Remembering what I had in my back pocket, I slipped my hand behind by back and produced a small can of mace. Aiming it at his face, I squeezed down on the latch. Domestic hollered and let me go. That's when the door to his office sprang open. It was Foreign.

She looked at me, then back to Domestic, who was aimlessly trying to wipe the pepper spray from his eyes. "What happened?" she asked softly.

"Look at my face. That's what happened." I stared her directly in the eyes hoping she wouldn't make the same choices I had made with this man.

Foreign rushed to his aid as I walked casually out of his office.

My face and neck throbbed in pain. Opening my car door, I got inside and locked the doors just in case he came out. Crying uncontrollably, I grabbed some napkins from the glovebox and wiped my face. A sudden knock on my window startled me. When I looked up it was Foreign. In search of Domestic, I scanned the lot. When I didn't see him, I cracked the window far enough for us to hear one another.

"I'm sorry. I know you don't know me, but are you okay?" She appeared to be sincere, but I didn't know her well enough to be one hundred percent sure.

"No, I'm not."

"Do you need an ambulance?"

"No, but let me give you some advice. If you're a smart girl, you'll leave him alone. Domestic is a very dangerous man, he's controlling and very abusive. You see what he did to me."

"I've never seen him act that way. I'm sorry he did this."

"I never saw it either. Then one day he snapped and beat the shit out of me. He promised he would never hit me again, but that was fifteen years ago. The last one was about a month ago. I advise you to be careful. He's not what he appears to be."

Foreign's expression revealed her ambiguity. That told me she didn't believe it could happen to her. I felt sorry for her because she was sadly mistaken.

"You don't know me either but take my word for it. Get away from him before it starts, and whatever you do, don't move in with him. That was my biggest mistake aside from having his baby. I love my son to death, but you have to be careful who you have kids by."

Domestic was headed in our direction. His hands were in the air as he shouted obscenities. "I have to go. Don't end up like me. Good luck." Before he could make it to my car, I was peeling out, leaving nothing but dust in my rearview. If I was going to leave, it needed to be now. So, I headed to Shawn's house with the quickness. But first I called Demerius to let him know not to go home or accept his father's calls.

CHAPTER 16
FOREIGN

The shit I witnessed Domestic do had me looking at him sideways. Not only did I see what he did to the mother of his child, I'd heard their entire conversation. Apparently, they were still sleeping together. The shit had me in my feelings because he was the only man I was sleeping with. We walked inside his office and closed the door.

Folding my arms, I stood in the middle of the floor with a mean-ass expression on my face. "You want to tell me what the hell all that was about?"

"I'd rather not." Domestic was wiping his eyes with a rag soaked in milk.

"I think I deserve an explanation of what I just witnessed."

He stopped wiping his face. "You wanna tell me why you out there talking to baby mama?"

"I was trying to make sure she was okay. Her face is badly bruised. What you did wasn't okay. That's your son's mother, Domestic."

"I don't give a fuck who the bitch is. She not about to disrespect me. Fuck outta here with that bullshit."

"That's what you do, beat women?"

His top lip curled and the fire in his eyes surfaced. "If it's warranted. That bitch is disrespectful. She deserved it."

"Why? Is it because she's sleeping with someone else? I'm trying to understand how the fuck that's your business. You fuckin' me so you shouldn't be worried about who she's giving her pussy to. That's not your concern."

"As long as I'm her provider, I run that."

"Oh really. So, you fuckin' me and her?"

"I was, but I stopped when we got serious. That's why she mad. But you don't get to question me about what I do. You still married remember? I don't know what you do with your husband when we not together."

His comment was like a punch to the gut. My anger was now raging, and I refused to let him talk to me like he was crazy. Aaron could never get away with talking to me any type of way and Domestic wasn't about to get a pass either.

"For the record, I haven't fucked my husband since I started fuckin' you. So, yes, I *do* get to question you. We don't use protection and I care about my fuckin' health. You don't know who she's sleeping with and now I don't know who else you sleeping with. I know one thing. I better not catch shit."

"Foreign," he bit down on his bottom lip, "don't fuckin' play with me."

"No." I held my arm out. "You don't play with me. All this time you've been lying to me. You know what I'm going through with my husband and you doing the same damn thing. Then you beat this girl at your place of business in front of me. You dead ass wrong and I don't respect you as a man."

"What?" he barked.

"You heard me. I don't respect—" Domestic reached out and popped me dead in the mouth. Fresh blood invaded my mouth and I was in complete shock.

"Stop playing with me, girl. I'm not your punk-ass husband. I'll never let you disrespect me. Fuck you talking 'bout."

Domestic was raging and I could've sworn I saw smoke steaming from his ears. One thing that I wasn't about to do was become victim number two, so I walked over to the desk in silence and grabbed my purse.

"Where are you going?"

"Home. I'm not doing this with you."

He grabbed my arm and pulled me close to him. "I'm sorry, baby. I didn't mean to do that. I'm already stressed out and you're not making it easier for me. You're nothing like Casey. That bitch not innocent."

"Stop calling her a bitch. That's disrespectful." Pulling away from him, I reached inside my purse and pulled out my keys. "I'm not going home with you tonight. I'm going home. You need time to cool off and so do I."

The Price You Pay for Love

On my way home, I kept replaying the event that occurred. That side of Domestic was one I never wanted to see again. The fact that he'd slapped me told me I was non-exempt. I didn't know if Casey was truthful about the things she'd said, but it definitely had me thinking that my knight in shining armor had a side to him I was unaware of. For that reason, I needed to tread lightly and rethink going through with the pregnancy.

After I'd driven around for two hours, I contemplated on calling his phone. Even though he had slapped me, I knew his mind was somewhere else when his baby mama had gone in and messed up our vibe. I wanted to head home and give him a few weeks to himself, but the more I drove around alone, the more I missed him. My thoughts definitely wasn't on going home to Aaron. He disgusted me more than Domestic at the time, and no matter how I judged the situation, Domestic had yet to treat me like shit in front of another bitch. He wasn't ramming cucumbers in hoes pussy at work, and when his baby mama came to speak with him, he still addressed me as his woman. Regardless of what had transpired, my mind couldn't let me forget how he stood beside me as if I were his wife.

Grabbing my phone, I decided to put my feelings to the side. Domestic's hard ass didn't look like he had the capability to pick up a phone and apologize about anything. His phone rang twice before I was greeted by the voicemail. Of course, I tried again and got the same thing. I hated the fact that we'd gotten into it about another woman.

The more I thought about it, the more it dawned on me that I didn't need to worry about the next woman who hadn't been successful with Domestic. There were numerous things people had the tendency to leave each other for. That reason alone told me to mind my business and focus on him instead of the mistakes he'd made with the next bitch. Too bad, so motherfucking sad.

Domestic didn't have time to focus on another woman, especially with the news I had for him. A baby was my dream. I couldn't fulfill that dream with Aaron which proved we were better off separated.

Ten minutes later, I found myself pulling back up to the carwash. Climbing out of my car, I headed inside. Tracy pointed towards his business room when she spotted my face. Walking over to his office, I knocked on the door frame before entering. He sat at the table with his head down. From the way his leg rocked I could tell he was still upset. I closed the door and walked over to him seductively. I didn't stop until my crouch area was directly by his face.

He could feel my presence because he gazed up into my face. Grabbing me by the waist, he placed his head on my stomach, as if he was a little child. "Just touching you makes me feel better," he expressed with sincerity. "Ever since you made your way into my world, it's been flipped upside down."

The comment made me give him a salty look. Of course, he quickly clarified his statement. "I don't mean it like that, baby, I mean for the better. Since I've been dealing with you, I've actually been happy. It's hard to make a man like me smile, but you do it with so much ease."

He caressed my ass up and down. "Aww, Domestic, that's my mission. I've actually been having mutual feelings. Since meeting you, I've grown to feel love on a different level. It's like I know you'll give me that hard, passionate relationship I've been yearning for. You were meant to find me. But I don't want be abused in the process."

"When will I be able to have you for good?" His hands gripped my hips like he was demanding an answer.

My pussy tingled and I knew then that this man had some type of spell on me. Whenever he got rough with me, the entire atmosphere slowed down, so I could lust over his healthy body and handsome face.

"You'll be able to have me forever, very soon. I'm placing that into effect right now. I'm getting a divorce. He's just being bitchy about signing the damn papers because he doesn't want me to leave."

"Maybe I could make him feel different."

I could tell by the sound of his voice, that wouldn't be a good idea. A clash between him and Aaron was what I didn't want or need. Time was my only concern. If I could make him see that we weren't meant to be, he would give me what I wanted and go on back to his whorish ways. It was the only way I could win. If he continued to do as he pleased and just sign the divorce papers, our problems would be settled. It wasn't like I needed his money. Hell, I had so much of that put up in the bank, I could start eight businesses if I chose to.

"I don't want to make things worse, Domestic, I'm trying to let him off easily without being too mean. He knows I'm dealing with another man because he keeps bringing it up.

"He should know." Domestic stood up, towering over me. Forcing me closer, I could feel his heartbeat coming through his button-up shirt.

"I love the way that pussy feels when I'm deep in it. She talks back to me, so I know I'm handling that business with our bed sessions. Everything else is pretty simple. I make you mine, you divorce him, and we'll live happily ever after. Imagine life without me, Foreign."

His lips snacked on my neck as if it was edible. The small bites and kisses poured three different types of feelings out of my coochie. There was no reason I shouldn't have Domestic later on tonight, so I wanted to be sure he knew what he wanted also.

"Am I the only woman you're having sex with?"

The question caught him off guard but he still kept his composure. "Foreign, you are the only woman I'm dropping all this beef in, baby." He placed my hand on his thick rod. I could feel him slowly bricking up.

"Why would I need something else when I got all this?" Slapping my booty, his chest heaved with anticipation. "You ready for my love right now?" His question was like a threat of pleasure and I knew he could definitely meet his goals when it came down to freaking my soul out of its shell.

Instead of getting half-a-freak fest in the office, I was going to wait until we reached our destination, so I could feel his shit beat the lining out my goodies.

"Not yet, but I can show you some love." Sinking down to my knees, I gripped his large print. Just the size of it made my mouth water. Loosening his belt, I flopped his piece out in front of me. The thick chocolate had me on the verge of saying fuck tonight. He could've fucked my spleen loose and I would've accepted it.

Gripping it with two hands, I shoved it down my throat and began to gag harshly. When his head flopped back in satisfaction, I grinned. Bobbing my head on the tip, I stroked from the bottom of his shaft to the center. I still couldn't find out the reason for loving sex in this man's office. I kind of felt it was the feeling of knowing I was fuckin' the boss. There would never be any consequences. Just that thought alone caused my slurps and moans to grow louder.

"Damn, babyyy! Eat that muthafucker."

Of course that nasty shit always worked. I held my own with that monster, taking it down past the tonsils. It was so big, I almost threw up on his slacks. Before I could, he tightened me up.

"You betta hold that shit. Don't spill not one drop," he grunted while fuckin' my mouth. After catching his load, I obliged and swallowed like a big girl.

"Stand up," he demanded and proceeded to pull my pants off.

Domestic lifted me up on his shoulders and cuffed my ass firmly. My pussy was lined up with his juicy lips and I was shivering before he could force one lick. After his tongue spread my lips, he posted me against the wall and sucked me into fucking submission. It felt like he was trying to detach the kitty from my body.

One of his fingers slid smoothly into my ass, making me arch my back like a waking child. He was a junkie for a minute of freak and skeet time. He showed me I was worth more and more each time I allowed him to enter me. Oral or vaginal, he fucked me like it was our last time together. I hated to say it, but I was fully in love with another man and I liked it.

Hearing a knock on the door, we froze like a deer in the midnight spotlight. "Mr. Payne, someone is here to see you."

"One minute," he replied quickly, before putting me down. "Put on your clothes. This is probably something important."

After sliding my pants back on, I checked myself in his mirror and took a deep breath. When I opened the door, the weird Spanish cop-bitch, I had spotted a few times before, was staring at me like I was under arrest. A young dude no more than nineteen or twenty stood behind her with his hands behind his back.

Brushing past me, the hoe moved over to Domestic's desk like she was the fucking co-owner. The young man stood with her, but remained quiet.

"Emilia. I told you five o' clock, not one. Why are you here so early?" Domestic sounded like he wanted to be rude but kept his business face on instead.

"First of all, if you must know all of my business, I have to go and arrest a few people today, so this shouldn't take long. You can excuse her, and we can handle this very quickly." Her crooked ass smile sent a surge through my body.

"Sweetheart, if you don't mind, I have to deal with this. You can wait in the lobby with Tracy. I'm sure that it won't take long."

"Okay." Even though I agreed, I made sure to shoot the bitch daggers before leaving.

Domestic . . .

"Let me tell you something, Emilia. Don't come up here aggravating my guests. Where are your business ethics? Have some self-control."

"I have no clue what you're talking about. I can't help that I'm the perfect woman up and down. Women get jealous too. I'm here for him," she pointed at the young man standing beside her, "he needs a job and you promised him one. It's all in the stipulations of his release."

Sitting back in my chair, I glanced over to the young kid who didn't look like he gave a fuck at all. "I just gave him twenty grand. He shouldn't have to work for nobody with a start like that."

"This isn't the block, Demerius. He needs a real job and I'm not talking about being your wash boy." Emilia crossed her arms before crossing her legs.

"Cool. I'll start him off behind the register with Tasha. Just go out to the front and tell her you need to be trained on how to work the prices and buttons. She'll take care of you."

"Thanks, big bro." He shook my hand before leaving.

After the door was closed, I was sure to straighten this woman in front of me. "Emilia, you know I'm very short with patience. Cut your little games and keep yourself together. If he screws up, it's your fault. I don't have any help to offer you after this. I wouldn't give a damn if he did thirty years for me."

"Well. Someone seems to be snappy today." I watched as the edge of her suit skirt rose up exposing her thick thigh. Her smooth olive skin glowed to perfection and it caused me to lick my lips.

"Listen. Just stop running to the carwash displaying your fucked up intentions. Leave them in the car. You're a detective for Christ's sake. Most people think you're a nut who's gotten hired to do the easiest cop work. You should be showing them different."

Standing up from her seat, she laughed. "Let me break something down to you, Demerius. I'm the best detective in this city. Whatever I want to see happen, it'll happen. I *am* Tampa. Therefore, people can say what they feel. Just don't get caught saying it. I'll be in touch."

Closely, I watched her turn and head for the door. Her plump ass jiggled with every strut. She was surely going to run Tampa with an iron fist, just not when it came down to me. My business was done and from that day on, there was no more complying unless it involved a dollar.

When I walked into the lobby, Foreign was sitting on the counter while Tracy ran her lips as usual. "Baby, are you ready to go?"

"Uh, yeah. I was just talking to Tracy for a second. She's so goofy." As she jumped off the counter, I handed her my keys. "I'll meet you at the car, love."

"Okay."

Turning my attention back to Tracy, she grinned. "You about to go have sex ain't you?"

"Mind ya' business, girl. Where's the new-jack?"

"I sent his ass to wash detail. He gotta put in a few days before he think he can just jump in my spot. You know I'm not into playing games with you 'bout my job now."

Laughing, I headed for the door. "Whatever you do, watch him to make sure all is well. I'm taking the rest of the day off."

Making it to the car with Foreign, we were sure to lock her car doors before heading out for our adventurous and steamy night.

CHAPTER 17
LEXI

After receiving fifty missed calls from Aaron this morning, I finally got out of the bed and made my way over to him. His depression was starting to become annoying. It was true indeed that a person would play with the fire until they got burnt. Now that Foreign was out getting piped down by Mr. Chocolate factory. His whole world began to tear down piece by piece. Foreign hadn't told me anything about stepping out on my brother, but you could always feel when a change of meat was on the brain of a woman. It was our natural aura to be distant when we were creeping. No sex. No talk. Just arrogance and silence. Those same actions of every woman had given the men intellect to finally catch on. Men were foolish and some may even accept a woman stepping out if she continued to play her role without making shit obvious. But when you drain the pussy well and cut all interactions for a slight second longer than usual, you've given up your creeping license.

This fool sat on the couch with his phone in hand like the girl was about to step through the receiver. "Aaron! You need to try and relax. Stressing will make you commit suicide. Think about all those girls you slayed and just call it even. Besides, you don't know what she's doing because you're not around her. Stop accusing if you have no proof."

"Proof? She's been staying out for the past month. I haven't even stuck a finger inside Foreign, let alone touched her. Not even for a hug, sis. I'm not dumb," he raged with his bottle of Avión in hand.

"Maybe you need to sit the bottle down for a second and watch a little T.V. Get your mind away from the gutter." I was trying to help the rebellious-ass nigga but he wouldn't listen.

"Every time I turn on the damn T.V, there's a secretly recorded video of me having sex with two women. This shit has hit every news stand and all social media. They're really using this tape to frame me for something I had no knowledge of. Foreign ain't about to come back to me with no stuff like this going on. You feel me?"

He was so close to my face like he didn't know his volume was on one thousand. I had to cover my nose from the alcohol that reeked on his tongue. "Aaron, your breath smells like you ate a baked peanut butter and shit sandwich. You're delivering some heavy blows right now and you just need to sit down. Please."

Taking a seat on the opposite couch, he started to tear up. I could tell he was about to explode and that was a side I hated to see him exhibit. Aaron became too emotional when he was mad. There was no telling what could happen when a man felt truly hurt and betrayed by his woman. My brother was my exact replica and he meant the world to me. I felt the need to break things down in a serious manner.

"Aaron, I don't know how to say this any clearer. The only reason you're going through this is because of your own actions. You have to face the fact that you were the one who cheated. A lot, might I add. Nobody forced you. With that being said, you have to accept the reality of Foreign's recent behavior."

"That's my wife, Lexi. What am I supposed to do without her?"

"You'll have to move on and try not to do the same stupid shit to the next one if you get lucky enough to find a next one. You're a man, act like it. You teased daddy so much about being a square, but fortunately for him, he *still* has mama by his side. It's been that way for thirty years. That's because he knows, nothing or no one is as important than mama. That's where you messed up. If she wants to move on, allow her to. You owe her that."

I realized he was contemplating taking my advice. Aaron's head hung low, but his tears had vanished. Leaning back on the couch, he wiped his face with the bottom of his shirt.

"Am I that bad that she should leave instead of trying to work things out? How could she say for better or for worst and peel like nothing was real? I made mistakes. I'm not perfect."

"The same reason you said you would cherish and love her with all your heart. You also made an oath and didn't fulfill your obligations. It's life."

The hard knocking that rang out on the front door paused my next thought. "Who the fuck is that?"

"I don't know. Foreign might have left her key," Aaron said rushing to the door. His posture changed after opening up his home for the twenty officers who flooded our living room with their guns drawn.

"Wait! What's going on?" Aaron asked, as they threw him to the floor.

My rage instantly shot through the roof. "If you fuckin' dirty-ass pigs don't remove your hands off my brother, I'll make sure every last one of you bitches loses your badge by the time you take your lunch break."

Before the man could counter, a female detective stepped through the door with a humungous smile. "Hi, darling. These officers aren't allowed to tell you anything. My name is Detective Flores and I'm here to arrest your brother."

"Emilia! What the hell is the meaning of this? You know I'm clean," Aaron shouted as he lay on his stomach. The officers cleared his pants pockets of all its items before lifting him back up, on his feet.

"What makes you think you're locking him up? There has to be a crime committed correct?" The bitch couldn't have known I was a live wire.

"Well, Ma'am . . . your brother is being arrested for sexual assault at a recent Super Bowl party. I'm sure he can explain the entire situation to you and your family." Next, the officer began quoting the Miranda Rights: "You have the right to remain silent. Anything you say can and will be used against you in the court of law, of course, you have the right to an attorney."

"Who issued this warrant with no sufficient evidence? He has the right to face his accuser. Who stated a claim against him because it certainly wasn't your victim, Samantha, right? The seventeen-year-old from Miami. I spoke to her mother two nights ago and she clearly stated she never touched my brother."

"We have other sources, Ma'am. There is a witness who works alongside your brother on the football field. It seems that Mr. Antwan wants to come clean and tell us about Mr. Young's despicable acts."

"You mean this Antwan?" I pulled out my cellphone and pressed play on the recording I had saved inside my gallery.

The argument that occurred a month back was clearly being played through the speaker. Aaron's voice was loud and recognizable. "Nigga, you set me up."

The sound of a fight breaking out could be heard. Emilia listened as if my recording meant nothing. After Antwan's voice appeared, she grabbed my phone to listen closer.

"Nigga, I leaked the tape! That's right. I did. I'm the one who invited that girl to the Super Bowl party too. I don't have to get rid of you because you killed yourself."

I stopped the clip and folded my arms with a stern expression. *What now, bitch?* I thought. "Release my brother from those cuffs. Antwan is the one you're looking for. You can keep the voice clip and Aaron will gladly come to court. But there is no case here and you know it."

I could see her skin turning blush-red. Emilia's eyes rotated to the officer standing beside her. "James, take a trip to Mr. Antwan Williams' home. Arrest him for false information and charges of sexual assault."

"Yes, Ma'am."

Pulling out the cuff keys, Emilia released the restraints from my brother's wrist. "Aaron, we'll be seeing you in court. I wouldn't get too excited about the evidence you have. Just giving you a warning. It seems Antwan is quite upset and according to him, you *did* assault Samantha. He's willing to testify."

"And he's going to be dismissed for false accusations once they see he's not credible to get on a stand to slander Aaron's character. Antwan is a liar. However, our lawyers will be in contact tonight." I had to stop the bitch because she seemed to have the shit pieced all together. They really wanted to take my brother's life away from him.

"I'm sure they will." She smiled before waving her finger for all of the officers to exit our home.

Moving behind them, I posted in the center of our doorway. "Excuse me, Ms. Flores."

This bitch had the nerves to turn on her heels like she was Mary Poppins or some shit. "Yes?" she answered smugly.

"Where's the warrant for my brother's arrest? Because we sure didn't see one?"

"You can ask for a copy at the hearing. I'm sure they'll be able to find it." Her evil smile spread before climbing back into the unmarked Dodge Charger.

Slamming the door, I gazed back at Aaron. "You need to clear your mind for what's ahead because this shit just got real. These people have a bullseye on your head and it's not good."

Aaron listened to me, but I could tell, his mind was still trying to process it all. My mind was always focused on the family. Shit was getting deep. Aaron was too hurt and too emotional to even focus. I didn't give a damn if I had to slide up to Miami myself. I was going to end it. Even if I had to do it alone.

Emilia . . .

Walking in the Tampa Police precinct, I strutted through the line of desks and marched into the Captain's office. From the look of the rookie officers standing around, I knew he would give me his weakest excuse for not having my warrant in a timely fashion. It felt so embarrassing to be viewed as the fool of the department. I rushed to handle my job and in return the old fuck stood me up with the evidence.

Knocking sternly on his office door, I noticed the lights were off.

"Hey, Flores. Is something wrong?" The Captain is handling business down in Jacksonville. Some type of meeting with their chief. He's not gonna be back until tomorrow.

I listened to Marshall speak and I could feel the wrinkles growing across my brow as my nostrils flared. "You're damn right!" I ordered a warrant for the arrest of Aaron Young and he's not even here? Luckily, I didn't run in the man's home before we knew a warrant wasn't available."

"Calm down, Flores. You shouldn't have any problems. Just give him 'til morning. I'm sure he's going to get the judge to sign off and then you can finish. It's only a few more hours."

He was flapping off at the mouth like he had something to do in Tampa besides be lazy at the office. Aaron was just happy he'd slipped through the cracks, but his bitchy sister was definitely going to be a problem when it came to sealing the deal on this case.

Turning my attention to the investigation room where Antwan was sitting, I walked off on Marshall defiantly. In order for my mission to be successful, I had to be sure of the information he was willing to give.

Entering the medium size room, his eyes landed on mine. Before he could speak, I raised my fingers to silence him. Closing the blinds, I headed over to the table and cut off the hidden recorder.

"Now, I'm sure you're wondering why I asked my team of men to go pick you up."

"You damn right. We had a deal. I give you Aaron and make these people leave me the hell alone. Do you know who I am?"

"Yes, you're Antwan Williams, a professional football player who happens to be involved in a rape case and crashed down horribly. You were found guilty from the harsh evidence of your teammate's sister's phone recording and received 25 years to the door. She has you on tape admitting how you'd leaked the video and brought that girl inside of Calvin's party. I think it's time to re-negotiate the agreement, Antwan."

It felt great to have my screws tightened. There was never a time where a man wanted to lose his fortune and fame for a grave mistake like this one. When it came to my job, anyone could be held accountable because I surely wasn't.

"Look, Ms. Flores, I'm pressing the issue about this situation. You can't possibly believe I would go through all of this just to lie about what we agreed on. I'm keeping it straight with you. My career is not about to fall for this bullshit! I got one of the best lawyers in the city. Aaron's word can't override mine," he shouted, as if I were moved by his tone.

"Calm down, lamb chop. Yelling doesn't scare me but losing does. This is one of the most talked about cases in the sport industry and I happen to be the one assigned to it. Listen to this before you say another word. In a few weeks, we're going to get this case in court. You're gonna be there. I need you to tell the judge exactly what you told me. If you can handle these small requests, I can assure you your freedom will be granted from this entire problem.

"What about Aaron? He's the fuckin' problem. Where does his slimy ass fit in this picture? He crossed me out and played the game raw. He needs to be deleted from the Tampa Bay Buccaneers. I wouldn't care if he caught a million years!" Antwan snapped.

Glancing back to the window, I made sure none of my fellow officers were eavesdropping. I didn't need any dirty information getting back to the Captain.

"We'll worry about that when the time comes. Until then, you need to remember your story like elementary kids recite the Pledge of Allegiance. It's a one-shot deal, Williams. One moment to talk yourself out of this mess."

Standing up, I adjusted my dress and checked the small watch on my right wrist. "I'll have someone come to escort you back home. You seem like a healthy big young man, so I know you don't need any witness protection, right?" I gave him a curious stare.

"Nobody is going to do shit to me. I'm ready to get this over with and be done. Simple."

Nodding, I exited the room. Just as I suspected, Marshall was standing at the door as if he was waiting for me to fall out in the lobby.

"Hey, Flores, any luck with your football star back there?"

Closing the door, I politely folded my arms. "No. I'm not about to pressure him into anything so soon. Eventually, he'll finish telling me what I need to know in order to put this case in the ground."

"Mhmm. Do you need me to book him in? I was about to head down to the county jail to transfer an inmate."

"No, thank you. I'm giving him time to prepare for court, so I'm gonna have Sarge drop him back off at home."

"Okay. Hey, I talked to Capt. He's getting the warrant official for you in the a.m."

This asshole was really pushing the limit when it came to snooping on my case. At first, he had no interest. Since finding out my case was going to be bigger than the sports entertainment itself, he began his little Inspector Gadget plots.

"There's no need. I'll call him myself and handle everything from here. Try and rest your neck, Marshall. This isn't your type of work." I patted him on the shoulder before heading down to my office.

I had waited for this day to come. Now was the time to grab my position in the department. My work had been looked over long enough and it was finally over. By the time I got ahold of Aaron, I would have this entire file wrapped up like a precious Christmas gift.

CHAPTER 18
CASEY

When I arrived at Shawn's house, by the grace of God his brothers weren't there. The last thing I wanted was for them to be all up in my business. It was bad enough that I'd have to be embarrassed by Shawn seeing me in this condition, but I didn't have a choice. He was the only one who could set me free.

Banging on the door, I rocked on my heels and waited on him to answer the door. Seconds later, the door flew open and the look of exasperation crossed Shawn's face.

"What the fuck happened to your face?"

The tainted look on his face pumped fear throughout my heart. "Lucifer. Better known as Domestic." At the mention of my son's father's name, Shawn's eyes turned into dark, tiny slits.

Biting down on his lip, he stepped back and let me in, slamming the door behind us. "What the fuck happened?"

"I went to see him to discuss our arrangement. Out of nowhere he flipped. He was bent all outta shape about me leaving Demerius home so I could go get fucked by you."

"Why is this nigga worried about me and you fuckin'? Ain't he fuckin' some bitch?"

"She was there."

"And he did all this in front of her? Where were you?"

"I went up to the carwash."

Shawn paced the floor with both hands on his head. "Why would you go there alone? I don't understand."

"Because I was trying to avoid a fight. I figured he wouldn't blow up at work, but I was wrong."

"Un-huh. I got something for that nigga."

Grabbing a hold of his arm, I was able to cease some of his movements. "No, all I want is for you to get me and my son out of here. I'm ready to leave. I can't take this anymore."

"After he get what's coming to him. You keep letting this nigga slide with hitting on you and I don't respect that shit."

All I could do was listen as Shawn continued to yell out of control, and that was the last thing I wanted to hear from him.

Jerking his arm, I attempted to get him quiet. "I get that you're upset, but so am I." He dropped his head and looked into my puffy eye. "I've been through enough. Just take me away from here. At the end of the day, my son still needs his father."

Shawn's hardened stare suddenly became deflated. The muscles in his cheeks became a bit more relaxed. It was like he finally understood my logic for not wanting to retaliate.

"Fine, but what are you gonna do until we leave? I don't feel comfortable with you going back to that house."

"I'm not going back there. We can stay at a hotel until we leave."

"Nah, y'all can stay here. We have more than enough room. DP can sleep in the spare room," he said, and grabbed me around my waist, pulling me into his warm embrace. "And *you* can sleep with me, of course."

"I don't want to invade your brother's personal space. That wouldn't be fair to them."

"They'll be cool with it. You know they fuck with you like that. Sometimes them niggas don't come home, so y'all good. Besides, I'll feel better knowing you and your son are safe."

Laying my head against his chest, I whispered, "Thank you."

"You don't have to thank me. You my girl now. I got you."

The words alone caused me to become emotional. To have a man be so gentle with me, one who genuinely cared about my feelings and the well-being of my child, was priceless. My grip on him was tight and I never wanted to let go. My eyelids were invaded by water, but I didn't want him to see me cry. However, that didn't last too much longer. Shawn raised my chin so I could see his face and placed his lips against mine. He kissed me slowly and passionately. When he finally pulled away, he wiped my bottom lip.

"Where is Demerius?"

"He's at a friend's house."

"You need to call him so we can go pick him up. Then we need to go to your house and get y'all stuff."

"I'll need a U-Haul."

"We can get that too. It won't take long and I'll pay for it."

"Thanks again, Shawn."

"I got you, baby. Let me grab my keys then we can go."

Everything was finally coming together and the madness seemed to be nearing the end. I could hardly wait to get away from Domestic. He was so cruel, so harsh, and so controlling.

In the beginning he was never like that, but after we moved in together, I started to see a different side of him, a darker version of him. Domestic had secrets that were buried. He'd done things I wished I could un-see, and said things I wish I could un-hear. Just the thought of my living experience with him sent a thrilling chill down my spine. The days and nights were like living through a horror movie.

"I'm ready, baby." The touch of Shawn's hand on my shoulder made me jump leading me to place my hand over my heart. "I didn't mean to scare you."

"I know. My nerves are just bad right now."

"You have nothing to worry about. I promise."

The sound of the locks clicking on the front door alerted us that we had company. Craig and Tim walked through the door laughing loudly.

"What y'all up to?" Tim asked. He took a seat on the sofa.

"We about to head out for a few," Shawn replied, as he took a hold of my hand.

"Wassup wit' you, sis?" Craig stood in front of me and I tried my best to keep from making eye contact with him.

"I'm good."

Before I could rush out the door, Craig noticed my face and stepped closer to examine the bruises. "Nah, hell nah. Bro, look at this shit."

Tim stood up and walked towards me. "That bitch-ass nigga did this to you, didn't he?"

Shawn spoke up before I could even open my mouth. "Yeah, but it's straight bruh. We about to go get her stuff now. She gon' stay here until we leave for Tennessee in a few days."

181

"I told you I don't want to invade y'all space."

"Fuck that! You staying here." Craig frowned. "Where that nigga at anyway? I want his head."

"I don't want y'all to kill him. He's still my son's father. All I want is to get away from him for good."

Craig nodded his head towards the door. "Let's ride then 'cause I'm not letting y'all go over there alone. Baby bro ain't 'bout that life, but we are. And, sis, I'm telling you now, if that nigga get outta pocket, I'ma do his ass. Real shit!"

All of us made our way out the door and into my car. On our way to the U-Haul company, I prayed that Domestic wouldn't show up. It definitely wouldn't be good for him considering how he'd portrayed himself as a woman-beater. Shawn had some crazy ass brothers and they didn't play about him. They didn't play about me either since we had been rocking for a while now. Both of them had welcomed me in with open arms.

***

It took a little over an hour to get the small moving truck and to pick up Demerius. We were on borrowed time, so I wanted to make our move as quickly as possible. All we had were a bunch of clothes, shoes, and electronics.

The house was empty just like I knew it would be. Domestic would normally come around seven, so we had roughly four and a half hours to get everything loaded onto the truck.

Craig backed the truck up in the driveway, while Demerius and I went inside the house to start packing. Once we were in his room, I took the time to talk to him one last time.

"Demerius . . ."

"Yeah." His nonchalant tone was unsettling and I didn't know how the conversation was about to pan out.

Sitting down on his bed, I rubbed my itchy eye. "We need to talk for a minute. Sit down."

"I'll stand." Demerius stood directly in front of me.

"Okay."

Nervousness took over by body. I started to twiddle my thumbs. The moment was heartbreaking to me. My son and his father shared a bond that began the moment we found out we'd conceived. Now, I was taking that away from him. Victimization had a funny way of making a person feel as though the abuse was their fault, and that's exactly how I felt.

"Before you pack your things, I want you to be sure this is what you wanna do. You're fourteen and I'm not gon' force you to up and relocate away from your father if that's not what you want. And I don't want you to think I'm doing this out of spite to hurt your dad. The feelings and love I have for your dad are not the same feelings he has for me. I did everything in my power to make sure you were raised in a two-parent home."

My confession was a lot harder than I expected. I teared up almost instantly, but I did my best to contain them.

"True enough, I love your dad. But love involves two people and not just one. Our relationship has ran its course and I can't allow him to hurt me any further. The fights and bruises are becoming harder to hide because you're older now and you understand what's going on."

No longer able to keep my raw emotions tucked away, I broke down and cried. "I can't do this anymore, and if I don't leave now, I'm afraid he's going to kill me."

"Fuck him. We can leave."

"Demerius, don't say that."

He was silent, but when I looked up at my son, his eyes were filled with tears and locked on me. He walked over to me and kneeled down in front of me. He wrapped his arms around my waist and squeezed me as tight as he could. He sniffled as he buried his face in my chest. It broke my heart in two.

"I love you, Ma," he said, and gathered himself.

Hugging him back, I took a deep breath and sighed, "I love you too, Son."

After our embrace ended, there was one last thing I needed to say. "Are you okay with moving away with Shawn?" That was the moment I had been waiting on and the most important question of them all.

Demerius rose to his feet. His height towered over me making me feel like I was the child instead of him. Then he replied, "Shawn is cool. He treats you better than dad."

I was finally relieved. I smiled so wide I thought my lips would split.

"Well, pack up your things. I don't want to be here when he arrives."

"Can I bring my four wheeler?"

"You can bring whatever we can fit inside that truck."

"Okay."

For the next two hours we packed up boxes and labeled them accordingly. One-by-one, Shawn and his brothers took them out. They had even loaded up Demerius' four wheeler. I was exhausted, but I couldn't stop now. We were almost at the finish line, which meant I was able to avoid a confrontation.

Picking up my phone, I glanced at the screen. It was 5:42 pm. I was cutting it close, but there wasn't much left to do. My heart started to race when my phone rang and Domestic's name flashed across the screen. I shoved it in my back pocket and ran to Demerius' room.

"Are you almost done? Your dad just called."

Demerius' happy expression turned into a frantic frown. "What did he say?"

"I didn't answer. We need to hurry up. Are you taking the computer?"

"Yes, and my desk," he replied.

"I'll buy you a desk. Pack up the computer and take it downstairs."

Rushing into my room, I grabbed the rest of the items that were on the dresser and scattered around in the closet. Some of the items I left behind were gifts from Domestic, things he bought me after he had beat my ass. Supposedly, tokens of his apology. That part of my life was over, and anything that reminded me of him was being left behind. Except for my son, of course, and he was the spitting image of his ass!

On our way into the living room, I dropped my small suitcase and duffle bag onto the floor. Craig and Tim were sitting on the sofa taking a break.

Shawn walked up to me and grabbed it. "Is that it?"

"And my computer," Demerius told him, as he sat the box on the floor.

"I'm about to—"

My words came to a halt when I heard a door slam. Rushing to the window, I peeked out and saw Domestic on his way inside. His pace was fast, the scowl on his face was nasty, and I knew there was going to be a problem.

"What's wrong?" Shawn asked.

"It's Domestic. He's here."

"Lil' man. Go upstairs." Craig and Tim stood up and pulled out their straps. "Don't be scared, sis. That nigga ain't gon' touch you. Not on our watch. His pussy-ass wanna fight, we can definitely get it crackin' up in this bitch." Craig smiled deviously and Tim winked at me. Shawn didn't appear to bothered in the least bit.

My heart palpitated and felt like it would burst right threw my chest. I didn't want to see my child's father die in front of me. If his temper exploded when he stepped across that threshold, Craig and Tim were going to match his aggression for sure. Hearing his keys jingle against the locks, I knew he would enter in a matter of seconds.

Destiny Skai

CHAPTER 19
DOMESTIC

I had called Casey's phone numerous times and she never answered or bothered to return my calls. I figured she was still mad about me putting her in her place when she'd showed up at the carwash earlier that day. But, still, it wasn't like her to ignore me 'cause she knew better. Due to my concern for my son, I decided to pull up and see what the problem was and why the bitch was trippin'.

For a minute, I thought my mind was playing tricks on me when I saw the U-Haul in my driveway. Even more so when I spotted a car I'd never seen parked behind it. Putting one and one together, it hit me. *This bitch done lost her rabbit-ass mind . . .* I thought. She was trying to sneak away. The crazy thing to me was the fact that we'd gone through this same thing once before. I ended up having to show her what the consequences of being an ungrateful bitch were. Especially, when I was the one providing her a place to stay and food to put in her mouth.

Parking my car in front of the house, I got out and slammed the door. My eyes glanced at the truck, loaded with the shit I'd purchased. The rage that started to build took over and I knew I was about to snap Casey's neck in half. Sticking my key in the keyhole, I barged in like a mad man, and I was ready to tear some shit up.

My son was standing behind two men with guns, while Casey stood beside Shawn's punk-ass. Closing the door gently, I cursed myself for not grabbing my gun out of the glove compartment. I cracked my neck from side to side as killer mode kicked in. A nigga like me didn't carry fear in his heart, and I could pop off at any given time, especially when provoked.

"Casey, you better pray to God, I don't kill you with the first punch I connect to your muthafuckin' face. Explain why the fuck these niggas in my shit, wit' guns around my son?" I barked, looking back and forth, from one face to another.

"Demerius, I just came to get my things and leave. I wasn't trying to disrespect you."

"All is well, my nigga. Won't be no problem, if you don't make one. We just here to remove her from the bullshit," Shawn spoke sternly.

I couldn't believe my eyes and ears. It was like a nightmare waiting to happen. Casey must've really been prepared to die on account of a stupid mistake. Balling my fist tightly, I glanced over at my son. "DP, are you okay? Did anybody touch you?"

"No, Dad. I'm fine."

His voice didn't sound too reassuring. I knew my son, and given the circumstances, I could tell his mind couldn't fully focus on me. He didn't keep eye contact, which let me know he was also guilty of something.

"Come over here with me. I held out my hand as a gesture to let him know everything would be okay."

Instead of moving, he looked as if these fake-ass killers were holding him against his will. My face twitched and my top lip curled. The fury inside me was ready to bubble over like a pot of boiling water.

Staring each man down one face at a time, I took a step forward. "Y'all niggas get the fuck out of my son's way and let him come to me. Don't do this shit 'cause I'm on my last strike and I don't mind losing it, bruh."

"Act like you wanna buck and get yo' ass popped!" one of the wanna-be thugs said, insinuating a dare. He returned my gaze like he was the gangsta of the century.

"Listen, Demerius, no one came here to disrespect you. I'm taking Casey and getting her away from this. She's my woman now and I refuse to let this happen to her again."

Shawn's bitch-ass was damn near ready to shed tears as I stared into his soul. I knew it was because of the unknown aftermath, of how this could ultimately play out for his family. It wasn't hard to hear about what I'd done in the streets. Back then, anybody who had ever crossed the line received the same fate. One slug. No mercy.

"You don't know me, Shawn. This is my muthafuckin' house. That's *my* damn son. You disrespected me when you stepped on my property with guns. DP, I said come over here with me. Now!"

"He doesn't want to be with you anymore, Domestic. My son is going with me. Ask him," Casey informed me, with malice in her tone.

"Bitch, don't you ever say no shit like that to me. You'll have to kill me dead before I let you take my boy. You think these niggas can protect you! Huh?"

Her comment caused my adrenaline to pump full force, and before anyone knew what happened, I crashed my fist into the glass window next to me. "Don't play with me, bitch!"

The fear in these niggas had finally showed itself because it was at that moment that I heard a bullet slide into the chamber of a gun. Remembering that my son was still present, my attitude turned down a notch. The audacity of Casey to pull a stunt like this was unbelievable. Looking into her eyes, I pointed a stern finger and said, "I'm going to make you wish you were dead. This was the last straw."

"No. The last straw was when you put your hands on me again, Domestic. I'm not your fuckin' punching bag. It's always about you, never about us being a family. Never what we want, only you. My brain is so drained from hearing the same shit. You don't even want me 'cause you told me you didn't. Our son is starting to hate you for what you've been doing to me. How could you say you love him, but you beat his mother?"

Rubbing my temple, I choked on my words. I knew DP was aware of me and his mother's scuffles, but I never tried to beat the hell out of her in front of him.

"DP, is this true? You starting to hate me." I sat back and waited for an answer.

He stumbled over his words before dropping a few tears on his shirts. "I don't like the things you do to my mama, Dad. You're hurting her. She wants to leave and I'm not letting her go without me. I love her," he said, before breaking down.

My son's pain shredded my fuckin' heart to pieces. My baby boy really didn't want to be with me anymore. Casey was filling his head up with so much fuckery that he'd really began believing she was the most perfect angel ever.

No one ever knew the reason she and I had fallen out. It had gotten to the point where we shared no love for one another. After cheating on me right before my son was born, I started doing disrespectful shit to her. Even though it crushed me, I felt like she deserved it. I was successful without her. Instead of finding a new life and letting me do the job of a father from a distance, she forced me to be part of her life. Casey was making me ponder on all the foolishness and it was beginning to show on my face.

"So you want to choose your mom over ya' old pops, huh? It's okay. I'm not even mad at you because you old enough to feel the way you want. But are you sure about leaving with her? Who's gonna give you all the new sneakers and clothes for school? 'Cause I'm the one who puts those clothes on yo' back, DP, not yo' mama."

"I'll make sure my son has whatever he needs. It's time for us to leave, Demerius." Casey walked past me with Shawn on her on her heels. "DP, come on baby. We need to leave now." She was dropping those same fake-ass tears she always dropped making him feel sorry for her.

Moving towards the door with the one of the men on each side of him, I slightly stepped out of the way to see if my boy was willing to abandon the one who loved him the most.

Walking over to Casey, he followed them out the door without uttering a single word to me. Strolling directly behind them, Shawn tried to secure the truck, as his brothers stood guard.

Breezing to my car, I quickly grabbed my gun from the glovebox. These niggas pulled a fast one with this bitch, but fuckin' wit' my seed was when shit got real. Drawing out my weapon, both men stopped and raised their guns.

"Is y'all fools dumb? What in the fuck make y'all think I'ma just let y'all push off with my son? You can go bitch, but my kid ain't leaving. Casey, you better get some sense into that brain and I mean quick."

"You need to lower your gun, bruh. We ain't doing no debating!"

Craig just relax, bro. We out here in the open," Shawn warned, before stepping in between us.

At that very moment, I wanted to put a slug directly in the center of his fuckin' skull. This nigga was moving my family out of my home like he was the director of the entire plan. My trigger finger was itching for a muthafucker to slip. Casey held my son behind her, giving him easy access to the truck. I took a step back just in case I needed to let off any shots.

"Casey, I'm not letting you run off with DP. He's all I got left. If you try and pull this fake-ass move, I'ma be sure to cause you hell. It doesn't matter where you go 'cause I'll find you."

Her gaze lowered when my eyes grew wide. "I'm not coming back, Demerius. Just ask your son if he wants to stay. If he agrees, I won't hold him."

Placing my attention back on my kid, I asked again hoping I received a different reaction. "What's up, DP? Stay with me, Son. Regardless of me and your mother's problems, I've done my job as a father to you."

"I love you, Dad," was all he said, before jumping inside the U-Haul.

I couldn't fathom something happening to my kid, but I realized that Casey had literally flipped him against me. As Shawn climbed into the driver's seat, he started up the engine and pulled out of the driveway. The other two men jumped in their cars and followed. I wanted to release my entire clip in the side of the car, but I continued to think about DP.

After they disappeared down the street, I made a call to a few of my personals. It was now official. Shawn and his brothers had to pay for the disrespect. When I wrapped my hands around Casey's throat, I was going to beat her unmercifully. My people played dirty in the streets daily, and these nigga's were like mini-snacks waitin' to be eaten.

***

Heading inside my crib, I posted up in the half-empty living room. Taking a deep breath, I found myself smashing my foot into the glass coffee table. Next came the walls and entertainment system. My mind was in a rage. All I could see was Casey's dead face. She would be the reason my old ways resurfaced. She only wanted to cause me pain and I was going to be sure on returning the same, just ten times harder.

Calling Foreign's phone, I listened to it ring in my ear while pacing around the room. Blood flowed freely between my fingers, from the deep cuts I'd caused during my small rampage. The sound of her voice calmed my spirit instantly.

"Hey, baby. Where are you? I was just on my way up to the carwash."

"No, don't go up there. I need you to meet me at my other house. I'm going to text you the address."

"Domestic, are you okay? Why do you sound like that?"

The time for questions was pointless and I didn't need any more thoughts to make me black out again. "I'm fine, Foreign. I need you with me right now. Please, just come. I really don't feel like explaining over the phone."

"I'm on the way now. Just text me the address, baby." Her tone was understanding and sincere.

Ending the call, I sent her the address and took a seat on the hardwood floor. The entire day was one that I would never forget. I had my son stripped away from my life and Casey was the one to blame. After all my hard work to provide, I still came up short. It wouldn't take long for me to find out where she would be resting her head. After those answers were revealed, she could kiss all her friends goodbye.

Foreign . . .

After getting a call from Domestic, I quickly gathered my stuff and headed out of the house. Aaron was gone to one of his fake sexual-healing classes, so I decided to stop at the house while I had the chance.

Picking up a few things, I grabbed my Louis Vuitton tote bag and headed downstairs. I thought I was hearing things when a noise came from inside the kitchen area. No one was home when I arrived, so I knew I wasn't over exaggerating.

Stepping through the living room, I reached the kitchen and locked eyes with Lexi who was sitting at the kitchen table. A plate of pancakes sat in front of her and she was tapping the bottom of a syrup bottle like it wasn't clear and empty.

"Lexi? What are you doing?"

"Bitch, what does it look like? I'm trying to eat these dry-ass pancakes, but you black-ass people are out of syrup. It seems that I'm just gonna have to use jelly instead."

"When did you get here? I didn't hear you come in." I took a seat at the table.

"Girl, I was here when you crept through like the Grinch. How's that new dick been treating you?"

She was still tapping on the bottle as if she hadn't just asked me some personal shit. "What are you talking about, Lexi?"

"I'm talking about that nigga who putting that cock in your back. You haven't been coming home, Foreign. Don't you think everyone can see you're having an affair?

My face screwed up at her last comment. "An affair? I think you got me confused with your brother's cheating ass."

"Girl, please. You cheating on him too. Quite frankly, I don't give a damn. But I feel that y'all need to go ahead and end this chapter in y'all's life before you start moving so sloppy with a man you barely know. That nigga could be a chain gang faggot for all you know."

"What?" I stood back to my feet. "What the hell does that supposed to mean, Lexi? You're the one who told me to go out and have some fun, remember?"

"I told you to go out and get some dick, honey. You've been acting like you're starting a new family. I have no parts of that, Foreign."

I couldn't believe Lexi. She was my friend, but her remarks were throwing me for a loop. She had encouraged me so many times to get the hell away from her brother, but now it seemed to be a problem.

"Look. Aaron doesn't make me happy anymore. I had my time with him, and I stood through a tragic-ass relationship while this man belittled me with all these thirsty-ass bitches. He doesn't even have respect for me. Why does it matters what I'm doing now?"

"Because what you're doing isn't you, Foreign. I wouldn't give a damn whether you got pumped sixteen times a day. You are still legally married to my brother. That means a lot to this family and there's a better way to hide what you're doing."

"I think your brother is in the same marriage, Lexi, and he doesn't give a damn about it."

Shaking her head, she took a bite of her pancakes before stopping me with a raised finger. "I'd have to disagree."

"Why?"

"Because he brings his ass home every night. Regardless of you guys' problems, you can't recall one night that he ever stayed away from this house. When you began to slumber in another's bed, it showed that the loyalty for home is no longer there. Flesh is weak, Foreign. I've never seen one man who can say they've never cheated. It's something all women are prepared for when they say the words *I do*. This man has obviously gotten you in your feelings because you can't even face your own husband. I love you and I'm not judging, but you were my friend before you became my sister in law. I can only tell you the truth and hope you don't slit my throat like the other bitches who don't wanna hear the truth."

Soaking in her opinion, I nodded humbly. Lexi was so in her brother's corner she'd forgotten all about the pain his trifling-ass caused me. I never imagined him doing this to me when he first popped the question. It was after the fame that he began to rip my soul right down the middle with his deceitful-ass cheating habit.

It didn't take a class for me to see if I was hurting my husband. All it took was a little effort to make our relationship work. When I caught him cheating the first time, I figured it was just a phase, a normal mistake for men of my husband's caliber. But after the repetitive cycle, I knew there was no care for the way I truly felt. It turned my heart cold as ice.

"If you aren't in my shoes. You can't tell me what I'm doing is wrong, Lexi. It's just not meant to be anymore."

Nodding, she took another bite of her food. "Maybe you're right, but what you're doing isn't going to help. You're gonna mix into a bowl of terror and you won't know how to escape it, especially if you're running your love ones off. That's up to you. Aaron will be back soon. Maybe you can just tell him everything and that'll make him sign the papers for you to be free."

"He'll receive them in the mail," I snapped, before storming off. I couldn't believe Aaron had Lexi treating me so distant like he'd been corrupted in this marriage and wanted someone to feel sorry for him and his actions. Sorry wasn't in my vocabulary and if the family felt it was my fault, to hell with them too.

Domestic needed my help and that's who my loyalty was going to be dedicated to from now on.

***

After arriving to Domestic's crib, I walked in his home and saw it had been destroyed. He was sitting in the corner with dried up blood all over his hands and floor.

As he filled me in on the situation, my heart ached for his predicament. I didn't know how it felt to have a child taken away. Especially, by the co-parent you'd provide for and sheltered. His mind was so distraught he couldn't even move from his seated spot, on the floor. It showed me just how much he cared for his kid. The news of our unborn child was still something I hadn't revealed, but I had yet to tell him. I knew the perfect time would present itself, but now wasn't the correct moment.

It took me a while to get him in the shower and back to talking about something different. After we'd bathed one another and exited the bathroom, I pulled him into the bed and cuddled up under him closely. The scent of his Axe shower shampoo gave me a tingle in my stomach for some love. I knew sex was the farthest thing from his mind right now. I could tell by the way he rubbed my shoulder and stared at the ceiling.

He climbed out of bed and rushed to the bathroom, closing the door behind him.

Domestic . . .

Stepping inside the bathroom, I kneeled over the toilet and puked violently. My stomach was turning knots and it felt like my heart was pumping out of my chest. The feeling was unbearable. After cleaning myself up, I made my way back to Foreign's side in the bed. She instantly caressed my chest and soothed my pain when I flopped down next to her.

"Are you okay, baby?" Foreign gazed in my eyes as if she could fix all my problems.

"Yeah, I just need some sleep."

Closing my eyes, I tried my best to forget about Casey and my son. Finally, I drifted off into a deep sleep. . .

Hearing the door handle to the dark closet shake, I jumped from my slumber. It felt like I spent days sweating and crying. My tummy hurt from the lack of food and I could feel her evil spirit outside of the thin wooden door.

In fear, I watched the door open. The bright sun light boomed through the window and nibbled on my skin. My eyes adjusted to her sinister facial expression beaming down on me. Her hands carried a glass of water and two pieces of bread.

Leaning down in front of me, she whispered in my ear. "You'll die in here or come out and obey your mommy like a good boy. Make a choice."

My voice was weak, and I couldn't think about anything, except my daddy saving me from the torture. "I just want my daddy, Mama." Tears flushed down my cheeks.

Her jaws began shaking and I could tell she was about to strike me. Instead, she pushed the water and bread into my arms and yelled in my face, "You're going to wish your daddy wasn't around when I'm done with you!"

CHAPTER 20
AARON

That bitch karma had a funny way of coming back and flipping a person's world upside down. I was in the prime of my career. My skills had brought home a championship ring for the second time in history, and now I was being investigated for having sex with an underage girl. One I hadn't touched, let alone know, for that matter. When everyone labeled you a hoe in the industry it was hard to make them believe your innocence. My actions had brought the devil knocking on my door. Not only did I let him in, but I allowed him to destroy my home. My marriage was in shambles and my wife was getting dicked-down by a dude I knew nothing about.

Moving like a half dead slug, I made my way to the bar and grabbed a bottle of Tequila. The fabulous life I dreamed of had turned into a nightmare on Elm Street. Flopping down on the sofa, I removed the cap from the bottle and turned it up to my lips. The hot liquid burned my throat on the way down, but it didn't compare to the heat that burned throughout my soul. Foreign was my life and I would give up everything if she would give me one last chance.

The thought alone summoned an ocean of tears to flood the gates of my lids and pour down my face. I had no one in my corner, except Lexi, and without her I would be lost. However, the love of just one person wasn't enough. Therefore, I sought help from something else.

Staring down at the baggie on my glass table, I picked it up and held it in front of my face. Earlier that day, I'd made a stop out to a familiar hood and copped a bag of cocaine. From what I'd heard, it would ease my pain. Drugs were not my thing, but I was willing to do whatever it took to make the pain stop— if only for a moment.

Opening the baggie, I dropped a tiny pile on a compact mirror. I had a rolled up one hundred dollar bill on standby. Honestly, I was afraid to try it. I hated the feeling of water when it got in my nose, so I didn't see how I would be able to ingest such a harsh substance through my nostrils.

"Fuck it," I mumbled and picked up the bill.

Taking two more shots of liquor, I sat the bottle down and put the bill over the tiny pile. Slowly, I took one sniff and the hair on the back of my neck stood up. Violent coughs bruised my throat and my eyes began to water.

"What the fuck?"

Dropping the mirror, the rest of the powder hit the rug underneath my feet, but I didn't care. That shit was horrible. In the movies they made it seem so easy. Quickly, I found out that was a lie. Hitting my chest, I coughed and gagged. Then I picked up the bottle and took another swig. A few minutes passed and I was finally able to breathe normally. Suddenly, a stern knock interrupted my pity party.

Grabbing the baggie, I slipped it underneath the cushion and picked up the mirror to check my face. There was no visible dust, so I went to see who the hell was on my doorstep unannounced.

Snatching the door open with a mean scowl on my face, it was the one bitch I didn't want to see. "What the fuck do you want, Emilia?"

She had this crooked smirk on her face. "You. Can I come in?"

"No. I ain't got shit to say to you after that bullshit-ass stunt you pulled. You really came to arrest me when you knew I hadn't done shit. Get the fuck off my property."

Just as I was about to close the door, she pushed it back open. "I don't think you want to do that."

"You have no idea what I want to do to you."

"If it involves sex count me in."

"I'm straight." Emilia reached out and grabbed my dick, but I slapped her hand away. "Stop playing with me."

"I don't think you understand me. So, allow me to make you aware of the shit you're about to be buried in. Right now, a warrant is about to be issued for your arrest. We have enough evidence to make it stick to you like flies on shit," she said smugly.

"We have a recording with Antwan confessing to those crimes," I reminded her.

She laughed. "What you have is a confession that was recorded without Antwan's permission. It will never hold up in a court of law, and I'll make sure of that. Unless . . . you give me what I want."

Not once did we think about that. It felt like I was back to square one with the bullshit that nigga had pulled. And now this bitch was threatening to make these fake-ass charges stick. "What do you want, Emilia?"

"You. I want *you*, Aaron." She reached out and grabbed my piece once more, but this time I didn't move her hand.

"You doing all this just so I'll have sex with you?"

"I want money too. One hundred thousand dollars to be exact." Emilia moved her hand and placed it on her hip. "The thing about you athletes is that you think you're above the law. Or that you're entitled to whoever and whatever you want. You thought you could fuck me one time and play me to the left like you did?"

"Emilia, I'm married, and you know that. You knew it was only sex. Nothing more. Nothing less."

"Too damn bad. *You're* married. Not me. You think you can just fuck me and disregard my feelings? It doesn't work that way, Aaron."

"Well, why did you act like you were okay with our arrangement?"

"That's simple. I figured the feelings would come later and eventually you would end up leaving your wife for me."

The broad was funny. Chuckling, I replied, "You knew I wasn't leaving my wife. Every female I fucked knew that, including you. Yo' ass just delusional."

"That's where you're wrong, Aaron. See, I was pregnant with your child. And, had I carried the baby full term, without a doubt, we would've been together."

That was news to me, but I certainly didn't believe her ass. "I don't believe you."

"You don't have to believe it, but I can assure you we're going to fuck today or you'll be arrested by midnight and then you can kiss your weak-ass life goodbye."

"Fine, I'm not doing this with you. Where am I meeting you? And after this I want you out of my life for good."

"No problem. Let me in, I'm ready now."

"Hell no, not in my home. My wife could come home at any moment now."

Emilia's laugh was loud, as she shook her head. "No, she's definitely not coming home to you any time soon."

Before I knew it, I had Emilia snatched up by the collar. "How do you know that? What did you do to her?"

She slapped my hands away but I didn't let her go. "I didn't do anything to her. Now let me go."

"Not until you tell me where she is." My bark was loud. If that bitch had done something to my wife, I was gonna choke her ass out right on my porch.

"She's with her boyfriend."

Her words hit me in the gut. The grip I had on her loosened instantly. "What the fuck you mean, her *boyfriend*?"

"Just what I said. Your wife has a boyfriend and I know him very well."

My gut had told me Foreign had a boyfriend but I couldn't let Emilia know that. "I don't believe you."

"Believe this then." She pulled out her cellphone and moved her fingers swiftly. Then she passed it to me. "That's your wife and her boyfriend, Domestic."

The photo of Foreign hugged up with some buff-ass nigga crushed my heart. My jaw hit the ground. The smile on her face was disgusting. She seemed so happy in his arms, as if she was in love with him, and that hurt. Regardless of my indiscretions, I had never given another woman my heart. I didn't love none of them hoes. They got the dick once or twice and that was it. Well, with exception of Emilia. We fucked for a whole month and that was only because Foreign had a miscarriage and we weren't having sex. Emilia had come along during that time and she'd taken up Foreign's slack.

Emilia took her phone back. "She's with him day and night, Aaron. I know you need some pussy since she's not giving you any.

She's too busy laying up with my associate." She stepped closer to me and rubbed my chest. "Let's go inside."

The emotional agony I felt made me want to hurt somebody terribly. Foreign was parading around town with a nigga like she didn't have a husband at home. I ain't never take them hoes nowhere. That shit had me hot. My blood was boiling like hot grits, and I had some built up pressure that needed releasing. Stepping back, I let Emilia inside and closed the door.

"Go to the couch," I demanded, as I removed my shirt and tossed it on the floor. My basketball shorts and boxers followed.

Emilia took off the tight fitting dress that clung to her hips and tossed it on the sofa. Facing me, she stood before me looking flawless in a sexy lace set. "Fix me a drink." She sat down to get comfortable.

"We don't have time to waste. So, stand up and bend over. You know how I like it."

"No, I'm in control. Like I said before, Foreign is with Domestic and she's not coming home. If she leaves him, I'll know. So, have a seat."

This crazy bitch really had some shit up her sleeves, but there was nothing I could do about it. Her plan was carefully thought out and she had me by the balls. Therefore, I sat down. Emilia picked up the bottle of tequila and drank from it. When she was done, she sat it back down and removed her underwear. Kneeling down in front of me, she took my semi-stiff rod inside her mouth and slurped me slowly. The warmth of her mouth made my shit rock up. Then, she straddled me. My eyes were on her shaved pussy. I watched my piece disappear inside of her inch by inch.

She rolled her hips slowly, in a circular motion. "Damn, Aaron." Her eyes rolled, as she pinched her nipples. I was pissed off, but I couldn't deny the fact that she was sexy as fuck.

My hands rested against her juicy ass, pushing her down onto me further. Together, we thrusted our hips against each other. Emilia rocked harder, then bounced up and down. Dropping her head, she buried her face in the crook of my neck. Her seductive moans stroked my ear drums.

With my arms wrapped around her waist, I rose to my feet and laid her on the couch. Never pulling out, I pushed one of her legs back and dug deep in her beige twat. If dick was what she wanted, I was gonna give it to her. By the time I finished beating her down, her shit was gonna be red. Thrusting hard and fast, I murdered her shit.

"Aaron! Aaron!" Her piercing screams flooded my ears, but I tuned her out. "Slow down."

"Shut up!" I barked and kept going.

A rough fuck was all she was getting from me. Minutes later, her screams turned into wails. Inside I was smiling, but there was a frown on my face. Pulling out, I held my dick in my hands and pulled on it to keep it hard. "Get up."

Emilia stood and I escorted her to the end of the sofa. "Hold on to the arm of the chair."

Doing as she was told, she planted her hands on the arm and I dipped back inside. Long stroking her from the back, I smacked her ass hard. She deserved a brutal fuck and I was the one to give it to her. The constant ass smacking left my handprint buried on her soft cheeks. Her juices coated me heavily. She was extra wet and gushy. In the midst of sliding out, I shoved it back in and punctured her asshole. She hollered and raised up with the quickness.

"Fuuck! That's my ass."

"Shut up!" Grabbing her at the back of her neck, I pushed her further onto the sofa and pounded that ass. My mission was to make sure she had a hard time walking out the door when she left.

One hour later, Emilia was all fucked out and damn near dead after I busted my third nut. "I hope you enjoyed it because this was the last time. I'll have your money in a few days."

Once we were cleaned up and dressed, I grabbed my wallet and keys before emerging from the house. Emilia walked like she'd just gotten hit by a train.

"Emilia," I called out causing her to stop in her tracks and turn around, "don't come back to my house. I'll call you and we can meet up. After that, I don't wanna ever hear from you again."

"In case you forgot, I'm running this show."

"Not if you want this money." Unlocking the doors on my SUV, I climbed inside and pulled off.

The news of Foreign's cheating had me in a fucked up state of mind. I didn't know what hurt more, the fact that she was cheating all together, or that she was running around with some thug-ass nigga. It looked like the nigga sold all the dope in Tampa. He was probably a kingpin or some shit, and that sort of lifestyle wasn't for her. She wasn't raised in the hood. Then it made me wonder how she'd met him. Lexi was adventurous and loved hood niggas, but I knew she hadn't introduced the two of them. My twin would never betray me like that.

Lucid thoughts invaded my mind about the situation. Images of Foreign having sex with that big ass nigga were disturbing. He was probably tearing the lining out of the pussy that once belonged to me. She was probably sucking his dick too. I was crushed and devastated, but I still wanted my wife back. Any other man would've probably left their wife at this point, not me though. I was the one who had caused her to go out and find another man in the first place; therefore, I had to forgive her.

I had to put a plan in full effect, ASAP, but I didn't know where to begin. Lexi said she would help me. That didn't seem to be working though because Foreign still didn't want me. My parents were upset with me, so they were out of the question. Calvin wasn't someone I could talk to about commitment or marriage so that was a dead end too. Then a lightbulb went off in my head. All wasn't lost after all. There were two people I hadn't confided in, so I headed to their home.

Thirty minutes later, I pulled up into the driveway and silenced the engine. An uneasy feeling came over me, as I contemplated on getting out. "Aaron, get out the truck and be a man. You have to do this if you want to save your marriage," I said aloud.

After giving myself a pep talk, I walked on the porch and rang the doorbell. Seconds passed and the door became ajar. "Hey, Son. You have a troubling look on your face. Is Foreign okay?" Mr. Hamilton asked.

"No." I nodded my head. "She wants to divorce me."

"Come inside, let's talk." Foreign's dad opened the door wide enough for me to enter. Since she wouldn't talk to me willingly, I was going to make her father do it. She valued his opinion more than anybody else's on earth.

CHAPTER 21
DOMESTIC

After waking from my slumber with Foreign, I got up and quickly headed into the bathroom. It didn't take long to tighten myself up with a clean shower and shave. Today felt better than yesterday, but the pain of my son being away was eating at my flesh like the walking dead. There was nothing I could do without DP. He was the one I strived so hard for. My prison bid showed me that leaving him wasn't in my thought process any longer.

It was deep to know Casey's bitch-ass was willing to crash me and my son's relationship for the satisfaction of some broke-nigga dick, a nigga who couldn't even pay somebody to move the shit I'd paid for. Her anger had gotten the best of her but I was zero tolerant for the bull.

It would only take a few weeks before she realized no one else would provide for her the way I had. She would fall back home on her knees and beg me to take her back in. It came with the parenting role. Of course, I would let her back in. And as soon as she crossed my threshold, she would feel the same pain I was placed in when she removed my child from my protection and possession.

Exiting the bathroom, Foreign was lying on her stomach. Her clothes were scattered over the floor from our late night session. As I stared at her gorgeous face, it dawned on me that she was what I'd needed the entire time. A woman who would listen and understand her place in my life. To be my wife and never go against my word. Within a small amount of time, she'd shown me that trait numerous times. Since then, my heart feigned for her love daily.

A trustworthy and loyal person was not one who was willing to always cause division between their loved ones, but one who was willing to comfort and love them through all the confusion.

Placing a kiss on her cheek, I headed in the kitchen to whip up a small breakfast. Salmon and biscuits was always the way to a woman's heart. I fixed up some cheese grits and started to brew up a pot of coffee. Thinking about the whereabouts of my kid, I picked up my phone and dialed Casey's number. It didn't take long for her to answer my call.

"Hello?"

"You have a lot of heart dragging my son away from me to be with another man. You know I'm not gonna forget this, right?" I could hear her huff and puff on the other end of the receiver like I wasn't talking about shit.

"Demerius, no one has dragged DP into anything. You felt you could beat my ass and treat me like dog. You never cared about me when I begged you to stop putting your dick in these women who didn't mean shit."

"Bitch! We have nothing! What don't you understand, Casey? My only job was to make sure my son and you had a place to live and eat. That's it! If you wanted to be a little freak for another man, you should have worked and saved up for your own. Unfortunately, you don't know what that feels like. It's sad to see you killing yourself like this because if I catch you, I'm going to beat you into a fuckin' coma. I want my son, Casey!"

"I don't care, Demerius. Fuck you punk-ass nigga. You think hitting on me is some real shit. You think it makes you a solid man. You've never beat up a man like that. You're a pussy and I can bet you were probably getting fucked behind those prison walls. You'll never see my son again. When he gets older, he'll find you if he chooses to. Please, stop calling my phone!" she screamed in my ear before hanging up.

This bitch had my blood boiling through the roof with her disrespect. Casey had really gained a small distance away from me and now she felt like she was untouchable. The thought of murdering her crossed my mind and I knew Shawn would be in the same box. I nearly crushed my phone thinking of how bad I wanted to break her jaw.

Hearing my phone ring, I glanced at the screen. Spotting the carwash business number, I quickly answered.

"This is Demerius."

"Uhh, Boss. You need to make your way to the wash soon. We got a problem."

Rubbing a hand on my temple, I sat down. "What's wrong now? The shit isn't hard to run. Handle the cars with care that's all you gotta do. How complicated is that?"

"It's not a customer problem, it's an office situation. The numbers aren't adding up.

Hearing her remark gave me clarification that my money wasn't being handled accordingly. Shaking my head, I hung up the phone and finished preparing Foreign's breakfast. As I stood in deep thought, my peripheral spotted her walking toward the kitchen.

"Are you okay, baby? I could hear you yelling in my sleep." Her eyes were slightly closed, and her beautiful face glowed to perfection.

"Yeah, just a little frustrated. I'll be okay though. I made you breakfast."

Moving over closer to me, she stood under my chin with those sexy eyes gazing up at me. Her aura was like a passionate spell not visually seen. She mesmerized my mind every time I touched her skin.

"What are your plans for me in the next twenty minutes?" Her tone was low and seductive.

I couldn't help but smile. She craved my loving and it enticed me more and more. Gripping that juicy ass roughly, I slid my tongue inside her mouth. She squirmed under my touch and I could feel myself getting excited from the feel of her soft breast. Pulling one out of her thin slip over, I sucked gently on the nipple. The sound of my phone vibrating reminded me I still had business to attend.

Breaking our lip lock, I placed a kiss on her forehead. "I gotta head over to the shop and see what's going on. Apparently, somebody has did something stupid and they need me to straighten it."

"Mhmm, I was hoping to get some more fun time, but I understand. I have to do a few things also. What time will you be back home?" she asked as I followed her to the room.

"Probably around five. I'm riding around for a routine checkup on all the stores. When shit starts to move funny, my face has to be seen. Why? You gon' be here waiting for me? If so, I want that face down and ass in the air."

Pecking my lips, she grabbed my piece. "Later, angry man."

Laughing, I waited for her to get dressed and we headed out together. Before she got in her car to leave, I gripped her pussy. "I want you home tonight. I can't rest without you." My lips locked on to her neck for a light smooch.

"I'll be here if you want me to be, love."

Nodding, I watched as she got inside her car and pulled away. Switching into business mode, I jumped in my Cadillac XT4. I usually didn't experience too many troubles when it came down to my business. Muthafuckers knew I was beyond serious when it came down to my shit and my money. After going through the process of bullshit once, I handled it with quickness and never had to worry about it again.

It only took me twenty-five minutes to arrive at my establishment. My employee's expressions switched when I entered the driveway. They stood around the entrance of the wash huddled in a circle. Climbing out of my car, they split like water and oil. When I walked inside, Tracy stood at the counter with a stupid smirk on her face.

"What's going on?" My voice alerted everyone who moved around who hadn't already acknowledged my presence. They froze in place and looked over to Tracy.

Coming from behind the counter, she walked up to me. "That little bastard-ass kid you wanted me to put behind the counter robbed you. His sneaky ass used the spare key from the office and cleared the entire safe."

Turning my head, the heat began to rise in my mind. The same slime-ass muthafucker I helped had crossed me out for my paper. The thought of Emilia's dumb ass invaded my head. She was the cause of this mishap and she was damn sure going to fix it.

"How much was in there?" I asked in a whisper in Tracy's ear.

"Forty."

The Price You Pay for Love

Taking a deep breath, I pulled out my cell and dialed that sheisty bitch Emilia's number. It took three rings before I got an answer. "I see you're alive and okay. What can I do for you, Demerius?"

"What you can do for me is pay me the forty grand that little punk ass nigga skated off with. You need to come see me right now," I spat before stepping outside.

"Excuse me? What the hell are you yelling for? I have no idea what you're speaking on in regard to any missing money. I don't do handouts for cash. Now calm down and tell me what's going on."

Sliding a hand across my goatee, I humbled myself. "Emilia, I'm going to say this as nice as possible. Today is not my day, bitch. Don't tempt me with that fake-ass gangsta talk. The young idiot you wanted me to help out so bad, robbed my safe and stole forty grand from me. When I told you I didn't want anything to do with the man, you still forced me to do it. Now who's reimbursing my shit?"

"First of all, I didn't take shit from you, Domestic. So kill the attitude. All I have to do is get someone to pick him up and find out where he stashed your money. You need to relax and—"

"Relax! How the fuck can I relax, and I just explained to you how that man just got me for forty G's? Do you really wanna play with me like this? You know how far I'm willing to take this shit."

"Yeah, and I also know you've got businesses you don't wanna lose. It all could be gone tomorrow, Demerius."

"There won't be a tomorrow without my funds," I said with aggression.

"Look, Demerius. Right now you're going to feel a certain way, but all you have to do is relax. If I'm telling you to, that means I'll look into it."

A slight chuckle escaped my lips as I watched the police cruise pass the carwash. "I'm gonna tell you something, Emilia. I'm a businessman and taking losses for the cause of a person like you is unacceptable. You're the reason I'm missing my money right now. You just don't understand, and it doesn't seem like you'll understand until it's too late."

Without another word, I disconnected the call and made my way back inside to Tracy. "Don't you have a picture ID of him in our computer?"

"I think so," she said, as she began to type on the keyboard. "Yep. We do!"

"Write down the address for me, please. I don't want you guys to worry about this issue. I'm going to handle it. Be sure to let everyone know this is not to be reported or talked about with anyone. We don't need any type of gossip running around the business."

"Okay, I got you."

Handing me the piece of paper, I shoved it into my pocket before heading out to my car. Pulling off into the intersecting street, I stopped at the red light and pressed the address from his identification card into my GPS. It wouldn't take long for me to find him in the streets of Tampa. A few dollars would make a nigga rat out his own grandmother in the hoods of Florida.

Fifteen minutes later, I found myself down in the trenches. The address led me to a small apartment complex that couldn't house more than a hundred people. Being that it was still in the a.m., movement was light.

Climbing out of my car with my pistol tucked, I walked along the bottom level until I reached apartment thirteen.

With a stern knock, I waited to see if I could hear a sound from the inside. I pressed my face against the window and I could see that the living room was empty, besides a TV mounted on the wall. I tried twisting the knob, but it wouldn't budge.

Backtracking down the walkway, I moved around to the backdoor. This time I was given access when I twisted the knob. Entering the smelly spot, I quietly closed the door and removed my gun. Checking the kitchen cabinets, I moved to the living area and still found nothing. The smell of weed polluted the air and bottles of Bud Ice beer lay scattered over the floor.

Opening one of the bedroom doors, I spotted a young nigga sprawled out ass-naked in the bed with a thin-bodied female. The room smelled like cooked fish, and the drug paraphernalia of powder sacks were scattered around, which explained why they hadn't heard me enter the room.

With rapid speed, I drew back and came forward with force, slapping the young dude across the face with my gun.

He caved over on the floor holding his bloody nose. "Shittt! What the fuck, dawg!" Keith rolled around like his body could no longer function.

His cunt-freak slid to the corner of the room with her eyes bulging out the sockets. Her lips were so dry she could start a fire with them. I realized after looking down in the young punk's face that I was dealing with a fuckin' junkie.

"Where the fuck is my money, chump-ass nigga? I give you a job and this is how you repay me? I'm the same one who shot you twenty bands to get your start in the free world and you *still* stole from me?"

I kicked his ass in the face urging him to speak. Keith held his hands up in an effort to catch his breath. "I didn't spend it all. It's in the book bag by the closet." He gasped for air as if he needed an asthma pump.

Glancing in the direction of the bag, I picked it up but kept my aim in case the fuck boy got any bright ideas. I unzipped it and instantly estimated about ten grand. That shit fueled my madness even more. The bitch had blown half of the funds within a ten hour time span.

"Where the fuck is my bread? 'Cause this damn sure ain't all of it. Explain! Where is my shit?" I pushed the barrel in the side of his temple.

"I spent it, man! I just needed to pay a little debt. I swear I was gonna replace it, boss. I didn't have a choice."

"You feel like you didn't have a choice on stealing my shit?" Grabbing a small switch blade from the table, I slashed him smoothly across the neck. His female friend began to scream, and I silenced her with one slug to the face. *Bloc!*

My chest pumped with rage. All I could see was blood flowing from his skin like a large waterfall. My adrenaline started to slow

211

down once I gathered my mind back from that dark place. The room ceased from spinning and the apartment grew extremely quiet.

Looking around at the disaster, I made a quick mental note of everything I had touched. It wasn't smart to move so fast because the game was easy to lose when it involved a life.

Making my way back to the kitchen, I found a bottle of bleach and a dish rag. Wiping all the knobs one by one, I eased out of the backdoor and got back to my car.

As I drove calmly away from the scene, I noticed a few neighbors standing on their porches. My only prayer was to hope none of them had heard the gunshot just minutes prior.

Once I'd made my way back across town, I bagged all my clothes and torched them inside of the grill outside my house. A warm shower was exactly what I needed before changing my apparel. After I felt fresh and clean again, I hid the Desert Eagle handgun up in the attic.

Just as I made my way back down, my phone started to ring causing me to jump. Ignoring it, I paced around the house until it began to sound off again.

Thinking about Emilia and the young idiot, I picked it up to see who was trying to reach me so badly. Foreign's name shined on my main screen, so I answered before she got a chance to hang up the phone.

"Baby?"

"Hey, I've been calling you. Is everything okay?"

"Yeah, why do you ask?" I replied in a paranoid tone.

"I just know you were a little upset before we left. You've been on my mind ever since we departed, love. How has your day been going so far?"

The images of the dead bodies caused me to pause on my reply. "It's been alright. Just a lil' shaky at the carwash. Somebody stole from the safe and it's got us all in an uproar."

"Oh my God! Did you ever get the money back?"

"Nah," I lied. I didn't need too many questions and answers being passed around until things blew over with my most recent issue. "What are you doing? Should I be expecting you back in my arms soon."

"Yes." She giggled through the line. "I'm about to go have lunch with my sister and handle a few more things, but you can expect me to be laying naked in your arms very soon, sir."

"That's good to hear. Enjoy lunch and I'll be right here waiting for your call when you're on your way back."

"Okay, handsome. See you soon," she uttered, before hanging up.

Grabbing my keys, I decided to head back up to the carwash in case anybody was wondering about my whereabouts. In the end, I was only focused on one person's movement and that was Emilia.

CHAPTER 22
FOREIGN

After leaving Domestic's place, I hit up Lexi and asked her to meet me for brunch. Of course, she obliged. A lot of the things she said were true and I just wanted to clear the air with her. We were best friends and I didn't want my dead end marriage to draw a wedge between our friendship.

Lexi was sitting out front of Bahama Breeze, focusing heavily on her phone when I walked up. "Look up, Lexi, and say cheese." I giggled.

"Hush, I saw you pull in." Lexi shoved her phone inside her purse and stood up. "You called right on time because I'm starving, and I need a damn drink."

"I'm starving too."

Inside, the hostess seated us at a table outside on the patio. The breeze was nice compared to the inside, which felt like a damn meat locker. Before I could spark up a conversation, the waiter showed up and introduced himself, while taking our drink and food orders. Lexi looked at me sideways.

"What?" My stare matched hers.

"Bitch, you ordered water. What happened to the alcohol? You always order a drink when we come here," she stated curiously.

"And what's wrong with that?" I asked avoiding direct eye contact.

"I'm your best friend, so that means I'm not stupid." Lexi rested her elbow on the table. "You pregnant again?"

Quick on my feet, I replied, "No. I just don't feel like drinking right now. I've got some errands to run when I leave here, and I need to be sober."

Lexi leaned back in her chair. "Yeah, okay."

"I'm serious."

"I believe you. So, what's going on?"

She didn't sound too convincing but that was cool. She had no proof and I wasn't ready to reveal the news just yet. Not with everything that had been going on. To keep me from being in the hot seat, I changed the subject.

"I've been thinking about what you said yesterday, and I just want to put some things in perspective. Everything you said was right."

"Say what," she interrupted with laughter.

"I'm serious, Lexi."

"Hell, me too."

"My moves have been reckless lately, but for good reason. I've decided that I want a divorce. The only problem is Aaron since he doesn't want to give it to me. We've been having this same argument for weeks now. Every time I bring it up, he gets upset and says he's not giving it to me."

"Damn," Lexi sighed. "I knew it was coming."

"Lexi, out of all people, you know I love your brother. I'm just tired." My eyes became watery, but I wiped them away before the tears had a chance to fall. "Aaron has done nothing but humiliate me publicly. It's been painful. I've had two miscarriages back to back and it's like he doesn't even care. You can't possibly know how that feels."

Lexi sat in place with a frown on her face. "I know and I'm sorry, sis. I really am. I just really wish y'all could've gotten past this phase, considering he's been seeking help."

"I get that, but it's too late. I'm sick of giving him chances. Like, how far does it have to go before enough is enough? Do I need to catch an STD first? Aids? I've been faithful to him all these years. He doesn't appreciate me. Therefore, he has to live without me now. That's the reason I don't go home. I figure if I continue being disrespectful, he'll grant me my wish."

"So, why don't you file to help speed up the process? Let him know you're serious."

"You know as well as I do. Aaron is not going to sign those papers. It would be a waste of time and money. I want him to do it. That way I know he's letting go for good."

"That's true but I don't want to get in the middle of the divorce. But I'll see where his mind is at." Lexi reached across the table and grabbed my hand. "You're still my sister no matter what happens. I've dried your tears for so long, so I get it. I just hate that he's so fuckin' stupid. He'll appreciate you when he ends up with a trifling ass, gold digging bitch."

"Right."

"I love you, sis."

"I love you too."

The waiter returned with our food after our heart to heart was over. As we chowed down on our food, we made small talk. My mind was on Domestic and the baby the entire time. All I wanted was to start a new life with the man I'd fallen for. I knew I could trust Domestic. He made me feel beautiful and wanted, something Aaron hadn't done since the beginning. The constant cheating made me feel like I was unworthy of being loved and treated like the queen I truly was.

About an hour and a half later, I was done eating and Lexi was finally finished drinking. I knew she was a little tipsy by the way she kept giggling.

"You good, girl?"

"Girl, those kiddie drinks? Hell yeah. I need a tune-up really bad. I'm talking about some ass-smacking and hair pulling. I need my shit split, split."

That made me giggle. Our bodies needed the same thing. A slight tingle crept through my vagina, as I thought about my man putting the smack down on my ass. "I guess that means you're going to see Antwan when you leave here?"

Lexi's smile instantly turned sour. "Hell no. Fuck that bitch-ass nigga. I'ma fuck Calvin."

"Well damn! What he did to you?" Her reaction caught me off guard.

"While you've been MIA, a lot of shit has been going down. So, apparently Antwan has a beef with Aaron that no one knew about. Tell me why this stupid muthafucka set my brother up. The chicks who recorded him had been promised fifty grand by Antwan if they could fuck Aaron and get it on tape. When Aaron refused to pay, they leaked the tape."

"That's fucked up on Antwan's behalf. But if Aaron would've kept his dick in his pants he wouldn't be in this predicament. Everything he's going through is his own fault."

"Damn, bitch, don't be so cruel. I love my brother."

"Well, bitch, that makes two of us. I'm just over being married to him. Maybe one day we can be friends after the dust settles."

"Yeah, I guess."

Picking up the billfold, I placed the money inside to cover our bill. "I'm going to the restroom. I'll be right back."

"Okay."

My bladder felt like it was about to burst as I hauled ass to the ladies room. All that water was running straight through my ass. Pushing through the stall, I pulled my jeans down and squatted over the toilet. The relief I felt was unexplainable. Wiping myself, I pulled my jeans up and washed my hands. On my way out through the door, my cellphone vibrated. Stopping in place, I removed it from my purse and checked the screen. It was *Scam Likely*, so I threw the phone back inside. Not paying attention, I bumped into a whole human.

"I'm sorry." When I looked up, I was up close and personal with a familiar face.

"Ms. Foreign. Long time no hear from." That smile was bright as the morning sun.

"Hi." I smiled.

"You don't remember me, do you?"

"Yes, I do."

"What's my name?" he questioned.

"Maurice. I met you at the Karaoke bar."

"You never used my number, I see."

"Yeah, I know. I got a new phone." The lie rolled off my tongue smoothly and without hesitation.

"Oh, well let me give you my number again. I would love to take you out for breakfast, lunch, dinner or coffee. Hell, anything for that matter." Maurice chuckled, while licking his lips seductively.

He was really sweet, and I appreciated the laughter, but I had a new boo and going out with him wasn't happening. However, I couldn't brush him off like that, so I took his number again.

"What is it?" My phone was now back in my hand.

Maurice recited his number and I locked him in. "Make sure you use it this time. I promise I'll be the perfect gentleman. I know you're married, so a friendship is cool with me."

"Will do. My sister is waiting on me. Have a good day."

"You as well."

Scurrying away, I ran into Lexi. She was standing at the end of the hall with her hand on her hips. "Um, who was that man? That's who you're cheating with?"

"No, girl. His name is Maurice. I met him that night I went to the karaoke bar alone . . . after I received the video of your brother fuckin' those hoes, remember?" Lexi had a disapproving stare, so I made sure I put emphasis on her dog ass brother.

"Yeah, I remember. Let's go 'cause I'm horny as fuck."

"Nasty ass."

"You a fine one to talk, heffa. I'm not going to harass you about the man you creeping with but I better get all the details sooner than later."

Although Lexi was laughing, she was dead ass serious. Now wasn't the time to go into great detail about my personal affairs. That conversation would have to take place another day. We left the restaurant and went our separate ways.

***

Now that my lunch date was over, I really didn't have anything on my agenda. Going home was out of the question. The last person I wanted to see was Aaron, so I decided I would drop by the shop to see if Domestic needed help with anything.

Silently, I drove on the highway and reflected back on my current situation with the men in my life. My pregnancy certainly wasn't planned and it had happened by default. One thing I knew for certain was that an abortion was out of the question. A baby was something I craved and being a mother was all I ever wanted.

Destiny Skai

Whenever, I decided to tell Aaron, I knew he would be crushed. Our families would be devastated. My parents were big on marriage and forgiveness. They had been married well- over thirty years and it wasn't always peaches and cream. There were certainly bad times, but they overcame every curve ball life threw at them.

Then my mind shifted to Domestic. The out-of-the-blue nightmare that he refused to speak on was still playing out in my mind. Out of all the times I'd stayed overnight with him I had never witnessed it. It could've been the Casey situation because he'd been down ever since.

Although he pretended to be okay, I knew that wasn't true at all. Earlier, I overheard him cursing loudly on the phone. I figured that was who he was talking to. Domestic had a good relationship with Demerius, so my heart went out to my baby. To keep Domestic calm I didn't question the situation.

The carwash appeared to be business as usual when I walked inside. However, that could've been a façade of what was truly happening behind the walls.

"Hey, Tracy."

"Hey, boss lady. Why you so late? You know I was waiting on my coffee and donut this morning." She smirked.

"I bet you were." I giggled, while leaning against the counter. "I went to brunch with my sister earlier. I'm not supposed to be here, but I decided to come anyway. Where's Domestic?" His car wasn't outside when I pulled up.

"At the bikini wash, but he should be back any minute now. He left a while ago. Apparently, something's going on over there."

"Like what?"

"I don't know. You have to ask him about it."

"Okay." Pivoting on my heels, I headed towards the office.

"Oh, Foreign," Tracy called out.

Stopping in my tracks, I turned back to face her. "Yeah."

"Boss man said he wrote down some things for you to do just in case you showed up. It's on the desk."

"Thanks. Tracy, where is your protégé'?"

220

Tracy rolled her eyes and sucked her teeth. "That ain't my protégé. I don't even like his ass."

That told me right then and there she was concerned about her position. Especially since Domestic had started him at the damn register first quarter, instead of outside as a wash boy. "I feel you on that."

"He didn't call in or nothing. I hope his ass get fired first quarter."

"Damn, already," I shrugged my shoulders, "I'm sure Domestic will handle it."

"I know that's right. I don't need no help manning my damn station. Boss man was crazy for hiring him in the first place. He should've put his ass outside."

"Well, now you don't have to share your workspace."

When I walked inside the office, there was a bouquet of roses sitting on the desk. A wide girly grin spread wide across my lips. Rushing over, I leaned down and sniffed them. There was a pink post-it note on the computer screen that caught my attention. There were several things he needed done and balancing the books was definitely one of them. For the next hour, I busied myself with the duties he'd lain out for me.

From my phone, the sweet melody of *Perfect Combination*, by Stacey Lattisaw and Johnny Gill, melted my heart. That was truly one of my favorite songs. It spoke on love and being committed to your spouse. I was a hopeless romantic, so I believed in love and everything it stood for. Too bad I couldn't get that in return.

"Hey, beautiful. I see you found your way to me after all." The sound of Domestic's strong voice instantly soaked my panties.

He had me smiling from ear to ear. "You know I can't stay away from you for too long."

"I know that's right." Domestic stepped in front of me and pecked me on the lips. "I hope you like the flowers."

"I most certainly do."

"Good." He sat halfway on the edge of his desk. "Did Tracy tell you what I said? I kind of figured you'd show up anyway."

"You know I'm bored out my mind at home. So, I have to keep myself busy while you're busy." My hand was now on his thigh. "I mean, until you're able to give me the attention I need."

"We have all night for that." He grinned. "Did you place the order for the supplies for me?"

"I can't. I need a card and there wasn't one in the cash box."

"Ugh! Right." Domestic stood up and reached inside his back pocket. "Use the American Express business card that's in there." He handed me his wallet. "I'll be right back."

"Okay."

Logging into the wholesale company site, I placed the items requested inside of the shopping cart. Once I was at the checkout section, I removed the credit card and completed the order. Shoving it back inside, my curiosity got the best of me. There were multiple credit cards, as well as debit cards.

"Ohhh, he got credit and more credit," I mumbled softly and smirked.

A few of his bills were lifted, so I shoved them down further into his wallet. For some strange reason, something was keeping me from straightening it out. Pulling the bills out, a small folded photo dropped on the desk. Picking it up, I unfolded it. The sound of my heart beating out loud made my chest rumble. It was a photo of me. My discovery was downright disturbing.

"How did he get this picture?" I mumbled a second time.

From the window I could see Domestic walking back towards the entrance. Quickly, I shoved it back inside and placed his bills neatly in the leather wallet. My nerves were shot. None of it made sense to me. This man was carrying a picture of me, and it was one I hadn't provided.

My cellphone startled me. Taking a deep breath, I snatched it up from the desk and swiped the green icon. "Hello, Father."

"How is my baby girl doing?"

"I'm good. How are you?"

"Not too good."

Panic dismissed the confusion I felt seconds ago. "Is everything okay? Is mom okay?"

"Mom is fine. I'm fine. But I need you to come over here right away."

"You're making me nervous. Just tell me."

"This is something we need to discuss in person."

"Okay, I'll be right over."

"See you then."

Just as I hung up the phone Domestic was walking back inside. Standing up, I grabbed my purse and car keys. "Where are you going?" he asked.

"My father just called. He needs me to come over right away. I'm not sure what it is, but it sounds pretty urgent."

"Will you be over tonight?"

"Yes, I'll call you as soon as I leave there." On my tippy toes, I placed a kiss on his lips. "See you, baby."

"Did you place the order?"

"Yes, the invoice is in your email."

"Okay, see you soon." Rushing out the door, I headed for my car. I didn't know what I was walking into but I hoped and prayed it wasn't too bad.

CHAPTER 23
FOREIGN

After getting the call from my daddy, I wasted no time heading over to my parent's house. I rarely got a chance to sit and spend time with him because of his overbearing business. I knew he loved being independent, so it was hard for me to blame him.

Driving through the late night breeze, I rolled up my windows and turned up the volume to my Keyshia Cole CD. Her song *Love* blasted through the speakers. Her words warmed my heart with every line she poured out on the track. It's the exact way I felt about Domestic. His hard loving and sweet tender ways were the way to my emotions.

After having the conversation with Lexi, I truly understood why she was feeling the way she was. Indeed, Aaron was my husband and I still loved him. Our relationship began to crumble when his feelings for me disappeared with the wind. I deserved to be treated like a queen, not the bottom hoe of a pimp stable. My emotions got in the mix when I met Domestic, and I began to spiral out of control a bit. His dick fucked my soul up. From the muscles to his handsome facial structure, he was a bitch's wet dream. For some reason, people didn't want to see my dream flourish with him.

Turning down my father's street, I pulled into his driveway. I stepped out of the car and observed Aaron's car, and instantly became aggravated. First, I wanted to know why he was at my dad's house without me. Second, I knew if he called me over here, Aaron must have come and ran his damn mouth.

Walking inside, both of their eyes landed directly on me.

"Foreign?" Aaron stood up with that weak-ass puppy dog face.

All I could do was stare him down with a look of death. I was still hurt from him mistreating me and it wasn't something that would just change overnight.

"Aaron, why are you here?"

My dad raised from his chair and walked over to me. After embracing me in a tight hug, he planted a kiss on my cheek. "First of all, it's great to see you, princess. I know you've been away for a while and Aaron came to speak with me about you guys' problems."

"There's no problem, Daddy. He's a cheater and a dirty ass dog. It's very easy to understand."

Before Aaron could speak my dad waved his hand for him to be silent. "Foreign, this is your father speaking from my own mouth, *not* your husband. I need you to have a little respect for him because regardless of what mistakes he's made, he is still the one you're bonded with for life. The first day you expressed your love for him to me, you were in high school. I stood behind you one hundred percent. I listened. All I'm asking you to do is give me the same chance. Hear me out, baby girl."

My dad was looking at me all sad and shit. It hurt my stomach to hear him sound the way he did. I valued his opinion more than anyone who walked on our corrupted-ass planet. He was my savior when I was a child, and he still was at the age of twenty-four.

Taking a seat on the opposite couch of Aaron, I purposely turned my back to him and faced my daddy.

"Now, I know you kids have enough on your plate but beating down each other's character will only make things worse. What's your side of this story, Aaron?" He turned to him like he was just a hurt victim of a rape case.

"Right now, I'm just trying to make amends with your daughter. She's my wife and nothing in this world means more than that. I've hurt her by sleeping with other women and there is no excuse for my actions. I'm becoming a better person, Mr. Hamilton. Baby, you have to believe me." He was bending down in front of me like I was about to fall for the begging and finessing.

Rolling my eyes, I pushed him away. "Aaron, get off me. You ain't sorry because you do the same thing over and over. You're only doing this because you feel like you're really losing me. Everybody wants to straighten up when they find out the tea ain't sweet enough for them. You're a compulsive liar and it's going to be hard just to forget about that."

"Foreign, you have to observe things from his point of view, princess. It's not only about your emotions, sweetie."

"Daddy! Don't defend him. He's trying to convince you that he's so sorry. Aaron has cheated with numerous women and showed me plenty of times that I'm not wanted. How hard is that to understand?"

"No one can convince me of anything. Not even you. My only solution to this is helping you both come to an agreement. This isn't a game. It's you guys' life. You have to make your decision right now. He's sitting right here, confessing his mistakes to you, and it takes a real man to do that. From my understanding, you've found a different friend also. Foreign, two wrongs do not make a right. Instead of committing the same act, you should've pulled yourself away and got yourself together. It shows me that you still love him. If your things are still in that home, you are still a part of his life."

"But—"

"No but's. We have to stop making excuses and realize no one is perfect except the good Lord. We can only push off each other's motivation and love. I can't see you two ending your marriage this way when y'all have come so far. Forget what the outside feels. It's all about what you two want."

I couldn't help but feel my daddy on his opinion. I hated the fact that Aaron and I were on a different page, unlike we'd been when we first met. There was a point and time when we were inseparable— best friends to be exact. Now, we bumped heads more than anything.

Aaron still pouted like he was ready to commit suicide and I couldn't think while staring in his face. Exhaling, I caught my daddy observing my anger rising and decided to calm down.

"To be honest, I still love you, Aaron, but I refuse to be treated like a freak from the streets. We're married, so act like you've got a wife and not a friend."

"Baby," he said, sliding in between my legs like a begging child. My father nodded his head as if he were coaching me to accept his apology right then and there. "You mean everything to me. You're my life. My world. I know I've made some bad decisions, but I don't want those decisions to drive you away from me. It's still me, baby. It's Aaron. I'm begging you for another chance to prove I deserve you. Please. Just one more chance, Foreign."

His teary eyes reflected the sincerity of his plea, but it was so hard for me to forgive him. I was always taught that once a person crossed you, you never give them the chance to do it a second time. It was my motto. Aaron had been my king when we were younger. He treated me like I was the last woman on earth, and nothing and no one could pull him away from me.

Tons of our happy times danced through my mind as I watched him cry. His performance in front of my dad was beyond overrated, but I could see he was genuinely hurting from our current beef.

"Why do you deserve another chance with me? Daddy, why did you call me over here if this was going to be the conversation? I came to spend time with you, and talk," I stated before standing up to leave.

"Foreign! Do not walk out of that door. I'm your father and this is still your husband, sweetheart. We called you over here to pull this family back together. You don't have to agree just yet but give him a chance to explain himself. I'll let you two step outside to have a little more privacy. Have patience for me, please."

My daddy always knew how to make me all mushy. True, I felt like he was going to help Aaron because the Buccaneers were, and had always been, his favorite football team. He always received free souvenirs and free tickets to whatever state Aaron was playing in. The whole nine. They were really close, and I could tell he didn't like the idea of me being with another man.

"You have ten minutes to say whatever you need to before I peel." I got up and headed out to the back patio.

Trailing behind me, Aaron stepped outside and lightly closed the glass door. I folded my arms and stared into space like I had better places to be.

"Baby, today I sat at home and realized my behavior towards you was unacceptable. My actions of cheating have drawn a wedge between us, and I don't like it. I know about the big buff dude you've been with."

My heart dropped hearing him describe Domestic. I was sure to keep my business with him discreet. Especially, when I was out in public. I wasn't quite sure where he was getting his information, but I knew he wasn't going to trick me into telling him anything.

"Aaron," I huffed, "you don't know what you're talking about."

"It's okay, because I'm not trying to go back and forth about who did what. I know the dude Dominic, Domestic, whatever the hell his name is, doesn't love you the way I do. He's looking at you for your beauty and trying to take advantage. You're in pain from my deceit and you have the right to be. I just ask one thing of you: allow me to have my life again. Without you, I'm only a football player with problems. Together, I'm Aaron Young. The husband of Foreign Young. You give me hope, baby. All I want for you to do is come home. I'm all alone," he mouthed, while twiddling his fingers.

Aaron's emotions were on the floor and the lack of my love was pushing him to the edge. I didn't mean to make him so depressed, but he was the reason for my actions with Domestic. Nothing was more powerful than the oath of marriage and once a person broke that covenant, the curse of disaster was bound to take over.

When he began to drop tears again, I prepared to put my pride to the side. "Aaron, stop."

Of course, he continued and pleaded with me about changing. Looking at his messy hair and unshaven beard, I knew he was ready to give up on life. Aaron was never the type to go around dirty without cleaning himself up. He was having a nervous breakdown. A part of me wanted to let him suffer, but my sweet side continued to tell me, he way my baby. He held onto my shirt allowing his head to rest against my breast.

"I can't lose you, bae. I'm lost without you."

"Aaron, you need to tighten up and listen to me. Get up."

Standing up straight, he wiped the snot from his nose. "Yes, baby?"

I wanted to laugh at his goofy ass. He'd done all that cheating and now he was out here crying like a kid who'd gotten his ice cream slapped out of his hand. Knowing this moment was serious,

I wanted to see what his reply to my question would be. If he didn't have the right one, I was bound to head back out to Domestic and get my tummy rearranged for the rest of the night.

"Why should I forgive you?"

"Foreign, I—"

"Answer the question, Aaron."

Lowering his gaze, he stared at the floorboard. "Because you still have a lot of things to accomplish as a married woman, and I'm willing to do whatever necessary to make sure you meet those goals. You're the only one who has ever said you loved me, Foreign. There still has to be some level of that love, level of that love, left in there for me."

Aaron's words almost crushed my heart. I hated when I was weak for his punk ass. It became a trait that was hard to break, and no matter how I felt at the time, he was right. My marriage wasn't a mistake. But it would only make it if I allowed it to. Thinking about his mother and father, I wondered how they would feel, even Lexi. The decision would hurt them being that I'd been accepted into his family since day one.

"I'm going to give you another chance, Aaron. One more," I stated with a finger in the air in case he didn't comprehend.

Wrapping me in a giant hug, he kissed my lips with excitement. "Baby, I promise, you won't have a problem out of me. I won't let you down."

"You better be sure, Aaron. I don't have time for a split decision when we can just go our separate ways right now."

"No, baby. I'm sure. I'm sure," he assured me, with a hand on my cheek.

Taking a deep breath, my mind flashed to Domestic. He was a great person, but my dad's opinion meant the world to me. All I could think about was the seed growing in my stomach and wonder how I would tell him. It wouldn't be easy, but the joy family wasn't either. I needed to do something in order to see if my life was worth leaving. My body told me that Domestic was my everything. However, the feeling without Aaron forever just didn't seem real. It would never be able to end that way. He was all I knew.

230

CHAPTER 24
FOREIGN

On our way from my parent's house, Aaron trailed me closely. There was no way I could be with Domestic tonight. In my heart, I dreaded making the call. There were no other options, so I put on my big girl panties and dialed his number.

"Hello."

"Hey, baby. Where are you?"

"About to leave the car wash and head home. How did it go with your parents?"

God, why was that his first question? Shaking my head, I kept my eyes on the road. Every so often I would check my rearview to see if Aaron was still behind me. He was. "Well," I exhaled heavily. "I was blitz attacked by my dad."

"How so?"

"Aaron was there. Apparently, he went over to report my current behavior to my parents. Of course, my dad gave me the third degree about not giving up on my marriage and sticking it out. It's kind of crazy because I never told his parents about his cheating ass."

"That ain't crazy. That's a bitch move."

"Tell me about it. Now, I'm being forced to go home and finish the conversation."

"You're a grown ass woman. Nobody can force you to do shit you don't wanna do. Tell that nigga you want a divorce and be done with it. You belong to me now."

Domestic's voice was low, yet stern. The seriousness in it told me he wouldn't take the news of me reconciling with my husband well. Thankfully, he didn't know where we lived. There was no way he could find me if I disappeared. Then the thought of my picture in his wallet crossed my mind again. As quickly as I thought about bringing it up, I changed my mind even quicker.

"You don't understand the type of parents I have. This is a really complicated situation for me. I just need some time to think things through."

"Well, we can discuss everything when you get over here. I'll run you a hot bubble bath and give you a full body massage."

"As tempting as that sounds baby, I have to decline the invitation. There are some things I need to wrap up with Aaron first. I have to get past this step in order to move forward with my life."

"Yeah, whateva!"

"Domestic, don't do that. He's still my husband and he deserves closure. That's the least I can do considering the disrespectful way I've been moving lately."

"Fuck that nigga!" Domestic screamed in my ear like he was chastising his child. "You don't owe him shit."

All the yelling and cursing was very unnecessary and truthfully speaking, I wasn't in the mood. There were a million things on my plate and fussing with Domestic wasn't one of them.

"I get that you're aggravated, but so am I. Before this turns into a big argument, I'm going to hang up now. Goodnight, Domestic."

Not giving him a chance to respond, I ended the call and tossed the phone on the seat. He called back right away, but I allowed him to speak to the voicemail. Pulling up in the driveway of our home, I got out of the car and headed towards the door. Aaron ran ahead of me to open it before I stepped onto the porch.

"Are you hungry?" he asked.

"No, I'm okay. I'm about to take a shower."

"Can I join you?"

"I'd rather shower alone tonight." The disappointment on his face tugged at my heart. "You can give me a massage when I get out though."

Aaron's eyes lit up. "I can do that. I'll fix us a drink too."

"I'll take some wine." On WebMD, I read it was okay to have one glass of wine. Tonight I needed it more than ever.

"Got it. I'll be waiting on you."

Standing completely naked in the mirror, I reexamined my stomach. It poked out a little. Not too much to where it was noticeable. Quickly, I hopped into the shower and cleaned myself up. Once I was completely dry, I slipped on my satin nightgown and walked into the bedroom.

Aaron was sitting on the edge of the bed and my glass of red wine was on the nightstand. Walking over, I picked it up and took a sip. My cellphone started to ring from inside my purse. It was Domestic again. Sending the call to voicemail, I realized I had nine missed calls from him. That was certainly going to be a problem, so I powered it off for the night.

"You ready?" Aaron was anxious to put his hands on me. My body was tense, therefore I *was* ready.

Getting comfortable, I laid on my stomach and closed my eyes. Aaron's hands traced my back and slid down my thin straps. Firmly, he squeezed my shoulders and rotated his fingers. After staying in the same spot for a minute or so, he made his way down to my back.

Cold drops of oil hit my skin, my thighs to be exact. Working his magic, he caressed my flesh, then he moved to my calves, and then my feet. Making his way back up to my thighs, Aaron eased his hands on my ass, while applying more oil. I was in heaven. This was the type of treatment I could get used to again. His hands worked my cheeks hard, then I could feel him raise my gown. It was now resting just above my waist.

All of his movement stopped, but I didn't bother to open my eyes because I was damn near comatose. "Keep going," I whispered.

"I am, baby. Hold on."

Seconds later, Aaron straddled my legs and continued to massage my ass. Now back into it, my body went into autopilot. His strong hands were what I needed. A little time had passed, and I could feel Aaron's fingers slide down the crack of my ass. Then, I felt him graze my lips before inserting them into my pussy. Gently, he pushed them in and out causing me to twirl my hips a little.

All day I had been craving sex. Unfortunately, Domestic and I couldn't finish what we started. Now, I was about to finish with Aaron climbing inside of me. Both of his hands were planted firmly on my cheeks. A cool breeze hit me between my legs. His warm tongue followed. That was his specialty when he was in the wrong. I was game, so he had better eat it right.

Arching up, I raised my ass so he could gain full access to my clit. His tongue worked me overtime. My first orgasm was surfacing. Gripping the sheets, I moaned, "she's cummin'."

Aaron continued to work his tongue until my release spilled out. The sound of his slurps filled my ears. Movement followed, then I felt his rock hard dick slip into me with no hesitation. Slowly, he thrust in and out of my juicy box, squeezing my hips in the process.

"I missed you, baby. I love you so much."

Easing up, I positioned myself on my knees and threw my ass back on him. He grabbed my hair, pulling my head in his direction. Slipping his tongue inside my mouth, we kissed sloppily, while he stroked my middle.

"Ooh, baby. Give it to me."

Thoughts of Domestic flashed in my mind while Aaron worked hard at beating my back out. He had something to prove, so he made sure to satisfy me. My ass collided with his stomach with each thrust. Burying my head in the pillow, I took deep breaths. Sliding my hand underneath me, I allowed my fingers to caress my clit. Every time he pulled out and went back in, I felt his rod graze my fingers. *Damn, that shit felt good!* The bottom of my stomach was filled with pleasurable aches and my second orgasm came gushing out. Aaron pumped harder and fingered my ass until I was in submission. Minutes later, he was busting inside of me.

Lying down beside me, he pulled me close to him. "Thank you for giving me another chance. Tomorrow is the new beginning to our forever. From this day forward you will never have to worry about me looking in another bitch's direction. I'm going to be the faithful husband I'm supposed to be. I allowed the fortune and fame to strip me from my morals and almost lost you for good."

His eyes were watery as he spoke. Using my fingers, I wiped his tears away. "Just keep your word and we'll be okay."

"The first thing I want to do is go to Paris. Since the season is over, we can go there for about a month maybe. I mean, if you don't mind staying that long."

"That's fine with me."

"I just figured that would give us a chance to start over. Once my name has been cleared from this bullshit-ass investigation we can go."

"And when is that?"

"In a few days. The detective on the case is looking into some things that will clear my name."

"Okay, that's fine."

Aaron held me tight in his arms. It was like he didn't want to let go. My mind was jumbled, and I didn't know who to turn to. The more I thought about my dilemma, salt-water filled my eyes. I was in love with two men, but I could only be with one.

Domestic . . .

For the tenth time, I called Foreign's phone. The voicemail danced through my ears once again. The time was starting to get late and I was eventually going to close the shop down for the night. I knew she'd said something about an urgent call from her father, but I was hoping things weren't too bad. Seeing her hurt from the destroyed marriage was enough. My only mission was to fuck her pussy into submission and be the best lover possible. Thinking of her sweet kitty forced me to try her line one last time. Still with no results, I began to prepare for closing.

Tracy stood at the register counting the last of our profits for the day. Her eyes met mine when I approached the counter.

"What?" she mumbled to me.

Of course, I stood there with a blank expression until she looked in my eyes. It was the only way she understood me. Removing her gum, she placed both hands on her hips.

"Let me guess. This one of yo' stuck nights, huh?"

Instead of responding, I stepped behind the counter and took a seat in the rolling office chair. Her eyes scanned my posture to see if I was serious.

"Demerius, I hope you know this is coming out of your paycheck. I'm not gonna be the last resolution when you can't satisfy that thick ass craving for sex, nigga."

Ignoring her statement, I unbuckled my slacks and released my dick. Just as she got on her knees, a set of headlights pulled inside of the carwash driveway. It was just my luck if Foreign was arriving when I was in the middle of a session with Tracy.

"Hold off on that. We got company." I pushed her head away and fixed my clothes.

"See how good God is. You can take all that anger out on ya' girlfriend." Tracy grabbed her purse and quickly clocked out.

Making my way to the parking lot, I noticed the unmarked Grand Marquise sitting with the engine still purring. Emilia's hand came out of the window. I could see her fingers waving for me to come over. The shop was closed and the only time this bitch came around was for money and fake ass rumors.

Stepping off the curb, I made my way over to her vehicle. Sticking my head inside of the rolled down window, she wore a nonchalant expression.

"Emilia, it's going on 12:00. What are you doing here?"

"We need to talk."

"We don't need to talk about shit. The carwash is closed and I'm off duty. Try and catch me tomorrow."

Before I could walk away, she stepped out. "Demerius, if you don't get in this car, I'll have all these businesses of yours shut down by morning. This shouldn't take long."

Scratching my forehead in anger, I took a few steps back. "Let me tell you something, Emilia. Since you've come back around, I've done everything you've asked. What the fuck do you want from me? 'Cause if its sex than we can go ahead and hit the office."

"Sex is the last thing on my mind, Demerius. I've had a long day and you can make it a little easier on me if you just get inside the damn car." Her tone said she was serious.

Whatever it was had to be important because she wasn't letting up. I watched Tracy head out of the shop and walk to her car. She gave me a silent nod as if she knew what was going on. Turning around, I got in the car and slammed the door shut.

"You don't have to slam my shit. Show some respect."

"Emilia, what do you want?"

"I wanna know what you've been up to these past few days. I haven't been available and it's my current time to check in. Where's the kid?"

"Who?" I had to play stupid. I wasn't prepared for him to be the topic of our conversation.

"Keith. How has work been with him?"

"I haven't seen that dude since I hired him. I have three businesses to run and I'm not about to chase a nigga to do his job."

"That's weird because I personally dropped him off here the other day."

Shrugging my shoulders, I adjusted my body in the seat and stared out of the window. Emilia was still a cop so getting the third degree with all the questions made me slightly uncomfortable.

"Is there anything you need to tell me, Demerius? We're partners right?"

"If that's what you want to call it."

"Keith called me the day I dropped him off and said he did something. If I'm not mistaken, it was something that would cause him to lose his job with you."

"What reason would I have to fire him? If this is what you got me sitting in your car for, you wasted your time."

"So what reason would you have to slit his throat and place a bullet in his junkie girlfriend's head?" She typed on her phone as if she didn't just question me about a murder. I was sure the police were about to swerve up in the lot at any second. I still remained calm and was careful not to let her see me crack a sweat.

"I don't know what the fuck you're talking about. He wasn't dead the last time I checked."

"I never said he was dead, Demerius."

At that time I knew she was trying to pull a fast one. Entertaining the conversation was enough to place me around Keith.

Shit had been perfect since I walked out of those prison walls and I wasn't going back. It didn't matter who I had to take out with me.

Cutting my eyes at her, I cracked my knuckles. "What the fuck are you trying to say, Emilia? Please, don't test me right now."

I could see the fear in her eyes. Emilia knew what I was capable of and it wasn't a bright idea to make me feel like I was the one in trouble. Keith played his cards the way he chose and lost.

"I'm not playing with you, Demerius. I know he stole money from you. I know exactly what happened. Did you forget that? Now before you say anything, I've stood behind you through all the dirt and criminal activity. Shit that could've landed you in a cell for eternity, so don't come at me like I'm the enemy. Calm your nerves and relax."

"I'm calm. Just don't play mind games with me. I don't know who to trust when it comes down to me going back to prison. When I step back in, it'll be for a damn good reason."

"I can't help the motor mouths you have working around you, Demerius. My job is to make sure the people of this county is safe. He's dead and I have two bodies on my hand that I can't explain. Why couldn't you just call me? I could've gotten the money back for you."

"He played himself and you knew that," I yelled out of anger. Emilia jumped from the sound of my voice. My reaction displayed my guilt. Not to mention, I just indirectly told on myself.

Turning to face her, I decided it was now or never with all the ignorant shit she'd been pulling. Grabbing her by the throat forcefully, I stuck my hands under her skirt to feel for a wire. I did the same with her black button up. Her bulky breast hung freely when I ripped her buttons.

"Demerius, let me go!"

Grabbing her pistol from her hip, I tossed it in the backseat. It didn't take long before she tried to fight me back. Of course, my strength was beyond strong. She was no match and I eventually proved that, once I turned her body towards me and climbed on top. That pretty pink pussy poked through her purple lace panties and I was going be sure to make her understand who the fuck was in charge. We struggled in the police cruiser until I ripped her panties and shoved my dick inside of her guts.

"Uhhh! I can't breathe, Domestic. You're choking me."

My hard pound game started to subside, and I eased off her throat. Now I was long stroking her warm walls with my giant frame. Her pussy released a sticky and loud sound as I watched it glide back and forth. All she could do was hold my neck while I handled the business. After five minutes of slaying, I busted my seed inside of her stomach. Kissing her lips, I leaned up and sat back in my seat. Hitting the button on her A/C, I watched as she panted heavily.

"I should arrest you for that shit. It's called rape you fuckin' bastard." Her pussy was still pulsating when she rose up.

"I had to make sure you weren't wearing a wire."

Of course I was lying. Truth be told, my mind just lost it when I came in contact with pussy. Good pussy at that. It was my way of control and there was no woman I'd ever met who was able to resist me.

"Get the hell out of my car, Demerius. From now on, keep your hands to yourself and try not to kill the rest of your employees. I can't help you if you don't listen."

Brushing off the comment, I stepped out and watched her pull away. A smile stretched across my face. I knew she couldn't deny a real man. My only problem was the way she knew my business. It was scary to have a person who knew your secrets. Someone who could get rid of you in the blink of an eye. Only one question traveled through my mind in the mist of all this shit . . . *Who in the fuck was running their mouth?*

CHAPTER 25
EMILIA

The next day . . .

The sun had just began to lower below the horizon, as I drove through the evening traffic. After discussing a few things with Demerius earlier, I had a new mission at hand. Ever since I'd discovered Keith's body in his home, my supervisor had been on my ass demanding answers. It looked very awkward that I had guided him upon his release from jail and not even a month later he'd ended up dead.

I had enough on my plate with Antwan, I needed my payday. A hundred grand didn't come easily. Neither did a conviction. All I had to do was keep the cards falling correctly and I would receive my end of the deal on both parts. Money and celebrity dick. It was all a plus.

A creepy feeling surfaced as I smiled turning down the next intersecting street. The luxurious homes were in need of a new face around the area, and I was about to be the first candidate. I had worked my ass off for the Tampa police department and still couldn't receive a promotion, a better pay grade. . . Nothing. After finding my flow in the streets of the dirty orange state, I started to apply my skills by pressing other people. If you didn't cut me in on the deal, you were going to get cut out. If you went behind me and continued to do the same thing, I would eliminate you from the streets until your death date.

Pulling inside the driveway, I holstered my weapon before killing the ignition. Stepping out, my heels clacked across the pavement with a sweet melody of happiness. This moment was surely one to remember. Ringing the doorbell of the elegant home, I waited patiently until she opened the door. When she looked into my face, her posture quickly changed.

Foreign . . .

Climbing out of my bed, I looked at the clock. It was nearly eight o'clock at night. The signs of the child was kicking hard. After my nasty session with Aaron last night, I passed out and didn't wake until this morning. I still didn't understand why I couldn't keep my eyes open, but sleeping my days away was not about to be my new objective.

Heading downstairs, I buttoned up my robe. I was craving for a fresh bowl of fruit and my stomach was turning circles just as I began to move. If Aaron kept the sex game straight like last night, he wouldn't have to worry about anything with the divorce. All in all, I still had time to straighten things out with Domestic.

The sound of my doorbell ringing grabbed my attention. Swiftly heading through the living room, I opened the door and paused when I saw the sheisty-ass cop chick.

"Can I help you?" I asked with sarcasm dripping from my tone. I wanted to know how the fuck the bitch got my address.

"Hey. Foreign, right?"

"Yeah. That's me. What do you need?"

"Well actually, I'm here to talk to you about your husband, Aaron. If it's not too much to ask, could I come in and have a second with you?" Her expression seemed like it could've been urgent.

Stepping to the side, I allowed her to enter. Leading her to the couch, I took a seat in the leather chair across from her. "Would you like anything to drink?"

"No, thank you. I didn't mean to just barge in, but I didn't know if you were alone or with him at the moment."

"What does it matter if I was? Is something wrong?" This bitch's vibe was definitely off key. She seemed a little too edgy.

"True indeed, it wouldn't have mattered whether he was here or not because I came to speak with you. Not him."

"What about? If this is about the football scandal with the little teen, I don't know anything. I'm only his wife."

"This isn't about the scandal. I've already gathered my evidence on that, and the truth will be revealed sooner or later. The trial date should be set. The reason I'm here tonight is more personal."

I had to look her up and down when she uttered *personal* from between her lips. I damn sure didn't have any smoke with her. Neither should Aaron. Regardless of the case approaching, the authorities had no reason to be snooping around our home.

"What is this about? I'm honestly not into the whole guessing game."

Emilia gave me a slight nod like she was about to expose my entire kindergarten history report. "Aaron has been cheating on you of course, and his affairs are starting to cause confusion in more than one home."

"Excuse me! What are you talking about?" Confusion in what home because this is the only crib Aaron lays his damn head in.

Her legs crossed hearing my remark. "Do you honestly feel that way?"

"So what the fuck are you saying? My husband is cheating with you. That's what you mean?"

"Not just me, plenty of other women too. I'm just the one he's spilling his seeds in. I know you may feel a certain type of way about this, but I felt like you deserved to know."

The pain of her statement left me with a scar so deep on my heart. Aaron was hanging on by a thread and out of nowhere this woman was telling me that he was playing house at another bitch's crib. Not just one, but numerous?

Leaning up in my chair, I eyed her with a devilish smirk. "This has to be a joke, right?"

"I'm afraid not," she replied with a straight face.

I laughed before standing to my feet. "Miss. You don't even know me or my husband, for that fact. I saw you snooping around at Demerius' carwash a few times. You sure that's not what this is about because it surely seems like he's close to you also."

"No, sweetie," she paused, "you and Demerius are close. I'm only doing my job when it comes down to you ever seeing me at that wash. You've been sneaking around on Aaron and it's quite obvious that you're in love with another man. Not to get off the subject, but I thought it may have been the reason for your husband's behavior."

This lady was calling out shit that no one else could possibly know. Her recent pop-ups at Demerius' business were sounding more like a spying mission. At the time, I didn't even know if I could trust the words coming out of her mouth.

"I don't know what you're talking about. I'm not cheating on my husband. I have a job at the carwash. It's the only reason you've ever laid your eyes on me. You've never seen me touch him so please don't speak on things you have no knowledge of."

Snickering, Emilia pulled out her phone and recited Aaron's number. "Do you think I'd be wrong if I could tell you what color your bedspreads are?"

I knew her bluffs were beyond accurate. The steam blowing inside my head told me to get up and beat this bitch to death. "It seems funny that you think you know anything about my husband. What if I beat your ass and called it self-defense due to you raging in my home?"

"What if I throw your ass in jail faster than a prostitute out of Dade County? I still have on a badge, sweetheart. Remain calm."

She was sitting like the Queen of England in my home and from the looks of it, she was beyond comfortable. Rocking my foot harder than a motor engine, I eased my tension. I should've made her stay on the other side of the door where I had all control of the situation. But things were about to fly off the handle once Aaron crossed the threshold of our home.

"Listen, Foreign, I didn't come to make you seem like the bad person here. I'm only making you aware of what's going on. You're sleeping with your enemy, baby. He's the one who's telling me a different story when he's at my house. I'm sure if you call him, he wouldn't be able to deny these accusations. You don't even have to mention me being here," she stated with confidence.

Testing her arrogance, I got up and grabbed my phone from the kitchen counter. Dialing Aaron's number, he answered after the fourth ring.

"Hey, baby?"

"Don't *hey baby* me, Aaron. Is there anything you need to tell me?"

"Foreign, I can't hear you. What did you say?"

"Oh, you heard me. I said is there anything you got to tell me?"

Hearing the phone beep, the call ended leaving me on the line alone.

"Maybe I should try back at another time," Emilia said before rising out of her seat. She headed for the door and left before I launched my phone into the wall. The tears that stained my eyes were for the last time. My mind was officially made up, I was leaving Aaron Young for good.

Aaron
Twenty minutes earlier . . .

Today was going to make the twelfth session in my sex class and I felt excellent. I could honestly say it felt great to open my eyes and realize that my girl could've left but stayed. She was ready to abandon the vows we'd made because of my horrible deception. The more time I sat in this class it began to come clearer. Foreign was hurt and the only way she could heal herself was to step away from me. Learning that love wasn't easy was the hard part for me. Through it all I was able to smile because I still had the love of my life by my side.

After Ms. Anderson cleared the class to leave. I approached her desk. "Hey, Aaron. Did you gain anything from the class tonight?" she asked, giving me her undivided attention.

I flashed her a positive grin before nodding. "I enjoyed it. The classes have been going great and I want to thank you personally for all the help."

"No problem. It's what I do. To be honest, I feel that you had it under control the entire time. Your heart shows that you want to change. When you've accepted change, you gain more because of your acceptance to something different. If it pushes you forward, go for it."

"True. I just wanted you to know that me and my wife are doing great again. We mended our differences. I can't say we've fully rekindled from my painful mistakes but were rebuilding."

"That's great, Aaron. Remember, time heals everything. The scar may still be visible, but the pain will eventually subside, if you change."

Grabbing a piece of paper, she scribbled something down on it before passing it over to me. Taking it, I viewed the address to her main office in Miami. We're having a main event for the center next month. It would be delightful if you and the wife could come and show support."

Agreeing to her wishes, I placed the info into my pocket and shook her hand. Walking out of the treatment class, I held my head high as the rain poured down heavily over the building. It took a strong person to admit things that could possibly destroy their character, fame, or relationship. It's what separated the pure from the cold hearted. If you're willing to risk everything you have for the one person you love, make sure they're willing to do the same for you. Foreign was my heart and nothing compared to her worth in my eyes.

Getting outside, I jumped in my car and sped off quickly. My mind, body and soul were ready to get back to her. Last night was magical. It had been a while since we bonded that hard and she definitely had me feigning.

Dialing Lexi's number on the phone, I stopped at the red traffic light. The sound of a Mustang engine pulled up directly beside me. Cutting my eyes at the car, I admired the dark black paint and midnight tinted windows.

"Hello?" Lexi yelled through the phone.

"What are you doing, sis?"

"Trying to find out who I'm screwing tonight. What do you want, Aaron? If you lost Foreign again, I'm not helping," she laughed into the receiver.

"Shut up. I just called to let you know I finished my class. Thank you for helping me, for real. I love you."

The light turned green and I continued across the intersection. I could see the bad ass Mustang that mashed the gas smoothly behind me.

"You're my twin, Aaron. That's my duty. I love you too."

246

Hearing my phone beep, Foreign's name flashed across my screen. "Lexi, she's on the other line now. I'm gonna call you back, okay?"

"Yeah, yeah. Make it tomorrow. Bye, boy."

Clicking over, I noticed the Mustang's speed had slightly increased. "Hey, baby."

"Don't hey me." The rest of her words began to slightly break up.

"Foreign? I can't hear you. What did you say?" I asked talking louder into the receiver.

The sound of the Mustang engine was now accelerating heavily. I glanced to my side and watched the car pull directly next to me like it wasn't a one way street. I jerked my car over slightly just to be cautious. Foreign's voice was still cracking in the phone and she didn't sound happy. Before I could reply, the car rammed into me and I couldn't grip the steering wheel fast enough.

My car flipped recklessly over the curb and the slow spin caused my life to flash before my eyes. All I could feel was the hard catastrophe of my car flipping uncontrollably across the ground. My neck connected with the windshield knocking the feeling out of my body, before crashing into the tree in front of me.

The smoke from my vehicle began to thicken and the sound of the Mustang's motor decreased, while I silently begged for help. I could hear the thump of my heartbeat slowing down through my ears before I blacked out.

To Be Continued...
The Price You Pay for Love 2
Coming Soon

Submission Guideline

Submit the first three chapters of your completed manuscript to ldpsubmissions@gmail.com, subject line: Your book's title. The manuscript must be in a .doc file and sent as an attachment. Document should be in Times New Roman, double spaced and in size 12 font. Also, provide your synopsis and full contact information. If sending multiple submissions, they must each be in a separate email.

Have a story but no way to send it electronically? You can still submit to LDP/Ca$h Presents. Send in the first three chapters, written or typed, of your completed manuscript to:

LDP: Submissions Dept
Po Box 870494
Mesquite, Tx 75187

DO NOT send original manuscript. Must be a duplicate.

Provide your synopsis and a cover letter containing your full contact information.

Thanks for considering LDP and Ca$h Presents.

The Price You Pay for Love

Coming Soon from Lock Down Publications/Ca$h Presents

BOW DOWN TO MY GANGSTA

By **Ca$h**

TORN BETWEEN TWO

By **Coffee**

BLOOD STAINS OF A SHOTTA **III**

By **Jamaica**

STEADY MOBBIN **III**

By **Marcellus Allen**

BLOOD OF A BOSS **VI**

SHADOWS OF THE GAME II

By **Askari**

LOYAL TO THE GAME **IV**

By **T.J. & Jelissa**

A DOPEBOY'S PRAYER **II**

By **Eddie "Wolf" Lee**

IF LOVING YOU IS WRONG... **III**

By **Jelissa**

TRUE SAVAGE **VII**

MIDNIGHT CARTEL

DOPE BOY MAGIC II

By **Chris Green**

BLAST FOR ME **III**

DUFFLE BAG CARTEL **IV**

HEARTLESS GOON **IV**

A SAVAGE DOPEBOY II

Destiny Skai

DRUG LORDS II

By **Ghost**

A HUSTLER'S DECEIT III

KILL ZONE **II**

BAE BELONGS TO ME III

SOUL OF A MONSTER III

By **Aryanna**

THE COST OF LOYALTY **III**

By **Kweli**

THE SAVAGE LIFE III

By **J-Blunt**

KING OF NEW YORK V

COKE KINGS IV

BORN HEARTLESS III

By **T.J. Edwards**

GORILLAZ IN THE BAY V

De'Kari

THE STREETS ARE CALLING II

Duquie Wilson

KINGPIN KILLAZ IV

STREET KINGS III

PAID IN BLOOD III

CARTEL KILLAZ IV

Hood Rich

SINS OF A HUSTLA II

ASAD

TRIGGADALE III

The Price You Pay for Love

Elijah R. Freeman

KINGZ OF THE GAME V

Playa Ray

SLAUGHTER GANG IV

RUTHLESS HEART II

By Willie Slaughter

THE HEART OF A SAVAGE II

By Jibril Williams

FUK SHYT II

By Blakk Diamond

THE DOPEMAN'S BODYGAURD II

By Tranay Adams

TRAP GOD II

By Troublesome

YAYO II

A SHOOTER'S AMBITION II

By S. Allen

GHOST MOB

Stilloan Robinson

KINGPIN DREAMS

By Paper Boi Rari

CREAM

By Yolanda Moore

SON OF A DOPE FIEND II

By Renta

FOREVER GANGSTA II

By Adrian Dulan

LOYALTY AIN'T PROMISED
By Keith Williams
THE PRICE YOU PAY FOR LOVE II
By Destiny Skai
THE LIFE OF A HOOD STAR
By Rashia Wilson
TOE TAGZ II
By Ah'Million

Available Now

RESTRAINING ORDER **I & II**
By **CA$H & Coffee**
LOVE KNOWS NO BOUNDARIES **I II & III**
By **Coffee**
RAISED AS A GOON I, II, III & IV
BRED BY THE SLUMS I, II, III
BLAST FOR ME I & II
ROTTEN TO THE CORE I II III
A BRONX TALE I, II, III
DUFFEL BAG CARTEL I II III
HEARTLESS GOON
A SAVAGE DOPEBOY
HEARTLESS GOON I II III
DRUG LORDS
By **Ghost**
LAY IT DOWN **I & II**

The Price You Pay for Love

LAST OF A DYING BREED

BLOOD STAINS OF A SHOTTA I & II

By **Jamaica**

LOYAL TO THE GAME

LOYAL TO THE GAME II

LOYAL TO THE GAME III

LIFE OF SIN I, II III

By **TJ & Jelissa**

BLOODY COMMAS I & II

SKI MASK CARTEL I II & III

KING OF NEW YORK I II,III IV

RISE TO POWER I II III

COKE KINGS I II III

BORN HEARTLESS I II

By **T.J. Edwards**

IF LOVING HIM IS WRONG...I & II

LOVE ME EVEN WHEN IT HURTS I II III

By **Jelissa**

WHEN THE STREETS CLAP BACK I & II III

By **Jibril Williams**

A DISTINGUISHED THUG STOLE MY HEART I II & III

LOVE SHOULDN'T HURT I II III IV

RENEGADE BOYS I II III IV

By **Meesha**

A GANGSTER'S CODE I &, II III

A GANGSTER'S SYN I II III

THE SAVAGE LIFE I II

Destiny Skai

The Price You Pay for Love

THE BOSS MAN'S DAUGHTERS II
THE BOSSMAN'S DAUGHTERS III
THE BOSSMAN'S DAUGHTERS IV
THE BOSS MAN'S DAUGHTERS **V**
A SAVAGE LOVE **I & II**
BAE BELONGS TO ME I II
A HUSTLER'S DECEIT I, II, III
WHAT BAD BITCHES DO I, II, III
SOUL OF A MONSTER I II
KILL ZONE
By **Aryanna**
A KINGPIN'S AMBITON
A KINGPIN'S AMBITION **II**
I MURDER FOR THE DOUGH
By **Ambitious**
TRUE SAVAGE
TRUE SAVAGE II
TRUE SAVAGE **III**
TRUE SAVAGE **IV**
TRUE SAVAGE **V**
TRUE SAVAGE **VI**
DOPE BOY MAGIC
MIDNIGHT CARTEL
By **Chris Green**
A DOPEBOY'S PRAYER
By **Eddie "Wolf" Lee**
THE KING CARTEL **I, II & III**

Destiny Skai

By **Frank Gresham**
THESE NIGGAS AIN'T LOYAL **I, II & III**
By **Nikki Tee**
GANGSTA SHYT **I II &III**
By **CATO**
THE ULTIMATE BETRAYAL
By **Phoenix**
BOSS'N UP **I , II & III**
By **Royal Nicole**
I LOVE YOU TO DEATH
By Destiny J
I RIDE FOR MY HITTA
I STILL RIDE FOR MY HITTA
By **Misty Holt**
LOVE & CHASIN' PAPER
By **Qay Crockett**
TO DIE IN VAIN
SINS OF A HUSTLA
By **ASAD**
BROOKLYN HUSTLAZ
By **Boogsy Morina**
BROOKLYN ON LOCK I & II
By **Sonovia**
GANGSTA CITY
By **Teddy Duke**
A DRUG KING AND HIS DIAMOND I & II III
A DOPEMAN'S RICHES

The Price You Pay for Love

HER MAN, MINE'S TOO I, II

CASH MONEY HO'S

By Nicole Goosby

TRAPHOUSE KING **I II & III**

KINGPIN KILLAZ I II III

STREET KINGS I II

PAID IN BLOOD **I II**

CARTEL KILLAZ I II III

By **Hood Rich**

LIPSTICK KILLAH **I, II, III**

CRIME OF PASSION I II & III

By **Mimi**

STEADY MOBBN' **I, II, III**

By **Marcellus Allen**

WHO SHOT YA **I, II, III**

SON OF A DOPE FIEND

Renta

GORILLAZ IN THE BAY **I II III IV**

DE'KARI

TRIGGADALE I II

Elijah R. Freeman

GOD BLESS THE TRAPPERS I, II, III

THESE SCANDALOUS STREETS I, II, III

FEAR MY GANGSTA I, II, III

THESE STREETS DON'T LOVE NOBODY I, II

BURY ME A G I, II, III, IV, V

A GANGSTA'S EMPIRE I, II, III, IV

THE DOPEMAN'S BODYGAURD

Tranay Adams

THE STREETS ARE CALLING

Duquie Wilson

MARRIED TO A BOSS... I II III

By Destiny Skai & Chris Green

KINGZ OF THE GAME I II III IV

Playa Ray

SLAUGHTER GANG I II III

RUTHLESS HEART

By Willie Slaughter

THE HEART OF A SAVAGE

By Jibril Williams

FUK SHYT

By Blakk Diamond

DON'T F#CK WITH MY HEART I II

By Linnea

ADDICTED TO THE DRAMA I II III

By Jamila

YAYO

A SHOOTER'S AMBITION

By S. Allen

TRAP GOD

By Troublesome

FOREVER GANGSTA

By Adrian Dulan

TOE TAGZ

The Price You Pay for Love

By Ah'Million

Destiny Skai

BOOKS BY LDP'S CEO, CA$H

TRUST IN NO MAN

TRUST IN NO MAN 2

TRUST IN NO MAN 3

BONDED BY BLOOD

SHORTY GOT A THUG

THUGS CRY

THUGS CRY 2

THUGS CRY 3

TRUST NO BITCH

TRUST NO BITCH 2

TRUST NO BITCH 3

TIL MY CASKET DROPS

RESTRAINING ORDER

RESTRAINING ORDER 2

IN LOVE WITH A CONVICT

Coming Soon

BONDED BY BLOOD 2

BOW DOWN TO MY GANGSTA

The Price You Pay for Love

CPSIA information can be obtained
at www.ICGtesting.com
Printed in the USA
LVHW021548061120
670969LV00010B/851